No Rules. No Limits.

Party girl Tyler Gillette has just one rule: no football players. As the daughter of the owner of the San Antonio Hawks, she grew up in the shadow of the sport and her father's enormous wealth. She was even named Tyler because he wanted a boy. Life couldn't have drawn up a better play for turning her into a wild child—until that same life is threatened by someone from the past . . .

Former Hawks running back Rafe Ortiz has a few rules of his own. First, no weaknesses. Second, no babysitting spoiled football princesses. But his new career as a bodyguard means he's responsible for protecting the beautiful Tyler Gillette from her mysterious stalker. But keeping his hands off her might be harder than keeping her safe . . .

Books by Desiree Holt

Finding Julia

Game On Series
Forward Pass
Line of Scrimmage
Pass Interference

Published by Kensington Publishing Corporation

Pass Interference

A Game on Romance

Desiree Holt

LYRICAL PRESS
Kensington Publishing Corp.
www.kensingtonbooks.com

Lyrical Press books are published by
Kensington Publishing Corp. 119 West 40th Street New York, NY 10018

All Kensington titles, imprints, and distributed lines are available at special quantity discounts for bulk purchases for sales promotion, premiums, fund-raising, and educational or institutional use.

To the extent that the image or images on the cover of this book depict a person or persons, such person or persons are merely models, and are not intended to portray any character or characters featured in the book.

Special book excerpts or customized printings can also be created to fit specific needs. For details, write or phone the office of the Kensington Special Sales Manager:
Kensington Publishing Corp.
119 West 40th Street
New York, NY 10018
Attn. Special Sales Department. Phone: 1-800-221-2647.

First Electronic Edition: MONTH YEAR
eISBN-13:
eISBN-10:

First Print Edition: MONTH YEAR
ISBN-13:
ISBN-10:

Printed in the United States of America

First, as always, to the man of my heart

* * *

But for this book there is a second dedication. In 2013, my daughters took me to the Gristmill in Gruen, Texas, to celebrate my birthday. We were waited on by the most gorgeous man, who went out of his way to make my celebration lunch a special one. I told him one day I would model a hero after him, and I took pictures. He was very gracious, even though I'm sure he thought I was crazy. Well, Joshua Ramos, here it is. Rafe Ortiz is you come to life. Thank you so much for being such a good sport.

Acknowledgements

First a thank you to my sister, Sonya Langden, who first introduced me to the excitement of football. To my late husband David, who shared my love of the sport. Loved those weekend bets we had! And of course my son, Steven, who is the most knowledgeable person about this sport that I know and answers my endless questions. Huge thanks to my fabulous beta reader, Margie Mendel Hager. Where would I be without you? Also my incredible daughter Suzanne, and my granddaughter, Kayla, my assistants extraordinaire. To my daughter Amy, who will tell people about Desiree Holt at the drop of a hat. Thanks to my bestie, award-winning, multi-published author Cerise Deland, who is so great at brainstorming. To Paige Christian, editor extraordinaire. I will always listen to you. To Renee Rocco, without whom I would not be here writing this. I love you, sweetie. To the people at Kensington Publishing who take such good care of me. And last but far from least, to all my wonderful readers out there. Thank you so much for buying my books, for reviewing them, for telling me how much you like them and for passing the word. They are really all for you.

Author's Foreword

Football has been not just my pleasure but my passion ever since I read a book on how to watch the game. And watching it has been my salvation through every crisis in my life. When I see the first kickoff of the season—be it college or pro—my brain stirs to life. Some of my best books were written during football season. I also have to mention the dean of sportswriters, Grantland Rice, whose book The Tumult and the Shouting gave me the quintessential look into the history and the psychology of the game. And to all the players who put their bodies out there week after week for six months of the year, thank you for bringing me a sport that I truly love.

Chapter 1

Tyler Gillette swirled the amber liquid in her cocktail glass and stared into it for a long moment before taking a slow sip. Savoring the bite of the alcohol, she looked around the bar. About her usual speed these days. Slightly seedy, but in the dark it carried an artificial veneer of polish. Small (but not exactly what she'd call cozy), with a long bar on one wall and the rest of the room filled with tables and chairs. A jukebox in one corner banged out tunes, but, thank the Lord, the volume on it was turned down. She'd had enough jukebox headaches in her life, and she wasn't in the mood for one tonight.

Of course she wasn't in the mood for much of anything tonight.

She caught the sudden cloying whiff of heavy aftershave seconds before someone slid onto the bar stool next to her.

"Is this seat taken?" His voice was raspy, like a smoker's.

Tyler turned her head and looked at the man who had moved next to her. Dark hair, curling at the ends, hung to the collar of his black polo shirt, framing a face dominated by a crooked nose and thin lips. Why did men always think it was sexy to wear black? Didn't they want a little color in their lives? She let her eyes skim over him and took in the muscular body just beginning to soften, maybe developing a little flab. Okay, so men did the black-makes-me-thinner thing, too.

"Well, is it?" he persisted, in what she was sure he thought was a sexy voice.

Tyler was tempted to just turn her back on him, toss down her drink, and get the hell out of there. But her persistent self-destructive streak made her look him up and down, curve her lips in a smile, and answer him in what she hoped was a seductive voice.

"It is now."

The answering smile he gave her was part ego and part *I think I'm getting lucky tonight.* He hitched his bar stool a little closer. "Great. Just great, babe."

Babe. Crap, she hated that little word. She'd heard it from too many lips and too many men just like this one. And far too many times, in places just like this.

"So." He trailed a finger down her bare arm. Her shiver had nothing to do with a sexual response and everything to do with revulsion for the touch. "I haven't seen you at Tequila Sunrise before. You here with anyone?"

"Just myself." She gave him a sly wink and took another sip of her drink. God, she had this routine down pat, every comment, every single body movement memorized like a long-running play she'd starred in. How could she even stand herself anymore?

"Well." He returned the wink. "Me, too. That's quite a coincidence, isn't it?" He drained the rest of the liquid in his rocks glass and nodded at her empty one. "How about a refill?"

"Sure. Why not?"

Why not indeed? Tequila Sunrise was just one more dingy bar in the many she'd spent time in over the past few years. One more stop on her downward spiral. She could hardly tell one from the other anymore, and that went for the men, too. But it seemed to be the only way her father ever realized she was alive, albeit to tear his hair out at her behavior.

Tough shit.

The bartender cleared the empties and set up the refills. Tyler picked up her glass and waited until the guy touched his to hers before taking a sip.

"So," he asked, smacking his lips, "you got a name?"

"Marie." She always used her middle name. It offered a small amount of damage control and gave her a measure of anonymity. For herself, not for her father. It allowed her to separate the person she was from the things she did.

"Marie," he repeated. "Nice name." He waited for her to ask for his. When she didn't, he said it anyway. "I'm Dewey."

"Here's to ya, Dewey." She lifted her cocktail glass and took a healthy swallow. The alcohol burned as it slid down her throat and into her body, searing away her unhappiness.

"You live around here?" he asked.

Good Lord, were all his lines so stale?

"Sort of." She took another sip.

"You're sure a sexy little piece. I didn't think I'd see any action in here on a week night, but lucky me. Here you are."

Yes, lucky him.

"So, what do you do when you aren't hanging out in places like Tequila Sunrise?"

She shrugged. "This and that."

What did she do, anyway? Not a hell of a lot. She'd studied many things during her scattered college career but never pursued any of them. She'd thought about what she'd do if she completed her degree but —She took another sip of her drink, pushing those thoughts from her mind.

Glancing around, she noticed some of the people had left but others had wandered in to take their place. All of them looked as seedy and desperate as Dewey. When he coasted the tips of his fingers over her knee and tried to ease them beneath the hem of her skirt, she jerked, sloshing some of her drink on her dress. She grabbed cocktail napkins from a stack on the bar and blotted up the liquid. As she did, she brushed Dewey's thick fingers away, too.

"Awww, don't be like that." He tried to touch her again, but she swung her body at an angle away from him. "You got really soft skin. Nice skin." He leered at her. "I'll bet it's just as soft all over."

Again he made an attempt to ease his hand up the inside of her thigh. Tyler gave a forced laugh as she grasped him by the wrist, her stomach roiling at the contact.

"No touching in public." She made herself laugh again. "I have rules."

"That so?" He took a deep swallow of his drink. "Any other rules I should know about?"

"Yes. No personal questions."

"Uh-huh." He studied her. "You got something to hide?"

"Doesn't everyone?" She dug up a friendly look from somewhere. "I'll bet you do. Right?"

He shrugged. "Maybe, but nothing all that interesting." He shifted on his bar stool in an attempt to lean closer again. "I'd rather talk about you."

She hated to think how many men like Dewey she'd been in this same situation with over the years. It was a game; one she played far too often. Tease but don't give in. They can look but don't touch. Don't get too close unless she was desperate. Thank God she hadn't been that desperate in a long time.

By the third drink, she was getting sloppy and Dewey was getting more aggressive. She needed to pull herself together because she had no intention of letting Dewey and his ego get any more private with her than the seats on the two bar stools.

Nor did she plan to leave with him or anyone else. She knew the prevailing assumption was she slept with anything that had a dick but they were so wrong. Oh, sure, she'd had a few lovers, but not nearly as many as people thought, and not for a long time. It was an act she'd perfected so no one could see who was beneath that slutty armor.

She'd begun to realize lately, though, that the slutty armor pinched. That even as a disguise, it didn't seem to fit her anymore. She wasn't comfortable with herself and that disturbed her. Had she gone so far over the edge she'd lost the core of Tyler?

Unexpectedly, he stopped trying to paw her. "Hey, Chuck." He signaled to the bartender and pointed to the television mounted up in one corner behind the bar. "Turn that thing up, will you?"

"Aw, no one wants to hear that crap tonight," Chuck argued. "They got the jukebox going."

"I said turn up the fucking television," Dewey challenged. "That is if you expect any kind of tip tonight."

"Asshole," Chuck muttered.

Tyler wanted to agree with him, but the man threw down his bar towel and reached for the remote. When she looked up at the screen to see what was so important to the jerk next to her, she *really* didn't want it turned up. Behind the sportscaster was a huge rendering of the new logo of the San Antonio Hawks. Up in the corner was an inset of Kurt Gillette's photo. Her *beloved* father.

"...still pouring in," the man was saying. "The public is still divided almost equally on whether they want the team to remain the Bisons or keep the new name, the San Antonio Hawks."

The female reporter laughed. "Like it or not, Kurt Gillette won't be changing it back. Since the big switch, with a new logo, new colors, and new uniforms, the team has rebounded from the slump it's been in since the loss of star quarterback Tate Manning."

"Gillette says they'll get used to it as the team keeps racking up wins. You have to admire the man for taking such a bold step, but it seems to be working."

God! It seemed no matter where she went, Tyler couldn't get away from her father or his precious effing football team. As the television reporters continued to discuss the topic, nausea roiled up into her throat. She needed to get out of here. Fast. Get away from both Dewey and yet another news blast about the vaunted Kurt Gillette.

She slid from the bar stool and grabbed the thin strap of her purse. "Be right back," she said, slurring just a little.

"Hey, wait." He grabbed her upper arm with his thick fingers. "You're not gonna run out on me, are you? I got drinks invested in you, Marie."

She forced a smile. "Would I do that? I just need to head to the little girls' room for a minute."

She glanced pointedly at where he held onto her. With a frown, he released her, but took the moment to stroke his fingers the length of her arm. Tyler managed to keep from spitting in his face. After all, the whole thing was really her fault. If she hadn't been here in the first place, having her usual pity party—

She shook herself. "I'll be right back. Promise."

"You'd better be." The tone of his voice had an unpleasant cast to it. "If you take too long, I might have to come after you."

She lifted her eyebrows. "In the ladies' room?"

"Wherever." He grabbed her arm again. "I don't let my women run out on me. Not until I get my money's worth."

"*Your* women? Damn, Dewey, all we had was a couple of drinks."

"You gave me the come-on, sweetie. Don't try to deny it."

She yanked her arm away again and took a step back. Arguing with him would get her nowhere so she dug up a smile. "I told you. I'll be right back. You just order us another round of drinks."

As if he needed one. She managed to make it to the restroom although inside she was shaking. Usually she was a pretty good judge of the guys she met. If they got a little too aggressive, she could back off and they looked somewhere else. Apparently Dewey didn't fit into that category.

Inside the ladies' room, she took a good look at herself in the mirror. What a mess. The hair she'd arranged so artfully to fall just so to her shoulders looked as if she'd been combing it with her fingers. Okay, so she had. BFD. The black dress that she'd thought so sexy when she got dressed now looked like a cheap come-on. Her makeup, well, it didn't look too bad, but her vision wasn't quite as sharp as it had been early in the evening. All in all, she was bordering on a mess.

She was doing herself in. At this rate, she'd be dead before Kurt Gillette had a change of heart.

She had another little problem to deal with, too, one she hadn't told a single soul about. Mostly because she had no idea who to bring it to. She really hoped it would just go away.

Yeah, right. Like that was going to happen.

Sighing, she took care of business, washed her hands, and pulled her cell phone from her purse. She'd taken a cab so she didn't have to worry about driving, but she needed an alternative now. She was pretty damn sure good old Dewey would put up a huge fuss if he saw her trying to get into a taxi. No, she needed a better solution to the mess she'd gotten herself into.

Taking out her cell, she dialed her friend, Betsy. She'd definitely come and bail her out. But all she got was Betsy's "Leave a message." She tried ten more numbers, people she felt comfortably asking to help her with this ugly situation, but she only got their voice mails.

Damn! Damn! Damn!

Did no one have their cell phones on tonight, when she desperately needed to reach someone?

Bam, bam, bam.

The heavy pounding on the door startled her.

"Hey, Buttercup. You comin' outta there tonight?" Dewey's voice was edged with anger, an anger no doubt fueled by his consumption of alcohol.

Holy crap. No way was she opening the door. Still, she couldn't spend the night in the ladies' room.

"Miss?" A strange man's voice. Oh, wait, it sounded like the bartender. "Miss, are you okay in there? You need to open the door."

Not for any amount of money. But she had to get herself out of this mess and away from a drunken Dewey.

She had one more number she could call. She referred to it in her mind as her when-the-sky-is-falling-and-no-one-else-is-around number. The number for a man she'd been lusting after for a long time, who was unfailingly polite to her whenever their paths crossed yet as much as possible avoided her. She had hoped she'd never have to use it, for a number of reasons. A woman didn't want to call the man she'd dreamed about for so very long to get her out of this kind of trouble, a mess of her own making. She didn't want to see the disgust and censure in his eyes. But the sky was definitely falling tonight and this number would reach the one person she knew would get her out of it swiftly and cleanly.

She'd probably have to pay for it by listening to a good lecture and beg him not to tell her father.

Swallowing her misgivings, she dialed the number with hands that trembled. No one knew she had his number, that she'd programmed it in just in case. This was definitely a just in case. She prayed that he wouldn't hang up on her. Surely he couldn't refuse a plea for help, right? After all, he worked for her father, so how could he say no?

* * * *

"Okay, Ortiz, what do you think of the big name change for the Bisons?" Cal Hopewell looked at his poker hand, pulled out two cards, and threw them down on the table.

Rafe Ortiz studied his hand while he tried to form an appropriate answer. As the head of security for the San Antonio Hawks as well as Southern Bank Stadium, he had to be careful what he said, even in the company of his closest friends.

He slipped a single card free and tossed it down. "I'll take one," he told Andy Milliken, who was dealing, as he took his time putting his thoughts together. This wasn't the first time he'd been asked this question.

"The name change," Cal prompted.

"I think Kurt is a smart businessman who wants to inspire both his team and his fans. Whatever you might think of this, it's working."

"Yeah, but you played for the Bisons," Andy reminded him. "Don't you feel a disconnect to this new, so-called revitalized team?"

"Not at all. Some of the guys I played with are still on the active roster, and I want success for them. My relationship is to the team, whatever it's called."

"Well, whatever the circumstances," Cal said, "we're glad Gillette didn't forget about you. He gave you a nice cushy job when you decided to retire."

"Cushy?" Rafe laughed. "Did you say cushy? You come down to the stadium any Sunday and watch my staff wrestle drunks, sore losers, and bullies. Or corral some of the team members when they're loose in a new city. Then tell me it's cushy."

Not that he was complaining. He loved his job, more money than he'd ever use and a circle of friends he was comfortable with. Friends who didn't care about the celebrity status that still dogged him.

"Come on," Andy teased. "How hard can it be to herd all those groupies?"

The ringing of Rafe's cell phone broke into the conversation, saving him from having to answer. Because of his position with Lone Star Security, he kept the phone on twenty-four/seven. He pulled it out of his pocket and looked at the readout, expecting it to be one of the players or, worst case, Kurt, with a problem. When he saw who it was, he cursed silently.

Shit!

Kurt's spoiled, pampered princess. The wild child of Texas.

And the woman he'd been secretly dreaming about for ten years.

Just what he needed.

He pressed the Talk button. "Ortiz."

"Um, Rafe?" Her voice was soft and a little unsteady.

His stomach clutched, nervous apprehension dancing up and down his spine. What trouble had Tyler gotten herself into now? And why was she calling him, of all people? She never called the security team, never had anything to do with the Hawks unless she was forced to. And certainly never with him. Whenever he'd run into her, he was very careful not to show any interest that could be misconstrued. It hadn't been just the reputation she seemed intent on building. No, it was actually the fact she was Kurt Gillette's daughter with a big out-of-bounds sign on her. Getting involved with the boss's daughter was a sure recipe for disaster.

So often he'd been struck with the feeling that her entire lifestyle was just one big masquerade. That beneath her outrageous exterior was a woman in a lot of pain, determined to tell the world to go to hell. But he wasn't about to get in the middle of whatever complicated relationship she and her father had. Nope, not at all.

So he'd kept his distance, despite feelings that he ruthlessly suppressed. Now here she was calling him in the middle of the night.

How in the fucking hell had she gotten this number, anyway?

"Yeah, it's me." He tried not to let his irritation show.

"This is Tyler. Tyler Gillette." Didn't she know her ID showed up on his screen?

"How did you get this number?" he demanded. *Rude much, Ortiz?*

"Can we please, please talk about that later? Right now I really need your help."

He could hear loud conversation and music in the background. Obviously she was at one of her usual dive bars. Her activities were legend. Rafe gritted his teeth. If she'd called *him* it must really be bad.

"What's up?"

There was a long pause and he wondered if he'd lost her. If she'd hung up. Then her voice came back, a little lower as if she didn't want anyone to overhear her. Although with all that noise, he wondered how she could hear herself.

"I—uh—I hate to bother you, but can you come and pick me up? Please?"

Pick her up? He held the phone out and stared at it for a moment.

"Where's your car?" he asked.

"I took a cab." She was practically whispering now. "I am so sorry to bother you, but I-I have a bit of a problem and I seem to be having trouble reaching people. I would really appreciate it if you could see your way clear to coming to get me." Slight pause. "Please. I'm in, uh, kind of a bind."

He just bet she was. Probably the reason she was being excessively polite. His gut told him there was real trouble, and she had focused on him as the solution. He heard a sudden *Bam! Bam! Bam!* Wherever she was, it sounded as if someone was banging on a door near her.

"What's going on, Tyler? Where are you? What's that noise?"

"I—I'm in the ladies' room at a bar. Uh, Rafe? Please?"

Rafe frowned. Come and get her? Swooping up Tyler Gillette wasn't on his roster of responsibilities and he'd made damn sure to keep it that way. He had the feeling that no matter what he did he'd end up in trouble.

"Why can't you take a cab home?" he asked, hating himself even as he heard the callous tone in his voice. *Nice, Rafe.* "If you're too blitzed, have the bartender call one for you."

"I can't. I—You don't understand."

Bam! Bam! Bam!

"You in there, bitch?"

Okay, that really did not sound good. What the hell was going on?

"Fine." He let out a heavy sigh. If something really did happen to her, he'd never forgive himself. "Give me the name of the bar and lock yourself in the ladies' until I get there. If the guy busts in just scream, and the bartender will come running. I'll get there as fast as I can."

He disconnected the call and tossed his cards on the table. "Wouldn't you know it. Two queens with an ace back." He shook his head in disgust. "You guys can divvy up my money; I gotta dash."

"Man." Cal shook his head. "You don't get too many late night calls like this. It must be pretty damn important for you to break out of the game. Or something."

"Or something," he repeated and headed for the door of Cal's town house. "Just deal me out. I think I'm in for a long night."

God, he really did not want to be doing this. He'd spent a lot of years keeping as much distance between himself and Tyler Gillette as possible. Long years of sticking his hormones in deep-freeze where she was concerned. From the first moment he saw her he'd wanted her, with the passion that only a twenty-two-year-old could have. His need had been hot, strong, and gripping. And for one fleeting moment when they'd been introduced, he saw an answering spark in her eyes.

"Stay away from that one," Moe Dempster, a linebacker, had warned him the first day. "She's poison."

But he hadn't needed to be told. He'd been a rookie who needed to prove himself to his new owner, and she was that owner's daughter. And young, besides. He'd known from the get go she was off-limits. She was brash, brassy, over the top, the continuing star of tabloids. She might as well have had trouble tattooed on her forehead. Anyway, her lifestyle was so foreign to the way he lived. He could never be with a woman who defied every rule of good behavior the way she did, even if he did have a sneaking suspicion it was all an act. It wasn't the way he was raised, and it wasn't the way he lived.

In the intervening years, each time they'd run into each other, the air fairly shimmered around them with sexual electricity. He knew she'd be willing. The signals were very easy to read, but there was too much holding him back, such as his career and her reputation. She was such a contradiction, that girl. Woman. Not girl. Defensive, go to hell, fuck the world, yet whenever he was with her, he saw the vulnerability beneath the facade.

If there was one woman he didn't need to hook up with, she was that person. Yet here he was, on his way to clean up whatever her latest mess was. And then what?

Yeah, then what, idiot?

Thankfully, there wasn't all that much traffic on the streets at this time of night. Still it took some time to get from the north end of San Antonio to a bar on the south side. Miraculously, he found a space across the street and jogged over to the Tequila Sunrise. The moment he opened the door, he knew there was trouble. Almost everyone in the place was crowded toward the little back hallway, and he heard men shouting at each other.

"Damn it, Dewey." A man with a nasal voice was speaking. "I said get the fuck away from there."

"Not until I get that bitch out of there." And that, no doubt, was the cause of the trouble Tyler was in.

"Excuse me."

Swallowing a sigh, Rafe pushed his way through the crowd. No one wanted to give up their spot watching the action, so it took a few elbow digs and a look that said, "Get the fuck out of my way." But then he was in the short hallway. Two men filled up the space between the door to the ladies' room and the wall, both of them large and beefy. One of them was still banging on the door, even as the other tried to pull him away.

"Come on, Dewey. Don't make me get my baseball bat out."

Rafe guessed it was the bartender speaking.

"I'm not leaving till I get my hands on this bitch," the other man shouted in a nasty, drunken voice.

"Did you call the cops?" Rafe asked the bartender.

The man's face reddened. "I try to keep the cops out of things whenever possible."

"Even if someone is in danger?"

"Aw." The man scratched his head. "She wasn't in any real danger. I could conk Dewey over the head and put us all out of our misery."

"Next time remember that," Rafe warned. He turned to the man still banging on the door and shouting. "My turn now."

The bartender looked at the former defensive lineman for San Antonio, saw the expression on Rafe's face, and backed away. Dewey wasn't quite that smart. He ignored the fact that while he and Rafe were about the same size, Dewey's flab would be no match for Rafe's still-solid muscle. He took a step backward and put up his fists.

Rafe sighed again. He really didn't want to have to do this, but the asshole wasn't leaving him any choice. He reached out and grabbed the man by the throat with his powerful fingers, pressing his thumb into the hollow and pushing him away from the door. When Dewey still tried to fight back, Rafe just coldcocked him, and the guy dropped to the floor in a big messy heap.

"Thank you," the bartender said. "Dewey just gets a little feisty sometimes when he's had a drop too much to drink."

"Seems like you should have cut him off before he got too—what did you say?—feisty." He knocked softly on the restroom door. "Tyler? It's me."

"Rafe?"

"Yeah. In the flesh."

There was a long moment of silence and then the door eased open a crack. Tyler peered out, fear in her eyes before relief washed over her face when she saw it really was him.

"You can come out now."

Tyler opened the door wider. When he got a good look at her, he swallowed back a bitter taste. Everything was a mess—hair, makeup, dress. How in hell did she do this to herself? And why?

He reached for her hand and tugged her out into the hallway. Despite the fact she had a rep for being a gigantic pain in the ass, despite the present circumstances, the moment their hands connected electricity arced between them. There it was, that invisible crackle that had never waned and still sizzled his nerve endings. More like his brain.

No. She was off-limits and a disaster to boot. He had to keep telling himself that. Keep dragging his eyes away from the swell of her breasts visible over the cut of her dress, away from the sweet curve of her ass so lovingly outlined by the fabric. Even with her tawny hair mussed and tumbled around her face and her makeup streaked, there was something so—

So what, asshole? She asked you here to get her out of trouble, not to act out your fantasies.

He could do this. He was famous for his incredible control in all situations. He just needed to keep it in place for this one. Holding tightly to her hand, he towed her through the crowd of onlookers, concentrating on getting out of danger rather than getting into her pants.

"Come on. We're getting the hell out of here."

Rafe was tense, alert, prepared for anything as they headed toward the exit. Situations like this could go sideways in a minute. However, apparently not looking for the same treatment he'd given Dewey, people moved out of their way to let them go. Still, he held his breath as he guided Tyler through the tiny side parking lot and across the street to his car. He made sure she was belted in before he cranked the engine and pulled out into the street.

They drove in silence for a long time, tension humming in the car like low-level electricity. Not touching her would be a real test of his self-discipline. He wanted to ask her what the hell she'd been doing in a place like Tequila Sunrise, but he really didn't have to. He'd heard all the rumors, read all the stories. He knew this was one of many dives where she hung out. It puzzled him why a woman who had absolutely everything she could ask for lowered herself like this, but it was none of his business and he didn't want it to be. He didn't want to know anything, just to deliver her to her doorstep and get the hell away from her.

He shot a quick glance at her huddled in the seat. At last she spoke up, in a very small, tired voice, a trace of fear still clinging to it. "Thank you. I'm sorry I had to bother you."

"I'm sorry you did, too. You should know better than to put yourself in that kind of situation. What the hell were you thinking, anyway?"

"Nothing," she snapped, obviously irritated by his response. "Thinking can get you into trouble."

"And exactly what do you suppose tonight was?"

From the corner of his eye, he saw her glance over at him. "So I guess the price of my rescue is a lecture?"

"No lecture. Just a word of warning." He glanced over at her to see if she was paying attention. Only the tightly curled hands fisted in her lap gave her away. "You live a very destructive lifestyle, Tyler. One of these days you'll get yourself in a situation that no one will be able to get you out of."

"Then everyone's problems will be over, right?" she snapped. "Yours, mine, and especially the holy king Kurt Gillette."

He had no idea what was going on between Tyler and her father nor did he want to find out. Everyone on the team speculated, but if anyone had any answers, they were keeping quiet about them. It was none of his business, and he intended to keep it that way, for his own sanity.

As they rode through the silent streets he noticed that she kept tugging on the hem of her dress, seemingly uncomfortable in her outfit. If she was so uncomfortable in it why did she wear it? Why dress like that? Did she really want to attract men like Dewey? What was really going on with her, beneath the image she showed the world?

Silence descended and filled the car until at last he pulled into the driveway of her town house. Before she could move, he was out of the car, around the other side and had her door open. He extended a hand to help her out and guided her to the front door with a hand at the small of her back.

On the little porch, she turned to him. "Thank you again for answering my call and coming to pick me up, Rafe. I know I had no right to ask you, but you can't imagine how much I appreciate it."

"Next time pick your entertainment in a safer place," he cautioned. He studied her face. "Just out of curiosity, why did you call me, of all people? We can barely stand each other."

Hurt flashed so quickly in her eyes he wasn't even sure he had seen it.

"Maybe you're the only one I know who could have gotten me out of there." She flicked her fingers against his chest. "Don't worry. I won't make that mistake again."

"Fine. Good night, Tyler. Stay out of trouble if you can."

Before he could turn away, she launched herself at him, reaching up and wrapping her arms around his neck as she plastered her body to his. He reacted automatically, holding her against him, inhaling the tantalizing scent of her perfume. She was warm and pliant and his body reacted before his mind caught up. Before he realized it she had him in a lip-lock, her tongue halfway down his throat. It took him a moment to recover himself, but when he did, when he realized what he was doing, he lifted her gently but forcefully away from him.

"You don't want to do that, Tyler. You're drunk and tomorrow you'll regret it and be embarrassed."

She looked up at him, something like pain glittering in her eyes. "And what if I don't regret it? What if I'm serious?" Her lips curved in a sloppy semblance of a come-hither smile. "I could give you a very good thank-you, Rafe Ortiz. Very good. It's what I do best."

He sighed. He seemed to be doing a lot of that tonight. "Go inside, Tyler. Go to sleep. You'll feel differently in the morning."

He took her keys from her hand, unlocked her door, and eased her inside. Dropping the keys on a little table in the foyer, he gave her one last searching look before he closed the door and headed back to his car. He didn't fire the engine right away. Instead, he sat back in his seat, eyes closed. He could still feel the softness of her round breasts pressed to his chest, the hard tips of her nipples poking into him. He was sure she hadn't been able to miss his swollen dick imprinting itself on her mound. That damned dress was just too thin.

He ran his fingers over his lips where the taste of her still lingered, her own sweetness mingled with the flavor of whatever she had been drinking. The combination should have been a turnoff, but instead it gave his hormones a mega jump-start. And her tongue. God, when she'd thrust it into his mouth all he'd wanted was to suck hard on it and wrap his own around it. He silently cursed the unwanted boner pushing at his fly.

Tyler Gillette was a hot mess, a disaster waiting to happen. He wondered how a man like Kurt Gillette had let his daughter get so out of control and why he didn't figure a way to rein her in. Yeah, that "trouble" tattoo seemed like a good idea.

He was allergic to women like her, especially when the woman was Kurt Gillette's daughter. The man would eviscerate him if he stepped out of line with her. That alone was enough to throw cold water on his feelings.

He was so preoccupied with his body and Tyler's effect on it that he barely noticed the dark sedan that followed him through the quiet residential streets and out to the interstate.

Chapter 2

The first thing Tyler noticed when she opened her eyes the next morning was how difficult the process was. Crap! That meant she'd fallen into bed with her makeup still on and her mascara was bonding her eyelashes together. The next thing she noticed was the headache pounding in her skull, a reminder of how quickly alcohol had an adverse effect on her these days. And finally, her lips curving in a tiny smile, she recalled that hot kiss with Rafe Ortiz.

Rafe! How many years now had she dreamed of getting him into bed for just one night of incendiary, soul-searing, no-holds-barred sex? It seemed as if that feeling had hovered at the edge of her awareness ever since he joined the team as a rookie at twenty-two. She'd crushed on him big time. Huge! She'd been just a college freshman then with a bad case of hero worship.

Of course, her father had laid down the only rule he'd ever been inflexible on: stay away from the players. She could have defied him out of meanness, but despite her feelings for Rafe, she hated the team enough not to go head-to-head with Kurt. She wanted nothing to do with any part of the operation, not the players, not anything else. Even as the years passed and Rafe morphed into a man so masculine, so sexy, he made every woman's mouth water and her panties get wet, she'd forced herself to ignore him. He was connected with the team and her father, a man she believed had ruined her life, so that meant Rafe was definitely off her to-do list. Her father hadn't had to forbid her to date the players. They held about as much attraction for her as a bad case of the flu.

All except Rafe.

Why had she never been able to kill her desire for him, or the longing that persisted to this day? Somehow, even as she had an excess of wild flings with men whose names she couldn't even remember, even as she nearly ruined her life with a very bad—and thankfully brief—marriage, when she closed her eyes at night it was Rafe Ortiz's face she always saw.

Well, damn. Just damn.

He was off-limits. She shouldn't have kissed him last night.

Yeah, well, there were a lot of things she shouldn't have done in the course of her very rocky thirty-two years. The list had grown to be endless.

Your choice, Tyler. Can the pity party.

She pushed herself out of bed, dragged her fingers through the wild tangle of her hair, and made her way to the bathroom. She chanced a look in the mirror over her vanity, and for the second time since she'd started the wild, crazy ride that was her life, she didn't like what she saw. Didn't like? Make that disgusted. Who was that cheap-looking person staring back at her? The one who ended up in that ugly situation with Dewey. She wanted to throw up. What had she done to herself on this vindictive road? The whole thing had certainly not done her any good. Her relationship with Kurt Gillette wasn't one bit better. Maybe worse, even. Poking the bear had only made him turn away from her even more.

What did she do with her life besides shop, spend time with her two best friends and hang out in bars? Talk about a waste case. At the rate she was going even her friends might wash their hands of her before too long. She couldn't get rid of the memory of drunken Dewey trying to break down the door of the ladies' room and her cowering inside, frantically trying to figure out who to call for rescue.

God! She was a disaster and heading toward complete self-destruction.

Scrubbing her face clean of the thick layer of makeup that still remained and brushing her teeth made her feel marginally better. Next on her list—a hot shower and shampoo. Maybe she could wash away the person she'd seen in the mirror. But first a cup of coffee.

Grabbing her phone, she made her way downstairs and started the coffee brewing. Next to the machine were three gigantic boxes of boutique chocolates courtesy of Nate Broder, her obnoxious ex. She hated throwing them out. That would be just so wasteful. Maybe she'd give them to her cleaning lady again. The woman had an unquenchable sweet tooth.

She was just filling her mug from her single-serve coffeemaker in the kitchen when she heard the staccato beat of drums that signaled an incoming call. Leaving her mug to finish filling, she grabbed her cell from the counter where she'd set it down, taking a moment to check the caller identification first. Nate. Crap. Didn't this guy ever give up?

For a while he had stopped calling. She'd figured since she'd been deleting all his calls without answering them, calls that used to come in two or three times a day, he'd gotten the message. But yet, here he was again. What the hell? Maybe it was time to state the message a little more clearly.

"I asked you nicely not to call me anymore," she opened with. "You took me at my word for a while. The situation hasn't changed. Not a bit."

Nate's irritating chuckle floated over the connection. "Good morning to you, too, sunshine."

Tyler gritted her teeth. "Listen to me, and please try to pay attention. I thought you'd gotten the message. We're done, Nate. Finished. I don't want to talk to you, text with you, have lunch with you... Nothing. We are finished. Don't call me again. I mean it."

He was silent for a moment. "Tyler," he said at last in his all too familiar drawl. "I was just checking to see—"

"See what? Nothing about my life concerns you anymore. I thought we had that taken care of." She resisted the urge to slam her fist on the counter. "Anyway, just so you know, I'm changing my number. Again."

"I don't know why we can't at least be friends." His voice had that oily, egotistical sound that she hated. "Maybe have lunch together once in a while. Enough time has passed I thought we could at least be friendly acquaintances. We did enjoy each other's company."

"I think only one of us had any enjoyment." Tyler looked at the phone and frowned. "How did you get this number, anyway? I just changed it again."

He laughed again. "I'm an attorney with connections. I can get anything I want."

"Except for me. You can't get me. We aren't friends. We aren't anything. Now go away and don't call again."

She pressed the End button with more force than necessary. They'd each had a reason for getting into the marriage, neither of which had anything to do with love. It was the one time she'd tried to do anything to make herself respectable in her father's eyes. A last-ditch effort for a man who made it all too obvious he despised her lifestyle. Nate had thought it would give him a seat at the right hand of her father.

That hadn't worked for either of them. Before three months were up, she'd known what a mistake it was and kicked him to the curb. For a while the persistent messages he left in her voice mail were rich with anger. Then began the deluge of flowers and candy and texts, a good indication that he wasn't about to give up.

She was still holding the phone when it chimed again. This time it was Chad Sinclair, media relations director for the Hawks. Another big effing pest.

"What is it, Chad?" She didn't need to ask him how he got the number. She was meticulous about leaving it with her father's secretary every time she changed it. She didn't need the ten tons of shit that came down when she didn't, although she had no idea why he even cared.

"No hello? Or, hi, Chad?" His voice was nearly as smooth as Nate's and irritated her just as much. She really hated the occasions when she had to spend time with him.

"I'm really busy. What do you want?"

"Okay. Okay." He dialed it back. "Just wanted to remind you of the event this Saturday night at the Conquistador Club."

She wrinkled her forehead. "This Saturday?"

"Yes. The big fundraiser for athletic scholarships. The Hawks are big benefactors."

"Oh, yeah, another command appearance." An obligation forced on her by her father—if she wanted to keep the money in her trust fund flowing.

But he never left the choice of escort up to her, probably thinking she'd bring someone from her skanky nightlife. So Chad got the nod and made sure she got to each and every one. Maybe she'd once hoped if she continued to attend, her father would see a different side of her, see she wanted to please him and maybe even…like her.

But it hadn't made even the tiniest dent in the situation. She'd finally got the message nothing she did would change things with her father, but couldn't seem to stop herself.

Did he think that by forcing her to attend these, she'd begin to bond with the Hawks? She hated the effing football team. She saw it as the child that had usurped all her father's affections.

"I'll pick you up at seven," Chad told her.

"Fine."

"So, I wondered if you'd like to have lunch with me today?"

This was only about the fiftieth time he'd asked her. She had no interest in spending time with him beyond what she had to.

"Thanks, but I already have plans." Or she would as soon as she made them.

"You know," he said, in what she assumed was his most seductive tone. "I'm really a nice guy if you'd get to know me outside of our obligatory dates."

"I'm sure you are. I'm just not interested. See you Saturday."

She clicked off and finally managed to get her mug from the coffee machine.

Chad was always the perfect escort, dancing attention, even after she started drinking too much, often making a real fool of herself. A few times when he brought her home, he'd actually had to half carry her into the house and up the stairs. She always had enough wits about her, though, to make sure he left before he could try to take things further.

When she heard the chimes for the third time, she let out a string of curses. Ed Spinelli. What did he want now?

Had she pissed someone off royally? Was that why the three men who annoyed her the most all just happened to call her this morning? Or was Mercury in retrograde or the stars out of alignment? Did that mean she could expect a call from her father, too?

Ed wrote a sports blog that was followed by half a million people. He'd hit on her at a Hawks barbecue where she'd given one of her many command appearances. She'd gone out with him for a couple of reasons. For one she was curious about someone who had a blog that people followed religiously. For another, he'd written a lot of unflattering things about the Hawks, so it had been another big *Fuck you* to Kurt.

The man was hardly her type, tall and skinny with an ego bigger than the stadium. She'd expected him to be funny, charming, full of exciting and interesting things to do. Instead she'd discovered that his entire personality was confined to the words he wrote on his computer.

She'd been stupid enough to date him more than once. She'd broken it off when she found out that his goal was to get in her pants as his way of giving her father the finger. Apparently he was the only person in San Antonio who didn't know Kurt Gillette didn't give two hoots what his daughter did.

He hadn't been too happy when she broke it off, but at least he hadn't stalked her via her cell phone, unlike her ex. When she'd sent Ed a text telling him to lose her number or she'd do a blog about him, he finally got the hint. She had seen him out a few times with other women and figured he couldn't be too heartbroken. She hadn't heard from him in ages now, and wondered what was up with him now.

She had barely tapped the button to send the call to voice mail when—damn it!—here came another one. She looked at the screen and couldn't decide whether to answer it or not. The number wasn't familiar but the readout also didn't say Unknown or Blocked like the other weird calls she'd been getting, so she took a chance.

"Hello." She waited but no one replied. "Hello," she repeated. Still silence. Not even any background noise. Her fingers tightened on her cell and her stomach cramped with tension. Would this never stop? "Hello." This time she shouted it as anger bubbled up inside her. "Listen, whoever you are, this is not fun. Don't call me again." She paused. "Do you hear me?"

When there was still no answer, not even heavy breathing, she disconnected the call and tossed the phone down on her bed, as if it had a disease.

Crap.

Damn it all to hell, anyway.

The calls had started three weeks ago, silence, then heavy breathing. In the beginning, they'd only come once a day, then it had escalated to two, then finally four. At first, she kept saying, "Hello? Hello?" but no one ever answered. All she heard was that damn heavy breathing. Then whoever it was would hang up.

She'd thought it was some guy who'd somehow gotten her number and was pranking her. Since she didn't make a habit of giving it out, the choices of who the caller could be should be limited. She'd changed her number twice since it started, to the irritation of her carrier, but too bad for them. They got paid, didn't they? So how did some stranger keep getting his hands on it?

She was pretty sure they hadn't gotten it from any of her friends. They were all very careful not to share each other's information with anyone. If it was Nate or Chad or even Ed, what would she do next? Who would she tell? Tyler Gillette, the wildest woman in San Antonio. As she'd told Betsy, everyone would just think all this was a by-product of her crazy lifestyle. She'd stitch her mouth shut before running to her father. Maybe Rafe would help her, but he was off-limits. Besides, after last night he'd probably never go near her again.

Her own damn fault, for playing out this outrageous charade all these years.

Taking a deep breath, she dialed the number from the readout. No luck, just as the other times she'd tried. All she got was "That is not a working number." As someone who didn't live under a toadstool, she was aware that telemarketers bought phone numbers that they could hide behind. But no one spoke up and tried to sell her anything.

Climbing the stairs, she reviewed other possibilities, ticking off more names.

Maybe someone from the Hawks who'd seen her and wigged out on her? Was it someone hanging around the fringes of her life, lusting after her or angry with her for something? She tried again to think of every man she'd picked up and walked away from. Or those she'd hung tight with for a few days, maybe even weeks, then ditched with little more than a verbal kick in the ass.

She gave herself a mental shake. Time to get dressed and get moving. Nothing would get solved this way. She just kept hoping whoever this was would finally get tired of the game.

She stood in the shower, spreading the body wash lavishly over her skin, hot water sluicing over her, and tried to remember every place she'd had her phone for the past couple of weeks where someone could palm it long enough to check the number. She had to admit sometimes she wasn't as careful about keeping it in her purse as she should be. Maybe it had happened before that, and whoever was doing this had just been biding his or her time. Who had she pissed off so much that they were making these kinds of calls to her?

Oh, well, Tyler, how much time do you have?

She hadn't made any friends in the dive bars she trolled. Besides, that had all been nothing but a ploy. What had she thought? That the famous Kurt Gillette would finally ask her what the hell this was all about? Clutch her to his heart and ask how he could help? Unfortunately, her plan bombed since she never got the reaction she wanted. She wondered who was more disgusted with the person she'd made herself into, her father or herself?

In any event, she was pretty sure it wasn't anyone from her nightlife. They were all highly unlikely to indulge in games like this. She could barely recall half of the idiots she'd strung along in the bars but none of them would have her number. Would they? And no one else jumped out at her.

Maybe, possibly, one of her friends had laid their phone on a bar or table and someone had managed to scroll the contacts list. Or... The list was longer than her driveway.

First thing today after she dressed, she was getting another phone with yet another new number. She'd keep this one for all those annoying calls and use the new one for personal calls. That way she'd have some control over the situation. Maybe the person would get tired of it and go away.

She dried herself off, her mind doing a quick flashback to the previous night and Rafe. Calling him had been a move of desperation for her. She hadn't known who else would rescue her from the rapidly deteriorating situation. She got the feeling he didn't have a very high opinion of her but not nearly as bad as how she saw herself. What the hell was she doing with her life, anyway?

In a short robe and still barefoot, she carried a fresh mug of coffee out to the deck and dropped down into one of the lounge chairs. Letting the sunlight warm her, she closed her eyes for a moment and there was Rafe's face again. That thick shock of midnight-black hair set off a dark face with a square jaw and high cheekbones. Eyelashes as black as his hair and as thick as a woman's curtained eyes of a shocking electric blue. Faint evening scruff shadowing his square jaw made him look devilishly sexy. And his lips. God, those full lips, so soft yet at the same time hard and demanding. Remembering the feel of them, she touched her fingertips to her mouth.

If she'd just pushed it, she was sure she could have had him. The swollen thickness of his cock had been unmistakable when she'd imprinted her body against his. And she hadn't imagined the heat of the kiss before he'd forced her away. His tongue had been just as much involved in that kiss as hers.

She didn't think it would have taken much more effort on her part to coax him inside the house, to peel off the soft-collar shirt that matched his eyes so perfectly and the jeans that hugged his muscular legs and very fine ass. Oh, yes, she'd noticed his ass.

Over time her crush had developed and blossomed, despite no interaction between them to help it along. She'd certainly tried to obliterate her feelings with her lifestyle, but there it was. She was plain and simply stuck on the man. And wasn't that just a bitch, because she had as much chance of making anything happen as she did of her father giving her a hug and telling her he loved her.

Inside, she rinsed her mug and set it beside the sink. Fetching her phone, she scrolled through until she found the number she wanted.

"Hope you're not all perky today." Betsy Timmerman punctuated her words with a loud yawn.

"I don't think perky exactly describes my situation," she told her friend. "I need to do some stuff, and I want company. Is today a free day for you?"

Betsy was a docent at the San Antonio Museum of Fine Art three days a week, a responsibility she took very seriously.

"Sure is," Betsy said. "What's on your plate?"

"I need to buy another phone, for one thing." Betsy was the only person she'd shared her problem with."

"Oh, Tyler." She heard the caring note in Betsy's voice. "Are you still getting those damn calls? You ought to report it."

"And say what?" she asked. "They'll want to know who it could be and they don't have enough time to hear all the names. I'll get halfway through the list and they'll tell me they're sorry but my lifestyle just leaves me open to stuff like this. It's my problem."

"Surely not," Betsy protested. "They're the police. They have to help everyone, no matter what they think."

Tyler gave a bitter laugh. "You keep right on thinking that, Betsy, if you want to. They like to write off people like you and me."

"But your father has a lot of influence," her friend said. "Get him on it."

"Are you kidding? He's the last person I want to tell. He already thinks I'm a wasted piece of trash."

Betsy was silent for a long moment. "Maybe it's time to bury the hatchet with him."

Tyler snorted. "Oh, right. What kind of pills are you popping?"

"I'm just sayin', you know? After all, you are his daughter."

"He hasn't cared about that all these years. He's not going to start now." She sighed. "No, I'll figure this out myself. So, are you up for some shopping and lunch at Al Dente?"

Betsy laughed. "Two of my favorite activities."

"Good. I'll pick you up in an hour."

Before she could climb back up the stairs, her doorbell rang. A deliveryman stood there holding a disgustingly atrocious display of flowers.

"Miss Gillette?" he asked.

She nodded. "Yes."

"These are for you. Glad you're home to receive them."

Tyler stared at them. "Who are they from?" she demanded.

The driver juggled the flowers and checked his digital tablet. "All it says here is *From the man who will always love you.* Wow! He must really love you a lot. I know what they cost."

Tyler stepped back into the hallway. "Please take them away. Right now."

"But—"

"Away. Now." She practically slammed the door in the poor man's face. This had to be Nate. No amount of flowers or candy would gloss over the disaster that was her marriage.

She sat down on the stairs for a few minutes to pull herself together. This just had to stop. And she had to quit letting it bother her. But the phone calls and the flowers and the—

Get it together, girl. If you fall apart, he wins. Whoever he is.

Finally she pulled herself together and stiffened her spine. She'd go to lunch and ignore this. But maybe today she'd go without all the typical Tyler glitz. Maybe it was time for a change. Because she was tired of wasting her life, throwing it away and getting nothing for it. She knew who she really was on the inside. Maybe it was time to show the world on the outside.

Eventually she settled on a pair of unadorned skinny jeans—she hadn't even known she had any—and a plain, pale green T-shirt with no embroidery or bedazzling on it. She didn't even remember buying it. She unwound the towel from her head and picked up her blow-dryer to style her hair, then stopped, changed the setting and just dried it enough so she could skin it back into a ponytail.

She opened her makeup drawer, decided on just a brush of mascara and a swipe of lip gloss. She felt almost naked without the heavy mask of makeup she usually wore, but damn if she didn't look a lot better. Younger, even. Well, well, well. Simple studs in her ears completed her outfit. Then she was ready to go.

When she picked up her cell, she looked at it for a long moment, sure she was about to make a stupid mistake.

Do not call Rafe. Do. Not. Call.

But it's just to say thank you, she told herself.

Uh-huh.

Her finger hovered over the keypad and before she could change her mind, she punched in the number. By the time she hung up, she was almost sorry she'd called. What had she expected, that he would ask her out?

Oh, right! Dream on.

Time to head out.

When she picked up Betsy, her friend slid into the passenger seat of Tyler's car and froze in place.

"What's the matter?" Tyler asked. "Something wrong?"

Betsy just stared at her. "I didn't recognize you. What's the deal?"

"With what?" But Tyler was sure she knew what she meant.

"The clean-face look. You lose your makeup box?" Betsy continued to stare at her.

"Maybe I'm incognito. Fasten your seat belt."

"I need a drink." Betsy fastened the safety clasp of the belt. "I can't stand the shock."

"Okay," Tyler grinned. "We'll have iced tea with lunch."

"Jesus, Tyler. What the hell is this all about?"

"Maybe it's just about me," Tyler said. "Maybe I just need a change."

"Uh-huh. We'll see." Betsy chuckled. "We'll just see." She paused. "Although I have to say, you look a hell of a lot better."

* * * *

The team headquarters was busy, probably because the Hawks had just returned from two weeks on the road. Rafe knew they hated playing back-to-back away games, much as he had before he retired. The National Football League, however, had its own method of scheduling and there wasn't much to do except go along with it. At least they now allowed for jet lag when putting the calendar together. Rafe sometimes traveled with the team depending on the location. This time he'd chosen to stay home, clean up loose ends, and get ready for the first game after their return. He saved the open file on his computer and pulled up his digital calendar.

An important game was coming up Sunday, a highly competitive game with the Austin Mustangs. For the stadium security team this meant more drinking to monitor, more tailgate parties to keep an eye on, more everything. Only a few more days to prepare for the next onslaught of trouble. For the most part, football fans, as crazy as they were, behaved themselves. They respected the sport and the players and wanted only to show their support. But there were always the exceptions. In recent years there seemed to be more and more of them, people looking to settle sports disagreements with their fists rather than their mouths, and often in more drastic measures.

Then there were the fans who had that one beer too many and got belligerent when told they would have to leave. Rafe drilled his men constantly on the best way to handle all these people with a minimum of fuss and disturbance to the people around them. It was important that those who paid to see their team play had the best experience possible.

He had met with his staff twice already this week, but he made a note on the calendar for one more meeting on Saturday. He wanted to review everything before he went through the game-day drill once more. Clicking on Invite, he sent the notice with the time and place to everyone on the stadium security team.

Finally he sat back in his chair, wishing like hell he could erase the previous night from his mind. Images of Tyler Gillette had plagued his dreams so intensely that he woke with a painful morning woody. He'd tried an icy shower to shrink his stubborn cock but not even what he felt was subzero temperature had helped. He'd ended up turning the water to full steam, soaping his hand, and stroking himself to completion, imagining a naked Tyler kneeling before him with her slender fingers gripped around him. When the hot cum erupted from him and slid thickly over his fingers, his body had shaken with the effects of the release.

He'd leaned against the shower wall until he could catch his breath again and his legs were steady. For a hand job, the orgasm had been so powerful it totally rocked him. Not only didn't he remembered the last time he'd had such a draining climax, he also couldn't remember the last time he'd needed his good right hand as a partner. Maybe when he was sixteen?

He glanced reflexively down at his crotch, startled to realize he'd placed his hand over his fly and the insistent bulge beneath it.

Damn, Rafe! Get your shit together.

Tyler Gillette was forbidden fruit on so many levels. When the Hawks drafted him right out of college, the gates of the future had opened wide for him. He'd had a successful playing career, choosing to retire while his body was still in one piece. With his degree in criminal justice, he'd had a lot of options to examine.

Then Anthony Castillo, owner of Lone Star Security, had stepped in with an offer he couldn't refuse—head of security for Southern Bank Stadium and for the team. Kurt Gillette and the Hawks would be his sole responsibility. He couldn't believe they had given him this assignment first thing out of the box, but he'd busted his ass not to let anyone down.

Which was a very good reason to stay away from a wild card like Tyler Gillette, no matter how many of his fantasies she'd starred in over the years.

At that moment, the phone on his desk buzzed and he hit the Intercom button.

"Who is it?" he asked.

"Tyler Gillette." He heard both amusement and curiosity in the voice of the team receptionist.

Was it possible his wandering mind had called her up just like that? Shit.

"Did she say what she wants?"

"Just asked if she could speak to you for a minute." Pause. "I did ask if she'd leave a message, but she said she wanted to speak to you personally."

Now what?

He heaved a sigh, something he seemed to do a lot of where this woman was concerned. "Okay. Put her through."

He heard the click of the connection: "Tyler?"

"Good morning, Rafe."

She sounded a little less sure of herself today for some reason. Without the slurring caused by the alcohol or the gruffness of a late-night voice, her voice was almost musical.

Musical? Where had that come from?

"What can I do for you?" The best thing was to get this conversation over with as quickly as possible. He did not need any more contact with this woman than absolutely necessary. He hoped she wasn't calling to pursue that hot kiss from last night. He'd need every bit of tact and diplomacy to get out of that bit of trouble.

"I just wanted to call and thank you for coming to get me last night." She cleared her throat. "I appreciate it."

Hmm. That was the last thing he'd expected.

"I'm just glad I could be of help." He waited, wondering if she expected him to say something else, but what?

"Okay." Her voice breaking the silence startled him. "Well, thanks again for the rescue and thanks for your time."

And she was gone.

Thanks for your time? What the hell did that mean? She had to know that one of these days, she'd get herself in a situation like last night and it wouldn't end quite as well. She was on a fast trip to self-destruction if she didn't wake up. Still, it wasn't his responsibility. She was Kurt Gillette's daughter. Maybe the old man should put a leash on her the way he did on his players.

Still, there was something about her that he just couldn't put his finger on. A feeling that she wore a disguise, that beneath it there just might be a woman he'd like to get to know. Getting involved with Gillette's daughter, though…

He gave himself a mental shake. Forget it.

"Got a minute?"

He looked up as a gravelly voice broke into his thoughts. Kurt Gillette himself, in dark tailored slacks and a dress shirt with the sleeves rolled up, stood in the doorway. The man pretty much filled the space. A former football player, he still had the bulky but toned appearance of a lineman. Unlike many other former players his age, he hadn't let his body go soft, despite the amount of time he spent at his desk or in meetings. It was common knowledge that "The Boss" regularly used the workout room when no one was in there.

"For you?" Rafe smiled. "As many as you want. What can I do for you?"

Kurt lumbered into the room and dropped into one of the chairs in front of the desk. "It's about Tyler."

Damn! Had his thoughts conjured up this visit with the man himself? Tyler Gillette was the last thing he wanted to discuss, especially with her father. The man would not like what he had to say. Every muscle in Rafe's body tensed. He forced himself to relax before he spoke.

"What about her?"

The man rubbed his jaw. " I was just wondering... I mean, I know..." He shook his head. "This is a bad idea."

"Maybe if you tell me what you want, I can tell you if it's bad or not."

"Okay. I just..."

Rafe knew there was a kicker in here somewhere. This man was never at a loss for words. In fact, sometimes it was next to impossible to shut him up. Oh, crap. Had he heard about last night? Rafe was not in the mood to dissect it.

"You know I'd never discuss my daughter with anyone but you, Rafe. Right?"

Oh, shit. Now what?

It was no secret the old man and his daughter had a damaged relationship. Was Gillette regretting it now, for some reason? Rafe didn't think the man ever regretted anything.

"Where is this going, Kurt?"

"Okay, here it is. I'll just say it straight out. It's been brought to my attention by...people...that my girl has a tendency to get herself into a little bit of trouble now and then. I've been hearing about it more and more."

Really? No shit. Talk about an understatement. And was he concerned about Tyler or about his own image? He certainly couldn't like his high-octane friends telling stories about Tyler.

"I'm sorry to hear that." Rafe put a half smile on his face. "I'm sure this concerns you, but I'm not sure what I can do about it."

Kurt shifted, as if the chair was uncomfortable. "I don't have any right to ask this, but I know you're out here and there some nights." He lifted a hand. "I don't mean you hang out in bars and stuff like that. You're a good man, Rafe. I always thought of you as the son I never had."

Oh, Jesus.

Gillette shook his head. "I know she won't listen to me. Listen, hell. She hardly talks to me." He rubbed his jaw. "Anyway, I'm suddenly getting feedback from people more than before, so I just wondered if you could kind of put the word out to keep an eye on her."

Ah. Feedback from people. That meant his cronies were asking him what was up with his wayward daughter. But why now? Had news of the debacle at Tequila Sunrise reached his ears? Had someone called him and said, "*Your* daughter *is a mess. Fix it.*"? Was this all about how it affected Kurt's reputation? Or had all the stars suddenly aligned and focused on her father, giving him a nudge? Not likely, but whatever. He'd do whatever he could. After last night, he figured it was necessary, anyway.

He frowned. "Put the word out where, exactly?"

Gillette shrugged. "Wherever you can would be appreciated."

"I don't know how much help I can be," he said. "I hate to say it, Kurt, but it's not like I can call every bartender in town and ask them to watch out for her."

"I know, I know." The man gnawed on his bottom lip for a moment. "Maybe you could just tell the guys on your security team if they see her any place to pay attention to what's going on."

Rafe swallowed a sigh. "Don't get upset, but my guys don't exactly go the same places she does. I can do one thing, but I'm not sure you'll like it."

"What is it? I don't have too many options."

"I know a lot of the cops in this town. I can quietly pass the word to the ones who cover the part of the city she hangs out in to keep an eye out."

Kurt heaved a loud sigh. "You're right, asking the cops to watch my daughter isn't something that I enjoy, but if that's my only alternative, then I'd appreciate you doing it."

"Consider it done."

"Thank you." Kurt pushed himself out of the chair, then stood there a moment, just shaking his head. "I guess I made a lot of mistakes with her, Rafe. But…I had no idea how to raise a daughter. Still don't. And I hate the way she lives her life. Despise it. But I sure don't want to see her get hurt. Which," he added, "she's liable to if she doesn't make some changes."

Rafe had to ask himself if there was a spark of genuine concern in there, or Kurt was just more worried about how people would view him if indeed something bad happened to Tyler. Either way, that was none of his business. He'd told the man what he could do and he'd do it.

Rafe stared at the doorway for long seconds after the man had left. He'd talk to the cops he knew well enough to approach and hope that maybe after last night she'd wised up a little. She seemed determined to destroy herself and people like that didn't want help. Dewey could have done serious damage to her. Didn't she realize that?

Maybe so. She hadn't seemed quite as feisty.

As if the devil himself were tempting him, he found himself wondering yet again what Tyler looked like naked and in the throes of passion. *Not good*, he told himself for the tenth time. Thoughts like that could only bring problems. Maybe it was the lack of steady female companionship that was screwing with his head. He'd dated Mike Lazarus's sister for a time, but they'd figured out in a hurry they were better as friends than lovers. Since then no one had rung his bells.

Last night, he'd responded to Tyler's call because he worked for her father. Because he felt a responsibility. Period. The same with the promise he'd just made. But beyond that he was done. The farther he stayed away from this woman, the better off he'd be. Her lifestyle irritated him, and her attitude annoyed him.

Yeah, keep telling yourself that, smartass. Her father had nothing to do with that kiss.

Lunch. Food. Anything to distract him from thoughts of Tyler Gillette.

Still, as he headed out of his office, he rubbed his lips with the tips of his fingers, trying to brush away the memory.

He'd better rub it away real good. Otherwise he could get his ass in a very big sling.

Chapter 3

"We were lucky to get this table," Betsy said as they slid into their seats.

Tyler nodded. They'd scored a seat on Al Dente's mezzanine overlooking the world famous Riverwalk. The entire wall of the restaurant was glass, giving them an unobstructed view.

"It is pretty crowded today," Tyler agreed, adjusting her chair and looking around.

"Yes, it is." Betsy gave Tyler a penetrating stare. "You look good, gal friend."

"Excuse me?" Tyler's eyebrows lifted almost to her hairline.

"You heard me. I like this look." She grinned. "Am I seeing the real Tyler Gillette?"

"I don't know." Tyler looked down at the table. "I'm not sure I even know who the real Tyler Gillette is anymore, Bets."

Betsy placed a gentle hand on her arm. "I think," she said in a soft voice, "it's the woman I'm looking at right now. The one without a chip on her shoulder." She grinned. "But still feisty."

"I feel strange," Tyler said.

"Do you feel naked this way?"

Tyler gave a tiny little laugh. "Not so long as no one sees me, I guess. Of course, I'll bet they'd never recognize me."

Betsy put her elbow on the table and leaned her chin on her palm. "Maybe it's time to make big changes in your life. Stop worrying about certain people and do this for yourself." She paused. "You want to tell me what brought this on?"

Tyler nibbled her lower lip, a habit of her childhood that had popped up lately. How could she tell her friend why she was doing this when she wasn't even sure herself? She felt odd with her naked face hanging out but it was something she'd felt impelled to do.

"I think," she said slowly, "I took a good look at myself and didn't like what I saw—someone I wouldn't even want to be friends with."

"Maybe it's time you were." Betsy opened her menu. "Let's see what sounds good today. I could eat a truckload of something."

Tyler looked at her own menu for a moment but she really didn't see what was printed there. What the hell was she doing? Who was she trying to be? "Do it for yourself," Betsy had said. But who was herself? She picked up her glass of ice water to take a sip and was just about to set it down when something made her look up and there, being seated at a table near them, was Rafe.

He pinned her with his penetrating gaze, and Tyler nearly dropped her drink.

"What's the matter?" Betsy frowned. "You have a weird look on your face."

A sudden feeling of panic clutched at her, and she pushed her chair back from the table.

"I'll be right back. If the waiter shows up, order me a dirty martini and that bruschetta appetizer."

Grabbing her purse from the back of her chair, she headed—almost ran—to the ladies' room. Thank the Lord there was no one inside. Quickly she pulled out the makeup case she always carried and began to paint her face. When she was done, she yanked the holder off her ponytail, bent over, and raked her fingers through her hair. When she stood up straight and tossed her head back, her hair fell to her shoulders in sexy, messy waves. Good. Just what she wanted. She felt safe behind what was probably her stage makeup. No way did she want Rafe to see her face naked and vulnerable.

"Well!" Betsy gave her a wide grin as she took her seat again. "What brought that on? I told you before, I think I like the other Tyler better."

"I just—I didn't—" She swallowed. "God, Betsy, I got scared. I didn't have my usual mask in place."

"Maybe it's like a twelve-step recovery," Betsy teased. "You have to do it in stages."

"Maybe." She buried her head in the menu again.

"It's okay, Tyler." Betsy voice was filled with understanding. "I'm here for you all the way. After lunch, we'll stop at one of the T-shirt shops on the Riverwalk, and get you something to wear with a crazy saying."

Crazy saying. Right. Her whole life was a crazy saying.

"Sounds good." Impulsively she reached over and squeezed the other woman's hand. "I'm so lucky to have you for a friend, Bets."

"Same goes. Now let's have a drink on that."

At that moment, the waiter appeared with their appetizers and drinks. Tyler lifted her martini glass and took a swallow. The liquor burned on its way down, but it was a familiar sensation and one she embraced. It let her know she was alive.

"So tell me," Betsy asked, "how long are you going to keep changing cell-phone numbers? The guy at your carrier store looked as if he thinks you're nuts. Three numbers now." She tilted her head and studied Tyler. "You need to tell someone about this, Tyler. I'm not kidding."

"I'm not telling anyone."

"Anyone?" Betsy leaned forward. "Honey, you need to tell someone. I'm worried about you, that's all."

"I'm fine. Truly. And I'm stingy with who gets the new number." She forced a grin. "I'll just have a contacts list of the people who are important to me."

"Wow!" Betsy grinned. "I feel honored to be one of your important people. So what's the new number?"

"Hold on. I'm dialing you so you'll have it."

In seconds, Betsy's phone, which she'd placed on the table, began to vibrate. The woman picked it up, answered, and added the number to her contacts list. Tyler spent a few minutes calling the people who most needed to have her new number, the few she felt comfortable sharing it with like Betsy and her other really close friend, Lynn. She'd worry about the others later.

Unable to help herself, she glanced sideways at Rafe's table and caught him watching her again, his face expressionless. She didn't dare meet his gaze knowing she'd see a look of censure there. She'd deliberately plastered everything on as outrageously as she could, her version of flipping him the bird.

"What is wrong with you?" Betsy wanted to know. She gave Tyler a hard look, then turned to see what was going on and spotted Rafe, sitting with another man. "Wow! Who is that?" She fanned her face. "Hot, hot, hot."

"No one," Tyler muttered.

"No one?" Betsy's eyebrows nearly rode to her scalp. "If he's nobody, why is he giving you that hungry look, and why are you trying to avoid him?"

"Rafe isn't giving me a hungry look. More like distaste."

"Rafe, is it? Well! Rafe who? And where have you been keeping him?"

"For God's sake." Tyler took another sip of her drink. "His name is Rafe Ortiz. He works for my father, and if he stepped on me, he'd just scrape me off the sole of his shoe."

"Wow." Betsy took a swallow of her own drink. "Whatever did you do to him?"

"Nothing. And I don't intend to." She ground her teeth. "Can we please change the subject?"

Betsy lifted one shoulder in a graceful, practiced gesture. "Sure, honey, whatever you say. But if you don't want him, can I have him?"

"Forget him. He's poison." She lifted a sliver of the bruschetta and took a small bite, chewed, and swallowed. "Let's just finish our appetizers and go someplace else. I've suddenly decided I'm not in the mood for Italian."

Or Hispanic.

They paid the check, and when they left, she made sure to walk to the other side of the area then turn back to the open stairway. The quicker she got out of here the better.

* * * *

Rafe cursed his decision to come to Al Dente for lunch. But he had run into Leo Campion, the director of player personnel for the Hawks, on his way out and couldn't figure out a polite way to tell him he wasn't interested in company. This was Leo's choice of restaurants, and he'd gone ahead to get a table. Rafe had nearly tripped over his feet when he spotted Tyler sitting at a table against the glass wall. It wasn't so much that he saw her, but what she looked like. It was the first time in longer than he could remember that she hadn't had ten pounds of makeup on her face and been dressed to expose as much skin as possible.

"You look like you swallowed something bad," Leo joked, sliding in opposite Rafe.

"No. It's just—No, nothing."

Leo gave a grunt of skepticism. "I'm telling you, big man, that look doesn't seem like nothing."

"Just drop it, please." He definitely did not want to discuss Tyler Gillette with a member of her father's executive staff. Nope. Not going there.

But Leo was like a dog with a bone, scanning the people seated in the mezzanine. Rafe knew the moment the man's eyes landed on Tyler.

"Aha!" Leo sounded as if he'd just struck gold. "Fixated on the boss's daughter, are we? Have I missed something?"

"There's nothing to miss."

"She won't go there, anyway." Leo's mouth ticked up in nasty smile. "She won't have anything to do with anyone even dimly connected to the Hawks. I don't know if it's her father's edict or the fact she hates anything to do with the team. But trust me, she's a snotty brat. Just ask me."

"Can you still be a brat at her age?" Rafe asked.

"She hasn't grown up much," Leo commented. "So yeah, brat probably still applies."

Rafe deliberately lifted his menu to study it, hoping Leo would get the message this conversation bit was over. Still, he managed to catch a glimpse of Tyler with a sideways glance. She looked like a totally different person without all that trash on her face, wearing none of her usual glitz.

He knew she'd seen him spot her and hoped she didn't think he was following her or anything. When she left the table, he let his gaze fall to the menu. But then, in what seemed like a moment, she was back, stunning him with the change she'd affected. The layers of makeup were back again, her T-shirt pulled out of her jeans and knotted in front to expose her midriff, and the hair that had been so smoothly contained in a ponytail now hung in a wild tumble of curls around her face.

He wanted badly to tell her how much better she'd looked without all that crap plastered on her face, but was sure she'd misunderstand. Even from the distance he'd been able to see she had beautiful skin and gorgeous hair. In fact, he wanted to run his fingers through it, but they'd probably throw him out of the restaurant if he tried.

Then she was gone and he was left with more questions than answers about what had just happened. Why did she hide herself? What was so awful that she'd turned herself into a caricature of a woman with too much money and too few morals? More importantly, why did he care? That was the question that wouldn't leave him in peace.

"Those are some deep thoughts." Leo's voice broke into his unexpected reverie.

"Oh. Sorry. Just running over some things in my mind."

"Some things?" Leo asked. "Or some*one*?"

"Enough." Rafe cut him off. "Is that all you can talk about?"

"Well, we could discuss the uptick the team has taken since the name change." Leo dipped a piece of the Italian bread and stuffed it into his mouth.

"According to what I've heard," Rafe said, "it seems people are split evenly between a good and bad decision. But you can't argue with the fact the team's been winning."

"They have," Leo agreed. "Best streak since Tate Manning got hurt and had to retire."

"Boy, that was a damn tragedy." Rafe shook his head. "It nearly destroyed his life."

"But it didn't. Amazing what the love of a good woman can do." Leo grinned. "Maybe that's what you need, Rafe. Then you wouldn't be such a sourpuss."

"Sourpuss?" Rafe lifted his eyebrows. "I consider myself serious, not sour."

Leo shrugged. "Whatever. I can only tell you since Jeannie and I got married my life has improved a thousand percent."

"Yeah, well, we can't all be that lucky with a woman." Rafe should know. He seemed to have made a series of bad choices. Lately he'd just decided to avoid women completely. As he'd rediscovered in his shower, his right hand did the job and didn't give him any problems.

But it doesn't replace a living, breathing woman.

Shut up, he told the voice in his brain. He was doing just fine.

Thank God Leo spent the rest of the meal discussing the team and the upcoming schedule. They chatted about some of the players who needed some extra work, those who might be aging out of the game, what the future held for the Hawks. Neither man wanted dessert, so they paid their checks and made their way down the open staircase and out of the restaurant.

Just at the doorway, Rafe stopped. A tiny chill had raced down his spine, the kind of feeling you get when someone is watching you or danger is near. But what kind of danger would there be in a restaurant? He looked around, scanning the diners, but nothing seemed to catch his eye. He just had the feeling—

He'd been watching too much television. Either that or he still carried the vestiges of his confrontation last night with Dewey. But Dewey wouldn't be having lunch at Al Dente. And this was just plain stupid. Idiotic.

He made his way out the door and into the crowd moving along the Riverwalk. Maybe he'd been braced for trouble at the stadium for too long, belligerent drunks and angry fans. Maybe he just needed a little time out of the office.

Maybe he just needed to get laid.

At that, he snorted and blended into the crowd moving along the walkway.

* * * *

Malevolent eyes followed Rafe as he headed out of the restaurant.

Asshole! Jackass! Bastard!

He wanted to spit on him, then pulverize him into the ground. The thought of the man with Tyler made him sick to his stomach. If he hadn't been keeping an eye on her, he would never have been aware of what happened the previous night. It was enough to enrage him.

Who the fuck did the rich princess think she was, anyway? Damn good thing she hadn't invited Rafe into her house when he brought her home. Watching that kiss had been bad enough. It should have been *his* mouth on hers. *His* hands touching her body. He would have made damn sure he got inside her place. And then got inside her.

Thinking about it now he had to stop himself from licking his lips. He was in a public place, for fuck's sake. He closed his eyes for a moment and took a deep breath, steadying himself. If he didn't stop having these thoughts about her, he'd have an erection that nothing he wore could hide.

He'd called her that morning, just wanting to hear her voice. Maybe, he'd thought, this time he'd say something. Let her know who was making these calls. How special she was to him. But the moment he'd heard her voice, he'd just shut up like a clam. Maybe this wasn't the time to let her know how he felt. Bring it out in the open. So he'd just listened to her angry voice until she hung up.

Taking a moment, he slipped into the men's room, saw that it was empty and pulled his cell out of his pocket. He punched speed dial for the familiar number and listened while it rang. This was dangerous. He never called her when he knew she was with someone else. But seeing her and Ortiz in the same place after last night had his blood boiling. He needed to start letting her know who was boss.

He waited, watching for anyone else to enter, but the phone just rang and rang. He realized with a start it didn't even go to voice mail. What the hell? He hung up and dialed again. Same result. He gave the instrument a hard look. What the fuck was going on? He nearly threw the phone against the wall in his anger but caught himself just in time. Instead he gripped it in his hand, clenching it tightly, and forcing a calm he was far from feeling. He could not afford to let anyone see him like this. Too many questions to answer.

Shit!

Work was calling. But as soon as he was free he'd send her a message that she better not fuck with him again. Even if he never said a word, she'd damn well better take his calls.

Finally settled enough to be around others, he exited the restroom. Maybe he could cut out of work early today. Find out where Tyler was.

And send her a new message.

* * * *

Tyler parked in her driveway, thinking in the back of her mind that she might go out later so the car would be right there in the driveway waiting for her. She let herself into her town house, juggling her mail and three shopping bags, and headed directly for the kitchen. After stashing the food, she took a half bottle of Riesling from the fridge. She grabbed a wine glass and poured a healthy drink for herself. Two swallows and her nerves began to settle. She took the bottle and the glass with her out to her patio, settled in her lounge chair, and filled her glass again. The sun had not yet begun to set but its late day rays bathed everything with a warm glow, soothing her jangled nerves.

For some reason this morning's phone call had unsettled her more than the others. She had basically ignored them in the beginning, thinking they were a wrong number. However, when they persisted, she'd begun to get irritated. It hadn't yet occurred to her to be nervous about them. Now she wondered if she should, if there was something sinister about them.

Dramatic much?

Again the thought popped into her head that some guy in one of the many bars she hung out in might have clipped her number when she left her phone sitting out. Lately after a few drinks, she found herself getting careless about things like that. That was not good. Not good at all. She realized she was falling into a dangerous pattern but wasn't sure how to change it. And here she was ready to head out again tonight and do the same thing.

Stay home, a little voice in her head told her. *Don't go out tonight. Stay away from those places and the men you find there.* At least she wasn't falling into bed so easily any more. Too many unpleasant experiences had effectively killed that urge a very long time ago. Now it was more show than go. Still, she couldn't remember the last time she actually felt the stirrings of real desire.

Then she thought about Rafe and all her girl parts suddenly woke up and began doing a happy dance. What was it about that damn man, anyway? Surely she still didn't have a hangover from her stupid teenage crush, right? She started to take another sip of wine, then stopped as something occurred to her.

She wondered what Rafe Ortiz would think if he knew her dirty little secret—that every time she brought herself to climax it was his face that flashed in her brain.

Suddenly remembering last night's kiss, Tyler pressed the tips of her fingers to her lips, as if she could still feel the imprint of Rafe's mouth there. She inhaled, imagining the drift of his clean male essence in the air. And his touch, his hands on her arms, his cock so thick and swollen pressed against the heat of her pussy. The thin dress had been practically no barrier at all. She smiled with satisfaction, knowing she had aroused him, obviously unwillingly. Good! She'd like to arouse him a little more. She'd like to—

Enough. In or out tonight? She thought about it for a long moment, finally deciding to ditch the cruddy-bar circuit for the night. When she finished the wine, the sun had dipped even lower and she headed inside. Movie and jammies, she decided. And a pizza. Just what she needed.

A long hot shower worked out the kinks. She scrubbed every bit of makeup from her face, wrapped a towel around her wet hair, and creamed every inch of her skin that was visible. After belting a terry robe at her waist, she picked up her phone to order the pizza and suddenly remembered she had left her car in the driveway. She hated to leave it out there all night. Not that she had to worry about more than the weather damaging the custom paint job. Her neighborhood was safe and all that, even if the rare communications from her father included messages to move to a gated community.

Whatever he asked, she always did the opposite. Grudgingly, she admitted to herself that was getting old, too.

Everything was getting old. But it wasn't too late to clean up her act.

Sighing, she stuck her feet into slippers, grabbed her keys from the counter, and automatically put her cell phone in her pocket. On the way to the driveway, she disarmed the security panel so she could get back in easily. The outdoor sconces that she flipped on shone enough light on the driveway for her to see—

She stopped. Stared. Stared even more, frozen in place.

Her tires were slashed. All four, she discovered as she circled the car in a daze. Not just slashed, but destroyed, with deep cuts all around. She might just as well have put a sign on the car that said, "Destroy me." She must have been totally oblivious not to hear anyone. And it was dark enough now that someone could sneak up to her place, crouch down, and get the job done before anyone took notice.

She leaned against the car, suddenly weak and shaky. This person, whoever it was, had been right here in her driveway. Could have walked around to where she sat on the patio. Broken in while she was in the shower. Done God knows what to her. For a moment, she could hardly breathe. Couldn't move. This was more than silent telephone calls.

Don't call the police. You don't need that kind of publicity.

Besides, she could hear her father's voice in her head telling her that was the smart thing to do, so of course she would do just the opposite.

So no police. She didn't need blue lights flashing, photographers capturing every action, the neighbors all standing around whispering about her. No, there was only one person she could call, much as she hated to. Two calls in two days? She could just imagine what he'd be thinking.

When she could make herself move, she unlocked the car and crawled into the driver's seat. She pulled her cell phone from her pocket and, swallowing any misgivings, she punched in the number, praying she'd get an answer.

Please let him answer.

"Ortiz."

Oh, thank God.

"Rafe?" She took a deep breath, let it out. "Hi. It's Tyler." On the off chance that he'd frozen her out of his brain or knew a lot of women with the same name, she added, "Gillette."

There was a long moment of silence. "What now, Tyler? What's going on? Did you get yourself into another mess again?"

Well, of course he'd think that. Why shouldn't he?

"I—Can you come to my house? I have a little problem."

She could almost feel him come to attention over the connection. "Is he there? That guy?"

"No, no, no." Oh, God. "He doesn't even know who I am or where I live."

"So you say." Another pause. Then he repeated, "What's going on?"

"I—Someone slashed my tires. In my driveway."

"Slashed your tires?"

She could tell he was trying not to sound irritated. In a minute, he'd probably tell her to just call a garage and leave him alone. Or wait until the morning and get hold of the dealer. After all, she really wasn't his responsibility. Something pinched inside her when she realized she really had no one who was her go-to person. She'd done a good job of alienating everyone who might fit the bill. She was sure Rafe was only doing this because he worked for her father, because she knew he had little to no use for her. Then he sighed, a sound so audible it carried over the connection.

"Where are you now?" he demanded.

"Inside my car, still outside." And afraid to get out.

"Go in the house and lock the door. I'll be right there. Did you call the cops?"

"No." She shook her head, even though he couldn't see her. "No cops. I mean it, Rafe."

Another long moment of silence stretched across the connection. "All right. Go inside. I'm on my way."

"Thank you." She said it in a small voice. She wasn't sure he heard because he disconnected the call.

Looking carefully all around her, she eased out of the car and let herself into the house. He was coming. He might be furious with her but at least he was coming.

As she stood in the hall, her phone chimed with an incoming text message. She prayed it would be Betsy or one of the few people she'd given the new number to. Fingers shaking, she opened the text.

"Hope you weren't planning 2 drive anywhere tonight. I can get 2 u anywhere."

She slammed the phone down and pulled in a deep breath, hoping she wasn't going to throw up.

Chapter 4

Rafe parked at the curb and sighed as he shut off the engine. So much for rescheduling last night's poker game. He climbed out of his car and walked slowly into the driveway. Tyler had left the outside lights on so the damage to her tires was plainly visible. He walked around the vehicle slowly, then took out his camera and did another circuit, snapping pictures of it. She was lucky the damage wasn't worse. Tires could be replaced. Whoever it was could have keyed her expensive car with the high-gloss finish. Or done something to her engine. Jimmied the brake line if he'd had the time and no one saw him.

Was that really panic he'd heard in her voice when she called? She was such a fucking good actress, she could be playing a scam on him, for whatever reason. Maybe she was pissed off because except for the one tiny lapse, he gave her a wide berth. Of course, that little lapse—the kiss that had scorched his balls—was giving him trouble, too.

There was a possibility this could just be kids making expensive mischief, but Rafe had a feeling that wasn't the answer. Tyler certainly had enough losers who'd passed through her life that one of them could be seeking revenge now. Whoever this was, he didn't think they wanted to harm her. Not yet. This was more about frightening her. Maybe driving her back to him, whoever *him* was, where he could offer safety and protection. And exactly who would that be? Not the losers she picked up in bars, a string of one-night stands he was sure was longer than the ticket line at Southern Bank Stadium. Anyone investigating this would definitely have a full-time job.

He had to figure out the best way to approach this. It was important to let Tyler know she had to take precautions, that she needed to make drastic changes to her lifestyle. The viciousness of the act made Rafe think this was not the first time this asshole had reached out to her. What else had happened? Would she tell him if he asked? Someone had to find out what was going on and take the proper steps with her and for her. He sure as hell didn't want it to be him. Not when that one kiss was an indication of the sexual chemistry waiting to explode between them

Shit.

A headache brewed as he felt himself getting sucked into the whole thing.

He was still standing in the driveway, trying to organize his thoughts, when the front door opened, and he looked up to see Tyler standing there. Immediately he felt an unexpected and certainly unwanted punch to the gut that just looking at her gave him. Big problem.

She blew out a breath. "Pretty bad, isn't it."

He was struck by the fact there was none of the usual bravado in her voice. *Oh, no*, he told himself. *Don't let sympathy take over here. She is what she is, no matter what. And that spells trouble.* He needed to wear his matter-of-fact cloak.

"But fixable," he assured her. "All it takes is your plastic to pay for it. Right? You didn't need me. You could have called a garage to tow it."

She jerked as if he'd slapped her. Her entire posture changed. She hugged her arms around herself as if in protective mode. "You think I called you to help me get new tires? Listen, I guess this wasn't such a good idea after all. Go on back to your own little world. I'll handle this."

Well, jackass, could you be any more hostile or insensitive?

She was his boss's daughter. No matter what he thought of her and her lifestyle, he needed to be courteous at least. Besides, he could see how shaken she was by this, even though she was desperately trying not to show it.

With a deliberate effort, he softened his tone. "Tyler, listen, I'm—"

"Never mind." She bit off each word, her chin lifted defiantly even as a semblance of something resembling pain flashed across her face. "You're absolutely right. I'm probably making too much out of nothing. I'll take care of it like you said. I apologize for interrupting your evening. You can just go on back to whatever you were doing when I called." She paused. "And whoever you were doing it with."

Guilt washed through him. Yeah, jackass was the right name for him.

"I'm sorry, Tyler." He tried to make his voice reassuring. Pleasant, even. "Really. I didn't mean that the way it came out. Just that you're lucky the tires are all that got damaged. That there was an immediate solution for it." He swallowed. "And I'll be happy to help you with that."

She didn't move, just looked at him for a long moment. Her defensive posture was so easy to read. In a minute, she'd tell him to go to hell just to protect herself.

"I think I just overreacted, because…"

He cocked an eyebrow. "Because what? Is something else going on here?"

She looked hard at him then sighed. "You might as well come in. I mean, if you want to."

"I do." He shoved his phone back in his pocket. "I'm coming. I just took some pictures of the tires. For your insurance company," he added.

She stood back to let him enter the town house. As he brushed past her, something delicate teased at his nostrils, the faint scent of wildflowers. Probably whatever soap or shampoo she used. He wondered fleetingly and foolishly what she looked like without any clothes on. Was her skin as creamy all over? Was it soft to the touch? His hormones that seemed to have a mind of their own where she was concerned stood up and did a jig, until he sent them a mental death ray. Maybe he should stick his balls in the freezer so his brain knew to chill out.

"Thank you for coming over." She spoke the words in a stilted, formal tone, jarring him back to the present. "I appreciate it."

"Of course." What was he supposed to say? Kurt Gillette might not have the best relationship with his daughter, but Rafe owed him enough to answer a call for help from Tyler.

"Would you like some coffee?" Still with the stiff voice. "I have a lot of different flavors."

"Sure. Thanks. That would be great. Just regular if you've got it." Drinking coffee might take some of the discomfort out of the situation, although if he were smart he'd get the fuck out of there.

He followed her into the kitchen, hitching himself up onto one of the stools at the serving counter while she busied herself filling mugs. He took a closer look at her in the light. Scrubbed free of makeup, her face had a clean, fresh look that surprised him. It was the same look he'd seen at Al Dente before she'd run to the restroom and slathered the goop on with a trowel. He liked this one a lot better. Her sun-streaked blond hair was pulled back in a careless ponytail, emphasizing skin that minus all the makeup was almost translucent.

The damp ends of her ponytail were an indication she had showered not long before he got there. She wore a short-sleeved faded T-shirt and flannel pants, both worn-looking. Hardly the outfit he'd expect the princess to wear at home. He couldn't help noticing the drape of the flannel pants against her hips and the curve of her ass before they flared over her legs. Without thought, his gaze was drawn to the way the soft material of the tee draped over her breasts. It was obvious she wore no bra, the way her hard nipples poked at the soft fabric. Were they rigid because of him? Did he do that to her? Was she reacting to his presence?

Shit! Again!

Think of ice cubes. Freezing weather. Dead fish. Anything to control the raging hard-on that popped up so suddenly it shocked him. This was Tyler, the woman trying to convince the world she was the sluttiest woman in the city. Maybe in the state, and Texas was a big state. The woman at the top of his Do Not Fuck list. He certainly didn't need her to see his disobedient cock poke at her with the mother of all boners. He shifted position enough to keep the free-standing counter as a barrier between them.

When she turned to hand him a filled mug, he was stunned at the look of vulnerability he saw on her face. Her clear gray eyes, framed by surprisingly dark lashes, held an unexpected sadness, as if life had disappointed her. Then it was gone, so suddenly he wondered if he'd just imagined it. Or hoped for it.

"Let's go into the living room and sit, okay?"

What could he say? I have to hide my misbehaving dick? Instead, he pulled in every thread of self-control and followed her into the large room. She perched on the edge of the couch, so he took the armchair opposite, crossing his legs so one ankle rested on the opposite knee. Camouflage. Okay. That worked.

"Do you have any idea when this happened?" he asked.

She shook her head. "Obviously after dark but I wasn't really paying attention." She cradled her mug in both hands. "I sat out on the patio for a long time."

"How come your car wasn't in the garage?"

She squirmed a little on the chair and took a sip of her coffee before answering him. "I thought I might go out later."

"Oh." Well, that was no surprise. Was there ever a night she stayed home? Not for the first time he wondered how a woman like Tyler Gillette, who had everything going for her, could throw away her life so easily.

"Don't say what you're thinking." She glared at him. "None of the... people I meet know where I live."

He chuffed a sigh of exasperation. "Tyler, you aren't exactly unknown. Your face has been in the media as many times as the mayor. Unless the guys you pick up are deaf, dumb, and blind, they know who you are. They can easily find out where you live."

For a moment pain slashed across her face. Then, as with the other expressions he'd seen, it disappeared, replaced by a carefully arranged mask.

"I'm sure you realize it's not my face they're looking at." She took another sip of her coffee before she focused her gaze straight at him. "Look. I'm sorry I bothered you. This was a bad mistake on my part. I just got a little freaked when I went outside and saw…what I saw. Yes, I can fix it with my credit card. Even get the dealer to send someone out with the tires and change them." She twisted her lips. "Like you said, I'm Tyler Gillette. I can just wave my plastic."

"I didn't mean—"

"No, no, no, it's all right." She looked down at her feet. "You're right. It's probably just some neighborhood kid. I panicked. Again, I'm very sorry I disturbed your evening."

Well now, didn't he just feel like shit? He could see she was desperately trying not to fall apart over this. Just having her tires slashed wouldn't be something she'd feel compelled to call him about. No, this was no neighborhood prank, no matter what she said. There was something going on here he didn't know about and had no idea how to get her to tell him.

Maybe if you'd quit being such a judgmental shithead it would help.

The image flashed into his brain of her standing in the open doorway hugging herself, as if she might fall apart. Now he noticed that her hands were trembling, even though she gripped her coffee mug tightly. Okay, this was more than just someone slashing her tires. He should have figured that out right away. She wouldn't allow herself to bother him if it was just this one incident.

Yes, dickwad. You're the smart security agent who's supposed to be able to read a situation. Maybe he needed virtual reading glasses.

"Have there been other incidents in the neighborhood?" he asked, trying to keep his tone even and calm.

She shrugged, but it didn't quite come off as nonchalant, if that was what she'd intended. "I don't exactly socialize with my neighbors, so I wouldn't know. You think that's what this is? Kids up to trouble around here?"

No, he didn't. And looking at her face intently he saw the tiny lick of fear in her eyes. He set his mug on the table beside his chair, uncrossed his legs, and leaned forward, elbows on knees.

"What's really going on here, Tyler? What else is happening that I don't know about?"

She wet her lower lip, a gentle swipe of a soft pink tongue that sent unwanted messages to his hormones. Somehow all those years of discipline were slowly eroding.

"What makes you think there's anything else?"

"Because you'd never have called your father's head of security," he answered, "if you thought this was just a kid's prank."

He watched her nibble on her lower lip, her forehead creased in thought. He'd been such an ass she probably regretted calling him at all. But if something bad was happening to her, he at least owed it to Gillette to find out what it was.

"Tyler?" he prodded when she still didn't say anything. "I'm asking you again, what's really going on here?"

She wet her lips again. Immediately he had a vision of that same tongue licking his cock. He had to deliberately suppress the surge of hunger that raced through him. *Jesus, Rafe. Get your shit together.* But the damn sizzle between them seemed to be growing hotter and brighter. And though she hadn't given any indication except that incendiary kiss, his gut told him she had the same reaction. Double damn.

"Um, well…" She clutched that coffee mug as if it were a lifeline.

Okay, there was definitely something going on here, besides unbridled lust on his part. Deliberately he yanked his eyes away from her nipples, now as big as gumdrops pressing against the flimsy fabric of her T-shirt. If he could just get his mouth around them—

Shit. Damn. Fuck. And any other curse words he could think of.

"Yes?" he urged again.

"I've, uh, had some hang-up calls."

"Hang-up calls?" Not good. Not good at all. "When and how many?"

She took a healthy swallow of her coffee, avoiding direct eye contact. "A bunch over the past couple of weeks."

He frowned. "What do you consider a bunch?"

She nibbled her lower lip, her forehead creased in a slight frown. "Um, it's not all that bad. I don't think."

"Well?" he prompted. "I didn't think the question was so hard."

Suddenly the words just tumbled out. "It started with just a couple of calls each day, then escalated to about four."

"A day?"

Was she fucking kidding? Did she even realize she had a stalker? Anger surged through him with a violent force. It took a supreme effort of will to maintain his calm. "That many in just two weeks? Jesus, Tyler. Why didn't you change your phone number?"

"I did. Three times. Got the new one just today. And I only gave it to the people I really trust. I'm being very cautious about who gets it."

"Did that work?" He wanted to know. He didn't like the sound of this.

She brushed a few loose strands of hair from her forehead. "Sort of. I mean, no calls, but, uh…"

"But uh what?" he prodded.

"Tonight he sent me a text."

Rafe wanted to bite nails. It was like trying to pull a barnacle from a ship. "Did you ever get a text before?"

She shook her head.

"But you got one tonight. At your brand-new number."

She nodded silently.

Rafe swallowed his irritation. This was like digging for worms. "How about you get the phone and show it to me."

She rose and headed toward the kitchen, Rafe right behind her. She picked up the phone from the counter and turned to hand it to him. He didn't move, so her face landed smack against his hard chest. That elusive scent of wildflowers invaded his nostrils again, sending its tendrils straight to his cock.

"Oh!" She peered up at him, startled.

Think icicles. Ice cubes. Waist-deep in snow.

When she looked up at him with those clear gray eyes and those pouty lips it was all he could do to keep from taking her mouth with a voracious, claiming kiss. Was it because of the situation or did she feel the same things he did? Nope, better not to ask.

With a deliberate exertion of will, he stepped back and took the phone from her hand.

"Pull up the text," she told him, her voice unsteady.

Grateful for the distraction, he hit the Messages app and the most recent one came up on the screen. That certainly killed any hint of lust. Rafe read it twice, forcibly tamping down the anger that surged inside him.

"This is the first one you've gotten? The first text?"

She nodded and stepped deliberately away from him. She dumped her cold coffee in the sink, then refilled the mug from the coffee machine. She probably wouldn't drink this one, either, he figured, although the heat would do her system good.

"Okay, this puts a whole new face on things."

"What do you mean?"

"First, he got your new number less than twenty-four hours after it was assigned to you, so he's got a way to do this. Secondly, he's escalating.

You can hang up on his calls, but you have to read the text before you delete it. Tyler, this is damn serious."

She sighed. "If I'm in for a lecture, let me get you some fresh coffee first."

Outwardly, she was doing her best to be calm, but his trained senses didn't miss the tremor in her voice or the panic in her eyes.

"First thing," he said when they were seated again in the living room, "is I need to take this phone with me."

"But what if he calls and I don't answer?" Fear radiated from her. "If that was him slashing my tires, he might do something worse."

"I'll have one of the guys from the agency sit on your house tonight." When she started to protest, he held up his hand. "That's a given. Either that or you check into a hotel until I get your phone back to you. And by the way, even that wouldn't protect you if he wanted to find you badly enough."

That last bit of color leeched from her face. "So I'm not safe any place."

"You'll be safe tonight with a guard watching you. Hold on."

He pulled out his cell and called the agency. It took less than two minutes to set up what he wanted. He was grateful that he was in a situation there that people didn't question him when he needed something. Disconnecting, he turned back to Tyler. "Tomorrow we'll look at other options."

"What options? What do you have in mind?"

Rafe made his voice as patient as possible, but he needed to get his message across. "We're dealing with someone who has access to sophisticated equipment or who can easily bribe people." It also meant this was no run-of-the-mill, junk-bar stalker. This put things in a different light. "I won't keep the phone long. If he's sending texts, I'm betting he doesn't expect you to answer him. From the tone of this, he's into shaking you up. Making you uncertain and afraid. On edge."

"He's certainly succeeding." She rubbed her arms as if chilled.

He gave her a crooked grin. "Tyler, I didn't think you were afraid of anything."

For a moment, that expression of elusive vulnerability washed over her face. Then it was gone just as quickly.

"Is that how you see me?" She stared hard at him. "As fearless?"

"Maybe more as a go-to-hell, I'm-not-afraid-of-anything attitude," he told her. "I got the feeling you just kicked life in the teeth."

"And not in a good way," she added. "Right?"

This wasn't good. She had a real problem, and he didn't need to make it worse with his sarcasm. She needed help and it was up to him to see that she got it.

"I'm sorry." He rubbed his face. "You've got a problem here, and we can't ignore it. A serious problem. I understand now why you called me tonight. That was smart."

Her posture relaxed just a fraction. "Thank you."

"And I'm glad you did, believe it or not. This is nothing to fool around with." He stuck the phone in his pocket. "I'll get your cell back to you tomorrow, but in the morning, I want to run it over to the agency office first thing. See if we can get a trace on the number from the text. Find out whose it is."

"You can do that?" She gave him a questioning look. "At that office?"

He nodded. "We have the equipment plus we can check with your provider. They store all the information on your calls, incoming and outgoing. And you definitely need to tell your father. I'm serious."

The more he realized how much of what people saw was an act, the more concerned he became for her. This was no hard-ass chick who could handle anything. The more time he spent with her, the more he realized this was a vulnerable woman who was now in real danger. He had to figure out how to make her be sensible about it.

"No." She slammed her coffee mug down on the table hard enough that some of the liquid sloshed over the rim. "I'm not telling my father anything. You can forget that."

"He needs to know," Rafe insisted. "Whatever the problems are between you two, he won't want you to be unprotected when there's danger."

"Not. Telling. My. Father." She enunciated each word carefully and distinctly.

God, the woman was impossible.

"You need protection," he went on. "I'm damn sure if I tell you to be careful you'll laugh in my face. Right?"

He watched her try to settle herself with a sip of her coffee. Even under the circumstances, every movement she made was so graceful. This was driving him nuts. *She* was driving him nuts. He needed to get as much information as he could, make sure she understood that the kind of calls she'd been receiving and things like slashed tires could turn very ugly, and hand her over to someone at Lone Star Security.

She glared at him. Apparently, her anger was stronger than her fear, especially when it came to her father. The last thing he wanted was to get in the middle of a family squabble. He'd never understood that relationship, anyway. But all his instincts told him she was in real danger. First the calls, then the tires and the text? This guy was escalating.

"Did you hear what I said?" he asked.

"I thought maybe you could just figure out a way to find out who it is, go see him, and throw a scare into him." She lifted one graceful shoulder and let it drop. "You know."

"Just like that." He sighed. "It's not that simple, Tyler."

She frowned. "Why not? You can just pay him a visit, make a few threats, and get him to stop doing this stuff."

He raked his fingers through his hair. "Because unless I have the kind of proof that will put him in jail, he'll just smile, kick me out of his place, and step up his game. I don't think he's going to scare quite as easy as you think."

"Step up his game?" she repeated. "But—"

"Whoever this is, he has a plan." Rafe dialed down his impatience and tried to make his voice as calm as possible. "The kind of person that does this isn't just in it to annoy you. He has a specific end game in mind. That can be anything from ruining your life to driving you into his arms to…"

"To what?" Her voice rose a little. "To what, Rafe? What does he want? Because I just thought it was some guy jerking off while he drove me nuts."

Rafe nodded. "And he could be doing that. Nothing more. But we can't ignore everything else. This could be some guy you've really pissed off, and he wants to have his revenge. Which is why I want to get Lone Star Security to assign someone to you until we track down who this is."

"No." She shook her head and waved her hand so violently it knocked her coffee mug off the little table where it was sitting. "No bodyguard or whatever. At least not where it's connected to my—my father. I don't want him in my business."

"Tyler." He put as much patience into his voice as he could. "You called your father's head of security. Didn't you think he'd be bound to find out?"

She shrugged. "I hoped you could keep it just between us."

He studied her while she mopped up the spill and cleaned it so it wouldn't stain. When she was finished, she just stood in the living room, looking down at her feet. Then she lifted her gaze to Rafe. In those few minutes, he saw a transformation in her, and not one that pleased him. The aura of fear was nearly gone, replaced by anger and something he was at a loss to define.

"I guess I made a mistake calling you," she told him in a low voice. "No need to do anything that would involve my father. Really. I think I made too much of this. I freaked and I'm sorry. I apologize for ruining your evening. Again. I won't bother you anymore."

Oh, no, she wasn't doing this to him. She might not have all her war paint on, and the skintight clothes, but the minute her father came into the picture the go-to-hell Tyler was back. Damn. Well, too bad. She'd dragged him into this. Now he wasn't letting her push him out until things were settled. In plain English, he told her as much.

She just shook her head. "Like I said, I never should have made the call. I didn't stop and think, idiot that I am. Of course you'd have to let my father know. I won't bother you again."

He raked his fingers through his hair in frustration. "Tyler, I can't just—"

"Just what? Walk away? Why not? I'm nothing to you, Rafe. And even less to the vaunted Kurt Gillette. I'll find someone to help me that isn't connected to him or you or the team."

He didn't believe a word she said, but this wasn't the time to argue with her.

"If that's how you want it."

"So good. Then we're done here. You can just leave." She pointed to her front door. "Now. Again, sorry for bothering you."

Rafe was amazed. Traces of fear and rage still swirled in her eyes, but now something else was mixed with it. Some indefinable emotion lurking behind the mask that Tyler Gillette showed to the world. He damn sure wished he knew what it was or how to find out.

"It wasn't a bother."

"Well, I'm sorry to disturb your evening anyway." She marched to the front door and held it open for him. "I won't bother you again."

Great. Could he have handled this any worse? He rose slowly from the chair he was sitting in, trying to figure out how to convince she needed some protection here. Unfortunately, he didn't think that was possible. He'd have to figure something else out, but obviously not tonight. He'd managed to fuck that up royally.

Still, didn't the damn woman know she wasn't safe?

"I'm going to get someone here, whether you want him or not," he insisted. "Let me do that, will you? Your safety is important, Tyler."

"Listen to me. No. Guard. None. Period. Not from you."

He could force it but she'd just keep arguing. His best strategy was to call in a favor from a friend and have him find a place to surveil her without her knowing.

"Fine. Lock everything and set your alarm after I leave."

"I'll be okay," she told him in a stiff voice. "Good night, Mr. Ortiz. Enjoy the rest of your evening."

He wanted to tell her this wasn't over, but he doubted she'd even hear him. He'd just go around her and couldn't that turn out to be a big fucking mess. He paused at the open door.

"We're not done here, Tyler. You're at risk, and you need to be protected."

"Not by you or anyone connected to the Hawks," she insisted again. "Stay out of my business, Rafe. I mean it."

"We'll see." Out on her porch he turned back to her. "Be sure to set the alarm."

"I'm not stupid. Stubborn, but not stupid. Good night."

The door closed with a slam. Rafe was not looking forward to the next day.

Chapter 5

Rafe was back the following day with her phone and not much good news about tracing the caller.

"It's a burner," he told her. "We're checking the serial number to see where it was sold. Maybe we can find something that way, but I don't hold out much hope."

"Thanks for trying." When he stood in the doorway, making no move to leave, she asked, "Was there something else?"

"As a matter of fact, yes." He looked at her as if he could see right through her, a look that made her shiver. "Your stalker called three times while I had the phone and sent another text."

"What?" Nausea rumbled up from deep inside her, and she swallowed hard. "Are you serious?"

"As a heart attack. I answered them but without saying a word. I hoped we could get a trace, pinpoint a location, while the connection was open." He shook his head. "No such luck."

She stuck the phone in her pocket, doing her best not to let him see how her hand trembled. And it wasn't just the terror of the situation. Days later, her lips still remembered the feel of that kiss, the heat that sizzled through her, the electricity that snapped in the air. She needed to erase the memory somehow. This man was absolute poison to her, disdainful of her as he was. But oh God, between panic attacks about her stalker, she'd wondered what his body would look like naked and—

"Tyler." His voice burst her mind bubble. "Are you okay?"

"What? Oh, yes. I'm fine." She gave a slightly hysterical little laugh. "Well, as good as can be under the circumstances. Thank you for trying to get information."

"Have you done anything about getting protection the way you said you would?"

She looked down at her feet. "Yes. I made some calls. It's being taken care of."

"Liar."

"I said I'd take care of it," she reminded him and forced a smile. "And again, you have my word I won't bother you again."

He studied her for so long she wondered what on earth he was thinking. "Got your tires all taken care of?" he asked finally.

Now that was the last thing she'd expected. "I did. First thing this morning. Just waved my plastic and made it happen the way you said."

"I apologize for that remark. You had a problem, and I was being a sarcastic idiot. Would it be okay with you if I checked them over?"

Damn. What was with this nice act? She dealt with him a lot better when they were at odds with each other.

She shrugged, hoping she looked nonchalant. "They're just tires, but if you want to, sure."

She opened the inside door to the garage and stood there while he walked all around the car, crouching down to check each tire.

"I got the correct ones, if that's what you're looking for," she told hm.

"I can see that. Just making sure." He stood up. "And that's not a sarcastic remark, by the way. Just habit."

Oh. Sure. Nothing special for the waste case Tyler Gillette.

"Well. Uh, thank you. I guess."

When she stood aside for him to move past her into the hallway, he brushed against her and that wonderful Rafe Ortiz leathery scent teased at her. The pulse between her thighs woke up and began to drum the "Anvil Chorus" and her nipples beaded harder than they had the night before. And hadn't that just been damn embarrassing. How could she have the hots for a man who wouldn't be seen at the garbage dump with her?

Rafe Ortiz was not a player. That had been the line on him from day one. He was a solid, substantial citizen, whose private life always flew under the radar.

"Tyler?"

She realized he was speaking to her and gave her brain a mental shove.

"Sorry. My mind must have wandered. Thank you for checking the phone and for bringing it back."

"I meant what I said." The look he gave her was intense, the blue of his irises now darkened to the navy of a storm-tossed sea. "You need to be careful. Stay out of trouble until we find this guy. Because I can promise you he is far from finished."

"Thank you for your concern, but it's all good now." If he thought so little of her, she'd make sure he didn't have to waste one second of his precious time on her. "I have my phone, I'll keep my doors locked, and I'll be fine."

He scowled, opened his mouth as if to say something then just shook his head. "Be careful, Tyler."

Then he was gone. She set the alarm, then leaned against the door, wishing her world would stop spinning. She needed to get her life back, such as it was. A life that did not include Rafe Ortiz. She had been incredibly foolish in calling him to begin with. She shouldn't have panicked when the massive mountain of man, Dewey, had cornered her in the ladies' room. The bartender would have handled it if she'd just been a little patient. And why had her natural inclination been to call Rafe anyway?

Because she had such a strong thing for him, it just wouldn't let go of her. Now she couldn't get the tantalizing scent of his cologne out of her nostrils or the imprint of his lips from her mouth. Sometimes without realizing it, she actually found herself rubbing her fingertips across her bottom lip.

He was a man who had matured well. The older he got, the sexier he got. Not that she had that much occasion to interact with him. But there were the obligatory Hawks events she attended. She had always tried to flirt with him a little, but he was not having any of it. Ever.

If only he wasn't such a hard-ass where she was concerned. Had she thought reaching out to him the other night would make a difference? Yeah, that had turned out really well.

Sighing, she pushed away from the door and headed to the kitchen. Coffee. That's what she needed. And maybe a brain transplant.

For the next twenty-four hours, she holed up in her town house, having her food delivered, and watching old movies on television. Both Betsy and Lynn were out of town, but they kept texting her to make sure she was okay.

"Watching old movies," she finally texted. *"All is good."*

"Make popcorn," Betsy texted back on their three-way message.

"Drink wine with it," Lynn added.

She hugged the phone to her body, warmed by their friendship and their concern.

She hadn't planned to go trolling at night again. Kept reminding herself of the episode with Dewey, of the hang-up calls, the text. The tires, for God's sake!

But she hadn't had any calls since Rafe returned her phone, so she thought it possible the jerk, whoever he was, had gotten tired of his game. Maybe he knew Rafe had tried to trace the calls and decided it wasn't worth the risk. And she was bored being closeted in the house by herself. She'd hate to let people know it, but she really didn't like her own company all that much. It was time to put on her usual war paint and uniform and get back into her scene.

When she took one last look at herself in the mirror, she was tempted just to say the hell with it, scrub her face clean, throw on some old sweats, and crawl into bed. But she was in such a turmoil over everything, and she'd been the Tyler the world knew for so long she was having trouble being anything different. So she'd just take the one she was coming to despise and drag her ass out into the night.

Dressed and primped, she hauled herself to Mickey's, another of her favorites on the south side of the city. But two hours on a bar stool later, she found herself wondering what she was doing there. She hadn't even had a taste of alcohol tonight, shocking both herself and the bartender. Instead she sat there with her third fake martini, wearing her skintight black dress cut down to *there* in the front and *there* in the back and giving the automatic come-on to the guy sitting on the bar stool next to her.

She thought this was how actresses must feel when they had played a part one too many times. She had the costume, she knew the lines, but the audience response just wasn't doing it for her. When she was younger, it had been more fun to see how many buttons she could push, how much unfavorable publicity could fall on the mighty Kurt Gillette because of his daughter's outrageous behavior. She'd made an art form out of pushing the envelope. But it seemed the wilder she became, the more he turned away from her. The Hawks were his baby, not her, and he'd made it known that she should have been a son to take over from him.

She'd been ten when her mother had died suddenly and her life had turned upside down. Her father had dealt with his grief by burying himself in the team operations. But she'd had grief, too. Right? Why had he never seen that? She'd tried desperately to please him all the time she'd been growing up, to show him that she could be as important to him as a son. Nothing worked. He didn't get angry with her. He didn't get anything. He ignored her. Sent her away. Gave her money and told her to keep busy. The fact that she had—to his way of thinking—insulted him by being a daughter instead of a son only made things worse. He had even given her a boy's name. Tyler. Who named their daughter Tyler?

Her outrageous behavior was the only thing that had ever gotten a response from him. At least she had him tearing his hair out. She supposed that was better than nothing.

Except she'd only wanted him to love her.

Grow up, Tyler. Get over yourself. It's a lost cause.

Yes, it was. She'd literally destroyed herself and for nothing. Nothing.

So here she was, in yet another seedy dive, looking to —What? What exactly was she looking for?

Taking a sip of her drink, she tried to focus on what the guy next to her was saying.

"So how about it?" Mr. Nobody asked, leaning a little closer.

Tyler's nose wrinkled as she inhaled the excess of cheap cologne. Obviously, she needed the alcohol to do this because cold sober she wanted to pick up the nearest heavy object and bash this guy over the head.

"Hey!" He poked her shoulder with his forefinger. "You're not smashed already, are you?" Then he gave a gravelly laugh. "Although I don't know, some broads do it better when they're drunk. Are you one of them?"

She could have told him she had no idea, since she hadn't "done it" for so long she wasn't sure she could even remember how. But when she did, it certainly wasn't going to be with the guy next to her. What was she doing here, anyway? Whoever the weirdo was that was calling her and slashing her tires could be watching her. Maybe he wasn't through with her after all. Maybe he'd followed her from her town house. Was he in this bar even now, watching her, waiting to make his next move? An itchy feeling suddenly crawled up her spine.

Tyler looked around the very dimly lit bar but no one popped out at her. How would she know it was him, anyway? This was crazy.

Shit.

Dumb, Tyler. Very dumb.

Maybe this hadn't been such a good idea after all. She needed to get out of here. Grabbing her little purse and opening it, she took out a twenty, which she slid beneath her nearly full glass on the bar.

"I think I'm done for the night," she told the bartender.

He winked at her. "Wish I could say the same. Take it easy out there."

As she slid off the bar stool, the guy next to her grabbed her upper arm. "Hey! Wait a minute, here. We was just getting started."

Tyler was tired and disgruntled and out of sorts, and not in the mood for his crap. Even though she had to admit, his crap was her fault. She just didn't have the stomach for it tonight, so she took the flesh of his upper arm and pinched it as hard as she could.

"Ouch! Hey!" He released her arm and rubbed his own. "You just had to say you weren't interested."

"I think she did," the bartender told him.

"Yeah?" The guy scowled. "Well, maybe I'm not ready to take no for an answer after all."

Tyler eased quickly past him just as he slapped some money down on the bar and hitched himself off the stool. As she headed out the door, she grabbed her keys from her purse, holding them like a weapon between her fingers as someone had taught her a long time ago. Her skinny heels clicked hard on the painted concrete floor as she pushed out into the night and hurried toward her car. The sound of his footfalls behind her made her speed up even more, or as much as she could with her tight skirt and stupid needle heels.

"Hey, wait!"

She turned at the sound of his yell, ready to stab him with the keys, when a dark shape materialized from the other size of her car. In a moment, a sizable fist had grabbed the big guy by the front of his shirt and held him in place.

"I don't think the lady wants your company tonight." Rafe's deep voice bounced the words off the man he was holding. "You'd be best served if you just went right back on into that bar."

Tyler couldn't believe her eyes. What was he doing here? She clutched her purse and her keys as she watched the scene in front of her unfold. She'd known from the way his clothes fit him that he kept himself in shape. There wasn't an ounce of fat anywhere on that body. In the near dark of the parking area, he was an ominous presence. Apparently, the jerk from Mike's realized it, too. He just nodded his head, made some kind of nasty remark, and headed back inside.

"Good riddance." Rafe said the words as if he were cursing.

Tyler still stood there as if frozen to the ground. God! The timbre of that voice sent shivers dancing down her spine. It also kicked up her pulse and made her nipples tingle. The sight of him in his dark jeans that outlined muscular legs and a yellow, soft-collar shirt that emphasized his broad shoulders actually made her mouth water. Damn it all anyway. Would she never get control of her hormones where this man was concerned?

She was just so damn glad to see him that she was ready to throw herself at him and see if she could steal another of those panty-melting kisses. But when he spoke to her all thoughts of sex fled from her mind.

"Close your mouth," he told her. "You're catching flies."

She finally found her voice. "What are you doing here?"

"Making sure trouble isn't following you." He glared at her. "It appears it's a damn good thing I did. I can't believe with a stalker on your ass you're out in the same old crummy scene."

She was halfway between grateful he was there and pissed off that he was lecturing her. Again. And how on earth had he known where she was?

"Are you now my appointed guardian?" She knew how bitchy she sounded, but she just didn't want him following her around and spreading his disapproval everywhere. She never should have called him the other night from Tequila Sunrise. Or when her tires got slashed. She was used to taking care of herself. She'd done it all her life. Her panic was a momentary lapse and she needed to get over it. If she couldn't entice him into bed, she needed to keep away from him.

"It sure looks like you need one."

"I'm taking care of myself just fine."

"Is that so?" He snorted. "Doesn't look like it to me."

Tyler glowered at him. What was that saying? Never let them see you sweat. Well, she wasn't going to let Rafe High-and-Mighty Ortiz see her sweat. Ever again.

"Look." She tucked her hair behind her ears. "This is my fault. I never should have called you the other night. I appreciate what you did, but you can go back to your regular life now. You don't need to chase me around. I can handle things."

"Yeah, I can see how well you're doing that." He nodded toward her car. "Go on, get in, before someone else tries to join the party."

"You don't give me orders." She tried to pull up her best defiant posture. "No one does. I take care of myself."

He drew his brows together in a scowl. "So you're not going home?"

"I *am* going home." She unlocked her car door. "But because *I* want to."

"Fine. Whatever. As long as you go."

She expected him to just watch her until she drove away, but instead he got in his car and started it up. When she pulled out into the street, he was right behind her, and stayed that way all the way back to her town house. She thought about trying to lose him, but he'd probably prove to be a better driver. Besides, why bother? She'd let him see she was safely home, then he could wash his hands of her and go back to—whatever he wanted to go back to.

As she drove through the streets of the city, Tyler turned on her radio. She hoped music would smooth out the unsettled feeling that had crept up on her, the reason she'd boogied out of the bar. Nothing appealed to her, though, and about the time she finished searching for something, she was pulling into her driveway.

How had he found her tonight? He hadn't answered that question. Was he going to be there every time she turned around? Her evil brain whispered, *Maybe you can convince him to have some fun.* Unfortunately, she didn't think Rafe wanted to have fun, at least with her. He was practically on her bumper while the garage door opened. When she got out of the car, he climbed out of his and came to stand next to her.

"Before you say a word," she said, holding out a hand as if to stop him from coming closer, "I want to know how you knew where I was tonight."

"Not important."

"So you say. Well, it is to me. Did you follow me to the bar? That's really creepy, Rafe."

"No. I didn't have to."

She glowered at him for a moment. "So how did you know where I was tonight?"

He grinned. "If I tell you, I'll have to kill you."

"Oh, no," she protested. "Not playing that game. Did you put something on my phone? On my car? I want an answer here. You'd better explain yourself."

For a very long moment, he said nothing. Then he heaved a long sigh. "When I checked your tires the other day, I put a GPS locator on your car."

Stars exploded in her brain as anger surged through her. "You *what*? Are you shitting me?"

He shook his head. "Not a bit. You have a stalker, Tyler. It's now official, as far as I'm concerned. You go looking for trouble, and it's easier for me to bail you out when I find you than it is to search the damn city."

"Bail me out? I don't need your bailing, thank you very much."

His perfect mouth kicked up in a humorless smile. "Is that a fact? What about the other night at Tequila Sunrise? And tonight at Mike's. You could say I saved your ass both times."

Yes, but she wasn't about to admit it.

"I want you to remove it right now. Or I'll get somebody else to." When he didn't move, she said, "I mean it, Rafe. Now."

He gave her a hard look then shrugged, walked around to the driver's side of the car, bent down, and when he stood up had something in his hand. He held it up for her to see.

"Done. But this is a mistake."

"The mistake," she stressed the word, "was calling you in the first place. It won't happen again."

"You know, Tyler, it's bad enough when you get twisted up with some of the trash in the places you hang out, but some idiot is after you. He's probably just getting started. These things escalate, and the least little thing sets them off."

"Like I said, it's been a few days without calls. He's probably gotten bored with me and moved on to someone else." And didn't she just hope so.

He studied her silently for a long moment that stretched out until she felt like squirming. Finally, he spoke again. "No more hang-up calls? No more tire-slashing incidents or anything like it?"

"Well," she snarked, "since I've been driving around on my new tires I'd say they're just fine. And no, no more calls."

He took a step toward her. "Tyler, you need to take this thing seriously. I still want you to talk to your father about it. He needs to know what's going on."

"No. Did I say no? And…no."

"Next time you get yourself into a situation like the last two," he warned, "I might not be handy to pull you out of them. Kurt needs to arrange for protection for you."

"Not happening, so forget it. Now if you don't mind, I want to go inside so I can get ready for bed."

He shook his head. "Whatever. You're in for the night, I hope." His voice was uninflected, even. Confident, as if he expected her to do what he said.

"Yes, Daddy. I'm going to tuck myself in bed." She gave him a devilish grin. "Unless you want to do the honors."

She saw a muscle twitch in his cheek, the only sign that she was getting to him.

"I think you can handle that."

For a moment, he didn't move. Then he stepped back so she could walk around her car to the inside door.

"I'm closing the garage door," she told him, finger poised over the automatic door button. "If you don't want to get locked inside here, you'd better move."

He looked at her, his expression dead serious. "You might hate my guts, Tyler, and I might not approve of your lifestyle, but I want you to remember what I'm going to tell you. You have my phone number. Don't hesitate to use it. When you're in trouble and need someone you can call me. Any time. No matter what."

Emotions clogged her throat. He was probably the only person she knew that she could really depend on, and she had no idea why he even made the offer. Like a wind blowing against her face, she felt the pressure of his mouth again, her fingers automatically touching her lips. That kiss was seared into her body and her mind, and for a moment, she wondered what he'd say if she stepped up to him and pulled him close for another one.

Before she could even take a step, he moved toward the driveway. "Don't forget to reset your alarm and be careful answering the phone." He turned and headed out to the driveway. "I'll be seeing you," he called over his shoulder as he walked away.

If only he'd at least sounded a little more enthusiastic about it.

Sighing, Tyler walked inside, made sure the alarm was reset, and headed into the kitchen. She wondered what things would have been like if she and Rafe had met under different conditions.

Needing something to settle herself down, she pulled a half-empty bottle of Riesling out of the fridge. She had just taken down a wineglass when her cell phone began jiggling on the counter and the staccato drumbeat pounded at her. Distracted, she reached for the phone and pressed Talk without even thinking or looking at the readout.

"Hello?"

No answer.

Tyler repeated, "Hello?"

Still nothing.

"Whoever you are, leave me alone." She almost shouted the words, then steadied herself with a deep breath. "I mean it. Quit calling. Quit sending me flowers. Quit everything. Don't bother me anymore. I have protection."

She started to press End when she heard a laugh, eerie, as if it were coming from the bottom of a barrel. Tyler dropped the phone as if it burned her hand. She just stared at it, waiting to see if any further sounds came from it. But when it was silent for a couple of minutes, she picked it up off the floor, holding it as if it were contagious. Well, that's what she got for being stupid enough to answer it. She should just get rid of the damn thing but to what end? He'd find out her new number eventually.

She carried the wine and glass into her bedroom and set them down while she undressed. Minutes later, she was dressed in flannel pants and a long-sleeved tee, huddled under her covers. The chill she felt didn't come from her air-conditioning. It emanated from deep inside her bones. Her hand shook as she lifted the glass of wine to her lips, some of it sloshing on the comforter. She gulped it as if it were water.

Who in hell was doing this to her? And why? She knew she'd pissed off a lot of people, but she couldn't imagine any of them as a nut job like this. It just was not their style. Maybe she should go away for a while. Get out of the area. Of course, if he was a person who could find her unlisted cell-phone numbers, he could find her any place she ran.

Damn.

Had she done this to herself, become the object of a stalker because of her years of outrageous behavior? Was that what she'd turned herself into? A bitter taste surged in her mouth and the agony of realization swept through her. Was this what she wanted for the rest of her life? She hadn't gotten the attention from her father she wanted and she'd become the object of pity for someone like Rafe Ortiz. She'd tossed away her life for nothing.

She took another deep swallow of wine. Maybe she could drink enough to knock herself out.

Well, one thing was for sure. She might be feeling unsettled and, okay, maybe even scared, but she was not going to run to Kurt Gillette. The man had all but washed his hands of her. All she'd get from him was a lecture and she wasn't about to listen to it.

Rafe had said she could call him, but had he really meant it? Something was brewing between them, and she didn't know if it was good or bad. Or if she had the courage to find out.

Draining the rest of the wine, she huddled under the covers, pulling them up to her chin. She just hoped she didn't dream about this scary stranger. And luckily, she didn't. Instead, just as she fell asleep, the image of a handsome, very sexy former football player with hair like black silk and a wicked gleam in his eyes floated just beneath her consciousness.

Chapter 6

Tyler still felt unsettled when she woke up in the morning. Her sleep had been restless, her dreams filled with a combination of images of Rafe and of a faceless man chasing her. At seven-thirty, she finally dragged herself out of bed, brushed her teeth, and headed downstairs to the kitchen for a mug of coffee. The first sip of the hot liquid rushed through her system and blasted away at the cobwebs in her brain left by the wine she drank before she fell asleep. Good thing she hadn't had any hard liquor, or she'd feel really bad.

Leaning against the counter, she clasped the mug with both hands and closed her eyes for a moment. Bad move. Immediately Rafe's face swam in front of her. She popped her eyes open. God. If she could only convince him to have one hot night with her, she could get him out of her system. But that wasn't Rafe's style. From day one of his rookie year, he hadn't been any kind of a playboy, a man who lusted after groupies. He'd never taken advantage of the veritable banquet of flesh available to the heroes of the gridiron. She seldom attended the games, only under duress, but she heard gossip at team events and certainly kept up with the social swim online.

Rafe Ortiz had always been known as serious, grounded. She knew he'd bought a house for his family and put his younger sister through college. That was as much as she knew. Solid, stable. A rule follower. Maybe that was another reason she was so hot to get him into bed. The more he resisted, the more she focused on it. But no matter how she tried to tempt him at team functions, or any other time she ran into him, he always smiled politely and excused himself.

Well, enough focusing on him. She had other concerns. She would never admit it to Rafe, not after his criticism of her, but she had to figure out what to do about her stalker. She had no idea what he'd do next. Maybe nothing, but maybe something worse. Again, she tried to come up with alternatives. She could invade Betsy's or Lynn's homes, but then she'd have to tell them the whole story and maybe put them in the line of fire. She realized with depressing clarity that except for her very tiny inner circle she really had no friends. Certainly none that she could go and visit, and she was fast becoming tired of her own company.

She thought about it while she showered and shampooed. While she lathered cream on her body and blow-dried her hair. She was still thinking about it when her brand-new phone, which she'd left on her nightstand while she showered, chimed an incoming text.

There weren't too many people it could be. Maybe Betsy or Lynn was texting her. Was it Rafe checking up on her? But when she looked at the screen the readout said Blocked, just like the other calls and the text, and nausea rumbled up from her stomach. She supposed she could get yet another number, even another phone, but what was the use? Apparently, he tracked her new setup down without any problem.

How in hell did he keep doing it? What was his source? If she ever figured that out, maybe she could discover who this was. Maybe she could ask Rafe—

Sick curiosity prompted her now to pick up the phone and press the message icon.

"I cld have hlpd you last night. U shld not ignore me."

She dropped the phone on the bed as if it were a bug that had bitten her. Ignore him? Who the hell was she ignoring? Plenty of people approached her when she was at different functions, figuring dating Kurt Gillette's daughter would get them close to the seat of power. He was one of the city's power brokers. Besides owning the Hawks and the stadium, he was involved in important projects and always on everyone's A-list. Ha! If they only knew how he felt. His daughter was an annoyance. She was surprised he hadn't asked her to change her name by now.

And last night? The only way whoever this was could have known about last night was if he was following her. The thought sent a chill skating over the surface of her skin.

Positive she was wasting her time—*it said Blocked, dummy*—nevertheless she typed a return message and hit Send. Undeliverable. Well, of course it was. She wasn't exactly sure how all that worked, but she had to try it, just to satisfy herself. She sat down on the bed, the phone held loosely in her hand, and rubbed her forehead. Now what should she do?

First of all, get dressed, she told herself, realizing she was still wearing her robe. She grabbed a pair of yoga pants and a T-shirt and dragged them on. Then she took a scrunchee out of the vanity drawer and pulled her hair that she'd styled so carefully into a careless ponytail. No fashion statement for her today.

Who are you? she asked the image in the mirror. Maybe it was time for her to find out. Time to quit pushing Kurt Gillette's buttons in the hope he'd give her *any* kind of attention. Time to face facts and move forward, and not as some tarted-up joke.

She thought about leaving the cell in her bedroom, but what if Betsy or one of the others actually tried calling her? Shoving the phone in her pocket, she refilled her coffee mug in the kitchen and was just trying to figure out what to do next when the doorbell rang. Tyler frowned. She wasn't expecting company and her close friends knew not to just drop in on her.

Damn! It was the freaking florist again. She yanked the door open.

"Take them back," she snapped. "And don't bring me any more. Ever."

The face that peeked at her around the enormous arrangement was young. The driver could not have been more than eighteen.

"I-I'm sorry, ma'am. I'm just doing the deliveries."

Tyler sighed. "I know. Does it say who it's from this time?"

"No, ma'am. But there's a card here."

She held out her hand. "Give it." She slipped it from the small white envelope. *I won't give up. I can shower you with flowers every day.*

Nausea roiled up from her stomach. In the beginning, Nate's clumsy attempts to effect a reconciliation had been both laughable and annoying. But this was beyond seductive, or whatever it was supposed to be. If it was from him, he needed to stop. And the phone calls, too, if he was also doing those.

Shivering, she closed the door and locked it, resetting the alarm. She was just about to take of coffee for herself when the doorbell rang again.

Fucking damn.

When she peeked out through the window beside the front door her stomach dropped, then bounced for good measure. It was bad enough that Rafe stood there, looking sinfully sexy in black slacks and a red Hawks polo shirt. She would have been licking her lips over him except for the bear of a man standing with him—her father.

Holy hell.

Shock immobilized her, and the little girl who still hid inside her was thrilled that her father had actually come to see her. He was here. Her father was right here. The man had never been to her town house in all the time she'd lived here. In fact, since she'd moved out of his McMansion and into her own place, he hadn't given her so much as a housewarming gift. *Now* he showed up?

Well, hell.

Then she gave herself a mental kick. This was not going to be a pleasant visit. He had his combative face on, and she knew what that meant. Had Rafe told the man about the episode at Tequila Sunrise or the one at Mike's? She'd have to kill him if he had, slowly and painfully.

She wanted to run and hide in the bedroom until they went away, but knowing the two of them—especially her father—that wouldn't work. If, after all this time, he was here at her front door, he wasn't about to leave quietly. Especially if Rafe was with him. Rafe, who had probably tattled on her thinking he was doing his civic duty or something.

She glanced at herself in the little mirror in the hall and suddenly wished for different clothes, different makeup, and hair artfully arranged. The disguise she always hid behind. Well, shit. What the hell, anyway? He didn't give a damn about her. Neither of them did.

After punching in the code for the alarm, she opened the door and stood there, arms folded across her chest.

"Oh, look. It's the guardian angel and daddy dearest. How sweet." She figured sarcasm was her best defense.

"Good morning, Tyler." This was Rafe. "We'd like to come in for a few minutes." He bent down and lifted something to the left of the door. "You'd better put these in water. Someone left them for you."

Tyler looked at the enormous arrangement of flowers and trembled all over. The damn delivery guy had apparently just left them. She wanted them gone.

"Just leave them out there," she said. "I don't want them in the house."

"They'll die out there without care."

"Good. Then I can throw them away."

Rafe looked at her intently then just set the flowers back outside.

Even as angry as she was with him, she couldn't help noticing how gorgeous he was and how incredibly sexy. She wanted to run her hands through the black silk of his hair and stroke the chiseled line of his jaw. Rub herself up against him and inhale the richly enticing scent of sun-warmed leather. Of course hell would freeze over first, she reminded herself. His choice.

She reached for every molecule of the go-to-hell cloak she wore and tugged it tightly around herself. She gave both men a look she hoped would fry them on the spot.

"Whatever you're selling, I'm not buying." She looked from one to the other. "From either of you. This is a wasted trip."

Rafe stood in front of her father, his shockingly blue eyes now the navy color they turned when he was serious. Uh-oh. She knew she wasn't going to like whatever this was about. Had he tattled to her father about her situation? Of course he had, Mr. I Do The Right Thing. Damn him, anyway.

"I think it's important for us all to talk." He glanced at the man next to him. "Your father has some things he'd like to say."

"Finally?" She snorted. "I'll just bet he does. No thanks."

She started to back up and close the door, but Rafe held it open with the flat of his hand.

"We can do this the easy way or the hard way, Tyler, but we're coming in. So how about we go into the kitchen, get some coffee, and have a little chat."

Tyler glared at him, torn between spitting in his face and standing on tiptoe to plant a kiss on that mouth that she still remembered so vividly. Finally, she blew out a breath and took a step back into the foyer.

"Okay. Come on in. This should be a lot of fun."

She turned and walked into the kitchen, hoping her shaky legs would support her. Behind her, she heard the sound of the front door closing and sensed rather than heard the two men follow her.

"You have a very nice place here," Kurt commented.

"You sound surprised. What did you expect, someplace that looked like a bordello?"

When he didn't say anything, she glanced back at him and saw that he was visibly controlling himself. Was that a flash of hurt she saw wash across his face? No. Impossible. He was only concerned about his football players.

"I want to know what's up with you." She gave her father a piercing look. "All of a sudden you're interested in my welfare? Is this some kind of a joke?"

"Let's not get confrontational before we have to." Rafe's voice smoothed out the wrinkles in the air. "I'll tell you the same thing I told your father. We have important things to discuss, so let's try to approach everything like the reasonable adults we are."

"I'm reasonable," she told him. "I'm a very reasonable person." Not. She pointed a finger at Kurt. "Much more than he is."

"Why don't we just wait until we all have our coffee," Rafe said in a mild tone. "Okay?"

Tyler drew in a deep breath and let it out slowly. "Fine," she spat out. "Fine," her father said.

An uncomfortable silence wrapped itself around them as Tyler rinsed her mug and set out two others then stood aside so the men could choose their poison from the carousel of single-serving cups.

"Help yourselves." She waved a hand at the setup.

Filled mugs in hand, they waited for her to seat herself before taking their places at the table.

"Okay," she said. "You came here to talk? Talk away."

"I thought," Rafe began, "that—"

But Kurt interrupted him. "Let me take the lead here, Rafe. I've put you in a difficult enough situation as it is."

Tyler frowned. "What's that supposed to mean? And yes, by the way, you have."

Her father gave her a direct look. "It means Rafe came to me with his concerns, and based on that I'm the one who insisted on this visit." He cleared his throat then looked down at his coffee mug. "I think we can all agree that I leave a lot to be desired in the parent department," he began.

Wow! That was a shock. A big one.

Tyler snorted. She tightened the cloak of snarkiness. That was her only defense, the only way she could get through this. "No shit."

Rafe put his hand on her arm, as if to settle her down. She yanked it away, but not before his touch scorched her and made her nipples swell like gumdrops.

"Hear him out," he said. "Please."

Too late, she wanted to say. Way too late. But they were here, they were drinking coffee, so she might as well listen. At least her curiosity about the visit would be satisfied.

Kurt took a healthy slug of his coffee. "Like I said, I won't ever win parent of the year. I made a lot of mistakes, Tyler, when you were little and again when you were growing up. I know that." He rubbed his jaw. "The reasons don't matter. Let's just leave it that I've been a lousy parent."

"True enough," she agreed, unable to keep the tinge of bitterness from her voice.

"But here's the thing," he went on, as if she hadn't spoken. "Lately I've realized just how badly I screwed up." He scrubbed his hand over his face, as if he could wash away the past years. "I know you probably won't believe me, but I worry about you, Tyler. I see all the stories in the media. I hear stuff."

"Oh?" she interrupted. "From who? Your country club cronies? Is that what this is all about? You've finally decided I've embarrassed you too much to ignore?"

"Tyler," Rafe said in a placating tone.

"It's okay," Kurt interrupted him. "I deserve it. Let's just get to the point. I worry that you're putting yourself in danger. That stuff gets out of hand. Now this new thing." He rubbed his face again. "Rafe came to me this morning and told me—"

"What gave you the right so go to my father?" Now her anger came surging to the surface and she practically shouted the words at Rafe, outraged. "After I specifically asked you—no, told you—not to do it?"

"Who else would he go to?" Kurt demanded. "You're in trouble, so he came to me."

"Maybe if you acted like a father it would make sense." She glared at Rafe. "Are you nuts? That is a total violation of my privacy."

"You don't seem to worry about privacy much with your hijinks," Kurt snapped, his face turning red.

Rafe gave him a hard look. "That attitude is not going to help things."

"That's the truth." Tyler pushed her chair back and stood up. "And that right there," she told Rafe, "is why I don't talk to him and why I don't want him here. Or you. So you can just leave right now."

"No." He shook his head, his voice calm and steady, despite the tension that rolled through the room in heavy waves. "Kurt, we discussed this. You wanted to be able to reach out to your daughter. You won't do it that way, so let me handle things the way we agreed."

Kurt took a deep breath, visibly pulling himself together. Tyler was torn between wanting to throw him out and curious as to why, after all this time, he suddenly wanted to reach out to her. It had to be more than this problem. He could have just sent someone to talk to her. Like Rafe.

"We're going to discuss this because there is a serious problem." Rafe looked at Kurt. "You told me you're worried about your daughter. That's why you wanted to come here. I'm worried, too. Tyler." He looked at her, his warm fingers still curled over her arm. "You're not stupid. You know this situation is nothing to laugh about, so we're going to figure out what to do about it."

"But—"

"No buts. I mean it. This is nothing to fool around with." His tone of voice said he meant it. "Now. First things first. Like I said, I told your father about the phone calls and the tire incident. I'm going to assume those flowers are from whoever this is. Has he done this before?"

She thought about lying but then who was she hurting except herself? In point of fact, the reason she was even sitting here listening to this discussion was because the text earlier had rattled her.

"Yes." She swallowed a sigh. "Several times." She lifted a shoulder and let it drop. "I thought it was Nate. He was bombarding me when we first split up."

"That jackass." Kurt spat the words. "I don't know why you ever—"

"Kurt." Rafe snapped the word out like a gunshot. "We agreed, remember?"

"Yeah," the older man grumbled. "Okay. Keep doing your thing."

"Any more calls or texts?" Rafe asked Tyler.

"A text. Today." She looked down at her lap.

"What?" Her father barked the question. "You should have told us the minute we walked in. You should—"

"Remember what you agreed," Rafe reminded him again. His voice was still calm when he spoke to Kurt but there was an underlying core of steel to it that said he meant business.

Kurt blew out a breath, then took a hefty gulp of his coffee.

"Let me see the phone," Rafe told Tyler.

She handed it to him, hoping he wouldn't notice the faint trembling of her hand. He brought up the text and read it wordlessly.

"Well?" Kurt asked, barely tamping down his impatience.

"Just as I thought. This is a good sign that he's escalating. The fact that he actually came here, to this town house, to wreck the tires means he's not afraid to get close."

"Then we need to take precautions," Kurt said. "Put safeguards in place." He looked at Tyler. "You need protection. A bodyguard."

Her automatic reaction was to object although with the latest text message, an indication that whoever this was seemed to be following her around, even she could see that she needed something. But the idea of a bodyguard turned her off, the same way it had when Rafe brought it up. Someone in her space all the time? And with her father, the absentee parent involved? She didn't know which choice was worse. Still, she wasn't giving in that easily.

"No," she insisted. "I told you that the first time you brought it up. That won't work. Find another solution."

"Tyler, I—" Kurt stopped, cleared his throat and looked at her across the table. "I don't scare easily, but when Rafe came to me this morning and told me what's going on, I was afraid for you. I'm not ashamed to say the thought of someone stalking you makes my skin crawl."

"So you thought after all this time you'd pop into my life, wave your magic wand, and wipe your hands of me again?" God, he was so insufferable. She'd be angrier if all this didn't just bring up the hurt she'd nurtured for so many years.

"So I have a solution. *We* have a solution," he corrected himself.

She looked at Rafe and saw him nodding. So the two of them had figured this all out without her?

"And the solution is the bodyguard," he went on.

Rafe nodded. "I agree."

"And Rafe?" Kurt looked at him. "That should be you."

"What?" Tyler shouted the word at the same time Rafe did.

Rafe recovered first. "Now wait just a minute, Kurt. You need someone who specializes in this, not me. The agency has a lot of good men it can provide."

"You're the only person I'd trust to do this," the older man said. "Whatever needs to be done, I have confidence you can figure it out."

"And what about my other responsibilities?" he protested. "The team and the stadium? I can't just walk away from them." He glanced at the man next to him. "This is a really bad idea, Kurt."

"But you agreed she needs a bodyguard."

Rafe nodded. "Just not me."

Kurt shrugged. "There are ways to work it out."

"Like what?" Rafe and Tyler demanded, again as with one voice.

"I refuse to have anyone from the team involved with me." Tyler spoke each word distinctly and clearly. "I want you to understand that."

"You can do some rearranging in your staff setup," Kurt told Rafe as if Tyler hadn't even spoken. "Figure out how often you really have to be on site. What you need your stadium office for and what can be done from a remote location. Right?"

"Not right." Tyler slammed her hands on the table. "That will just not work. Did you even hear what I said? No one from the Hawks. Especially not one of your precious football players."

Rafe gave her a half smile. "I retired three years ago."

"I don't care." She stuck out her jaw. "It's not happening. It's my life."

But again her father went right on as if neither of them had said a word. "Rafe, you can set up a temporary office here in the town house, right?"

Tyler felt the indignation bubbling up inside her. An office here? In her home? How dare they?

"Move in here?" Tyler wanted to scream in frustration. Wasn't anyone listening to her? "No. No one from the team and no one moving in with me."

"I asked because if you're going to move in here," Kurt continued, still ignoring her words, "you need to have an office to work from."

"I keep saying it's not happening," she snapped. "Forget it. I mean it, both of you. I'll take care of things myself. I don't need anyone moving into this place with me. No. The answer is no. And may I just say a big fat no."

"And exactly how will you do that?" Rafe asked, his voice the calm in the storm of anger surging in the air. "Take care of yourself, that is."

"I-I'll—" She waved a hand in the air. Yes, what would she do? But she wasn't going to admit to them she had no idea.

"Exactly."

At that precise moment, as if to remind her that the problem was very real, her phone blasted the now too familiar drumbeat. Tyler took it out of her pocket to answer, but Rafe grabbed it from her hand.

"Not so fast. I need to check it first." He looked at the readout. "Who's Betsy?"

"Oh, for the love of God. She's my best friend. And harmless. Give me the phone." She pressed Answer. "Hi, Bets. I'm a little tied up right now. Let me call you back, okay?" She slammed the phone down on the table and glared at the two men.

"Tyler." Kurt leaned across the table toward her. "Curse me all you want. I probably deserve it. But no matter how terrible a parent I've been, I can't stand the thought of something bad happening to you. Maybe it—" He shrugged. "Maybe it's a chance for me to try and make up to you for all the other years."

She looked at him with curiosity. What the hell? "Really? Can I just ask you why now, all of a sudden?"

He drained his coffee mug, taking his time as if gathering his thoughts. "Maybe when all this is over for you and we can sit down and talk, I can tell you. Right now, I don't want to take the time confessing my sins. It's important to me to make sure my daughter is protected from some maniac."

It was pathetic how badly she wanted to believe him, to accept that fact that maybe he was changing. That he wasn't resenting her as a daughter rather than a son any more. That maybe, after all this time, they could have a relationship.

Don't be a fool. He just doesn't want the bad publicity if something happens and he could have stopped it.

"I hear you, but you have to listen to me. I don't need or want a babysitter twenty-four/seven. Period."

"Tyler." Rafe put his hand on her arm again.

Oh, Lord. Having this man staying in her house, *if* she agreed to it, was going to be a temptation she might not be able to resist. Or it just might be the opportunity to convince him they should get naked together. A chance for her to see if this thing that simmered between them was more than pure lust. Hmm. Maybe she should rethink this whole thing.

She looked from one man to the other. "Okay. I have a question."

"What?" Kurt asked.

"What is it?" Rafe asked at the same time.

"What happens on the days Rafe has to be at the stadium, like on game days?" She shifted her gaze to Kurt. "I can't see you letting someone else oversee that."

"No problem. You'll just come with him."

Tyler jerked upright in her chair. "To the stadium? To a football game?"

Rafe actually laughed. "In case you hadn't heard, that's where the games are played. You might actually enjoy it."

"Not for one second." She blinked. "Wait. Are you saying you're actually going for this? You're moving into my house for...for...who knows how long?"

"I didn't say that. Yet." He looked at Kurt. "I still think this is a really bad idea. A full-time bodyguard from Lone Star would be a better bet."

"I want someone I know personally," Kurt told him, "not just some muscle-bound idiot. You want me to pull rank? Okay, if you don't do this, I'll pull the whole contract with Lone Star."

Tyler's jaw dropped. "Don't be ridiculous. That's idiotic. And I won't let you put Rafe in that position." She scowled. "You can throw your weight around with your players but not with me. And I won't let you do it with Rafe."

"Okay, stop." Rafe held up a hand. "Is this an ideal situation? No. Is it critical? Tyler, you have to agree that it is. So, Kurt, if you're willing to cut me some slack in some areas, I think we can work this out."

Kurt smiled and leaned back in his chair. "I love it when a plan comes together." Then he looked from Rafe to Tyler and back again. "Tyler, you do everything he tells you, exactly as he tells you. Your safety comes first."

"But—"

"She will," Rafe broke in. "She knows this guy can be dangerous." He slid a glance at her. "Right, Tyler?"

She slumped in her chair, all the fight suddenly drained from her, replaced by the fear that had niggled at her since this started. He was right, that she had to admit. "Right." She spat the word out grudgingly.

"Good." Kurt rubbed his hands together. "Excellent." He gave Tyler a smile. "Maybe I can make up a little for the past."

She wanted to tell him he'd have a boatload of making up to do, but she was already tired of this conversation. She didn't even have any idea what had brought all this on, and she wasn't even sure she trusted it. If there was one bright spot, it was the fact that Rafe would be here, with her, in her home. And maybe she could finally fulfill her secret fantasies.

Before she could get over the shock of his words, her cell phone chimed, signaling another text incoming. She reached to pick it up, but Rafe put a hand on her wrist and shook his head.

"Let me."

He brought the message up on the screen, scowling as he read it.

"What does it say?" Tyler craned her neck trying to see. Her stomach knotted when she got a look at it.

"u don't need them. u need me."

"Oh my God." Fear was a bitter taste in her mouth. "Is he watching me?" She swiveled her head as if he were right there in the room. "Where is he?" She jumped up, knocking her chair over. "Maybe he's out front."

Rafe stood up and closed his fingers over her upper arms, holding her in place. As it always did, his touch sent heat coursing through her. How on earth could one man do this to her? And why was she even thinking about that when all this was going on?

"Do not go look outside. If he is there, he'll see you peering out at him."

Her pulse thumped at the hollow of her throat. This was more than just heavy-breathing phone calls. Whoever this person was, he was *right here.* Just as he'd been right here when he'd slashed her tires.

"I can't believe he could be just sitting there in broad daylight." She looked up at Rafe. "Could he?"

"I don't think he'd be parked there." He gave her arms a light squeeze and stepped away. "That would be too suspicious. You live in a very upscale neighborhood, and I'm guessing anyone home during the day would call the cops on a strange car just hanging around. But he could be cruising the block, pretending to look for an address."

"I'm stunned no one saw him the other night."

"It was dark," he reminded her. "You told me you had your outside lights off. If he's smart, he could have done this without detection."

"Okay, we need to move forward." Kurt Gillette rose from the table. "Rafe, how soon can you get yourself moved in here?"

Rafe blew out a breath. "Let's see what's needed. Tyler, do you have a room I can use as an office?"

"I do. There's a den downstairs here that I hardly ever use for anything."

"I'll need to look at it." He turned to Kurt. "Then a visit to the stadium to take what I need from there, a meeting with the security team to let them know I'll be working a lot from a remote location. And a visit to my place to pick up some clothes."

Kurt rubbed his hands together. "Okay, then. Let's get started." He shifted his focus to Tyler. "You need to go with him. You can't stay here by yourself."

"What?" She was sure her eyebrows reached her hairline. "I'll lock all the doors, set the alarm, and not answer the phone. Okay?"

"Not okay."

"Your father's right." Rafe put his two cents in. "Show me the den and then we can leave. I'll drive your father back to the stadium and take care of business there at the same time."

Tyler looked down at herself. "I am not going out in public like this. Sloppy clothes and no makeup? Are you kidding?"

Her father opened his mouth to say something, but Rafe held up a hand. "All you need to throw on is a pair of jeans and a T-shirt. You have those, right?"

"Of course I do."

"Stick on big sunglasses and a ball cap and no one will know you." He smiled. "Besides, I like you without makeup."

Oookay. No makeup. If he kept using that same hot tone of voice, she'd go without clothes, too.

Her father stood there, watching her intently and nodding his head.

"Fine." She didn't have the energy to fight both of them. "Jeans and tee. Ball cap. Got it. Let's hit the den first."

She left the two men looking at the room while she raced upstairs to change clothes. Making a quick decision, she pulled on the plainest pair of jeans she owned and a navy tee. From the back of her closet, she unearthed a Port Aransas ball cap from a wild weekend she'd gone on. Looking at herself in the mirror, she gave the image a nod of satisfaction. Better. Much better. She should have done this a long time ago.

I might really like you, Tyler Gillette.

Her father and Rafe were waiting in the foyer when she came down the stairs. Her father seemed to pay her no attention at all. Rafe's glance took her in from head to toe and though he said nothing she could swear there was a tiny look of surprise in his eyes.

"Rafe says the den will work out just fine for him," Kurt said. "One more thing. The scholarship benefit Saturday night."

"I don't have to go," she told him quickly. "I don't mind."

"Yes, you do," Kurt insisted. "We upped our donation this year, and we need to have a presence. One change, though. Chad can go on his own. Rafe will take you."

"What?" She and Rafe uttered the word at the same time.

"No arguments." Kurt already had his hand on the doorknob. "Rafe, you go every year anyway, right? It's your friend Joe's pet project. The Athletes Scholarship Fund."

Rafe nodded. "Joe Reilly. Quarterback for the Coyotes when we won the state championships. He was a star in the NFL, too, for a long time until he injured his knee. He's reached out to all of us who were on the team with him."

"Then this should work out fine."

"Sure. No problem."

Tyler heard the resigned acceptance in Rafe's voice. She took a small measure of delight in knowing that if she had to suffer, he did, too. Her cheeks heated as she recalled her outrageous behavior every year, a big fuck-you to both her father and Chad. This year people would see a new Tyler Gillette. She could never embarrass Rafe the way she'd dissed Chad. Maybe they'd be shocked, maybe they wouldn't even like her, but at least she'd feel better about herself.

"I'll get a message to Chad." Kurt looked from one to the other. "So we're good to go?"

She thought of giving him a snarky answer, her automatic response. Instead she clamped her lips shut and nodded her head. Nothing good comes easily, she reminded herself.

"Then let's move it." Rafe put his hand beneath her elbow, setting off those electrical impulses again. "I need to get going."

She stopped, deciding to give him one last chance to beg out of this. "Rafe. If this is going to throw your schedule off too much—"

"It's fine, Tyler. Let's get going here or it won't be."

When they walked out to the car, she saw a car slowing down as it passed her place. Her muscles tightened until she saw it was Betsy. The woman sped up again but not before she gave the "Call me" signal. Yeah, right. That would be an interesting conversation.

"Friend of yours?" Rafe asked.

"Betsy Timmerman. My friend, the one who called earlier. She probably was going to stop in until she saw us leaving."

"Does she know what's happening?"

"Yes." Tyler smoothed her damp hands down her jeans. "But she's the only one. I didn't, um, want to tell any of my other friends about this."

He lifted an eyebrow. "Why not?"

"Because what if they somehow got sucked into it? Besides…" She looked away.

"Besides what?" Rafe prompted.

She looked down at her hands. "I was…embarrassed about it."

"Embarrassed?" The word cut through the air. "Because some weirdo wants to hurt you? I don't get it."

"It doesn't matter. Just let it go. Please?"

"But—"

"Please." How could she tell him the embarrassment came from the realization that her outrageous lifestyle was probably the cause of the whole thing? She was having enough trouble coming to terms with this sudden knowledge herself.

"You were right not to involve her, whatever the reason. You should distance yourself from her until we catch this guy." He gave her a hard look. "I mean it, Tyler."

"But why?" Not talk to Betsy? She'd lose her mind if she only had Rafe to talk to.

"Because she could be in danger, too."

Tyler felt sick to her stomach. If only she could hide in a closet until this was all over.

Rafe stood there for a moment scanning the street up and down before unlocking his car and opening the passenger-side doors.

She insisted on riding in the back seat on the way to the team headquarters facility. Rafe and her father chatted away about the team, the upcoming game, the road trip just ending, everything except the elephant in the room. Until this idiot was caught, she and Rafe would be alone in her town house.

She thought of the old saying that something good always comes out of something bad. Even in the midst of this ugly situation, she had a something good in mind, involving her and Rafe naked in her bed. This might be her one and only chance to make it happen.

Chapter 7

At the team headquarters, Kurt climbed out of the car, waited until she exited, and then stood there staring at her for a long moment. He seemed to be searching for words. Finally, he just said, "Rafe will keep you safe." Then he nodded once to Rafe and walked toward the facility. He had his cell phone out and clapped to his ear before he'd taken a dozen steps.

"He couldn't get away fast enough." Tyler just shook her head. She supposed she should be glad he'd reached out to her, but she'd give up a week of barhopping to know why now, after all this time.

"He's a busy man," Rafe reminded her. "It was his idea in the first place to come to your place and talk. I'd say that's a major reach-out on his part."

"And exactly how excited are you about having to move into my place for the foreseeable future?" She hoped he heard the sarcasm in her voice.

"I'm fine with it. The important thing is Kurt's happy and you're safe."

Rafe stepped up the pace so she had to hurry to keep up with him. Of course, she'd run the other way if she could. Being here at the stadium made her uncomfortable. Glancing over at him, she saw a muscle twitch in his cheek. So he was still not so happy about it, but he was going to do his damnedest to make it work. Well, she had plans for Mr. Rafe Ortiz, if she had the nerve to follow through on them. Big talk was easy. It was the follow through she needed the courage for.

She'd waited so long for this opportunity she didn't want to screw it up. She'd have to be careful about how she did this. If she didn't smack him first for his obnoxious remarks.

"I know you don't want to be my babysitter, but—"

"I also don't want you scared to death or harmed by some nut. I'll do what's necessary. Leave it at that."

He opened the door to the building for her and waited for her to precede him into the lobby.

"Where's your phone now?" he asked.

"In my jeans pocket." She slipped it out and showed it to him.

"Two things." He followed her into the elevator and pressed the button for the floor he wanted. "You don't answer a call or text from anyone you don't know and love. And you check every incoming before accepting it."

"Yes, sir." She saluted at the bill of her ball cap. "Whatever you say, sir."

He gave her a hard look across the elevator car. "This is no laughing matter, Tyler."

"Do I look like I'm laughing? I don't need you to give me orders. I'm not stupid, Rafe. I'm not looking for some idiot to get hold of me for God-knows-what reason."

"Good. Just making sure. When we get back to your house, I want you to help me make a list of anyone you think this might be." He narrowed his gaze. "And, Tyler, I mean anyone. You never know what trips someone's trigger."

"I guess I don't want to believe that anyone I know would do this to me. I mean, come on, Rafe."

"Come on, Tyler," he mimicked. Then his face sobered. "This is a personal crime. The sooner we nail down the person the sooner it will be over. End of discussion."

The elevator doors opened, and as they stepped out into the wide corridor, she heard someone call her name.

"Tyler? Hey, hold up a minute."

Ed Spinelli. Great. Just what she needed today. Not.

Rafe looked at the man through narrowed eyes. "What can we do for you?"

Tyler saw irritation tighten Ed's features for a moment before he pulled out a smile. "Hey, man, no offense, but it's Tyler I want to talk to." He looked at her. "Don't get to see you here at all. This a special occasion? Maybe we can have coffee."

"Thanks, anyway," Tyler said, "but no."

Rafe cupped her elbow. "She's busy right now. Excuse us, okay?"

"Us?" Ed's voice followed them down the hall. "There something going on here I should know about? Write about?"

Tyler just waved a hand back at him and let Rafe guide her to his office.

"Another of your admirers?" he asked.

She shook her head. "Just a pest."

"We're putting pests on the list," he reminded her. "I'll want to know all about him and your contact with him."

"Fine," she grumped.

"I won't be long."

She plunked herself down in a chair in the corner of Rafe's office, knees pulled up, and took her phone out of her jeans pocket again.

Rafe studied her for a long moment, his face inscrutable, then went to work gathering his stuff.

He was totally involved in what he was doing, and between phone calls and e-mails and gathering what he needed, he was fully occupied. Tyler settled down and set about answering texts from her friends while he pulled together whatever he needed to take with him. She was happy she didn't have to make conversation, although she was surprised there wasn't more traffic in and out.

"*R u ever going to cl me bck?*" From Betsy.

"*Ys. Can't tlk now.*"

"*What's Mr Gorgeous doing at yr hse?*"

"*Tl u ltr.*"

"*U bttr. Lynn wants 2 know 2.*"

Well, hell. So she'd discussed this with Lynn already? Of course she had. When they got back to the house and she had some privacy, she'd call them, although she had no idea what she'd tell them. Certainly not the truth. They'd be at her house and in her face as fast as they could drive, insisting she call the cops. Who she was sure, would just ignore the whole thing. They'd never catch the guy. He'd just bide his time until things died down. No, if anyone was going to take charge of it, Rafe was the lesser of two evils.

She'd like to explore more than a few evils with that man.

She was still answering texts when she heard a knock on the doorjamb and looked up to see Chad Sinclair.

"Hey, Rafe. Someone mentioned I'd find the princess in here." He looked around. "Where did she go?"

"Right here, Chad." She peered at him from beneath the ball cap. "What's up?"

Chad gave her a wide-eyed look of disbelief. "Tyler? Is that you? What are you in costume for?"

She slammed her feet to the floor and sat up straight in the chair. "Yes, it's me. What's wrong? Do I look like an alien or something?"

"No, you look"—he gave her a searching look—"normal."

She bounced up out of the chair and looked up at him, all six foot four of him. "What's that supposed to mean?"

Rafe stopped what he was doing and held up his hand. "Okay, calm down, Tyler. I think Chad is just commenting on your, uh, new look. Complimenting it."

"That's right." Chad gave her a huge grin, tiny dimples winking at the corners of his mouth and laugh lines crinkling at his slate-gray eyes. "I'll feel like I'm going out with a brand-new woman."

Tyler frowned. In all the time she'd known him, there had never been the least spark of chemistry between them. At least on her part. He was good-looking enough, with a thick head of dark blond hair and chiseled features. Although he hadn't played football since college, he still had the big, muscular football players' body, which he kept in great shape. He was funny and had always been unfailingly polite when he'd accompanied her to events at her father's direction, no matter how outrageously she'd behaved.

But where just looking at Rafe made her pulse pound, her panties get damp, and her mouth get dry, she had zero reaction to Chad. Less than zero. She hated dancing with him because he held her just a little too close, pressed his body against hers a little too hard. She knew his game, just like her ex-husband's. Hook up with Kurt Gillette's daughter and feather his nest. She was positive deep down he despised both her and her lifestyle, but she knew some men would do anything to push themselves up that success ladder.

She focused her gaze on him, trying to read what was in his eyes. Was it possible he was the stalker? Would he go that far? Was he angry enough with her to do something like that? She shook herself out of her mental side trip as his words finally registered with her.

"Going out?" she asked.

"Going out?" Rafe repeated.

Chad shifted his gaze to Rafe then back to Tyler. "I called to remind you, remember? Big fundraiser event this Saturday night at the Conquistador Club. The Annual High School Athletes Scholarship Fundraiser." He inclined his head toward Rafe. "It's a pet project for one of the golden boy's former teammates from Granite Falls."

"I, um, won't be going with you this year," Tyler said. "You can make your own plans this time."

"Excuse me?" He stared at her.

"Anyway," she continued, "I believe the situation has changed. Didn't anyone tell you?"

Chad frowned. "Yeah, I got some kind of crazy message that Kurt made arrangements for Rafe to take you Saturday night, but I'm sure that's a mix-up. I can't find Kurt to check with him. Then someone told me you were here in Rafe's office."

"I am." She nodded. "And you got the message right." She watched Chad carefully. He was obviously displeased. If he was the one stalking her—

No. He couldn't be. Could he?

He frowned. "Are you sure? We've been going to these things together for a long time. It's a habit I've gotten used to and look forward to." He winked at her. "You know I am always your loyal and faithful escort."

"You're off the hook for the party this year," Rafe said.

"And this way you can take a date of your own choosing," Tyler pointed out, sat down again, and turned back to her phone. "You'll have much more fun."

"Tyler." The smile was gone from his face and his tone of voice. "You don't mean you'd rather go with Rafe than me. You hardly ever see him."

"I told you. My father set it up. It's his personal request."

"Now why in the hell would he do that? Are you guys trying to put something over on me?" He looked at Rafe. "Why are you involved anyway? I know what you think about the princess here—"

Tyler glared at him. "Princess, Chad? I take it from your tone of voice that's not a compliment."

"Did I say—"

"Enough." Rafe slammed his hand on his desk. "You can stop right there. It's a done deal." He tipped a corner of his mouth in a half smile. "It's alright. You don't need to be on duty, Chad. I'm fine taking her to the event."

"Yeah?" A muscle twitched in his cheek. "I still can't figure out why you would be taking her." He stopped. "Wait a minute." He looked from one to the other, irritation plain on his face. "Is there something going on here I don't know about?"

"I'm not sure that's any of your business," Rafe answered, his voice filled with infinite patience. "Whatever is between Tyler and me is our business, not yours."

"Really." The word was laced with bitter sarcasm.

Tyler noticed that every bit of good humor had disappeared from Chad's face.

"Come on, Chad." She forced a smile. "You know you think I'm a pain in the ass. I'd think you'd be glad to get rid of me."

"Maybe you don't even need to go now," Rafe interjected. "I mean if you don't want to."

Tyler looked from one man to the other. There was certainly a lot of testosterone floating in the room from two men who she was sure didn't give two hoots for her sexually. Rafe gave her a hard look, something dark flashing in his eyes. What was that all about? Then it was gone and she wasn't sure it had even been there.

"Oh, I get it." Anger tinged Chad's words. "You think if you suck up to the boss by hooking up with the princess here, you'll be the son he never had. His anointed heir. Did I get that right, asshole?"

Tyler blanched at his words. Was that how he saw this? Saw himself? Saw her?

Rafe stood up slowly, a dark flush staining his sharp cheekbones, rage flashing in his eyes.

"That was a nasty thing to say, you unmitigated jackass, and totally uncalled for. You'd better get out of here before I take you apart."

Chad looked at Tyler. "I'll apologize to you, Tyler. I didn't mean that at all. You know I think you're special. I always have."

"No one cares." Rafe still had his gaze fixed on Chad. "And we're done here."

"I'm not taking your word for this. Or the word of whoever gave me the message."

"How about my word?" Tyler snapped. "I'm the one who was supposed to be your date, the operative word being *was.* Isn't my word good enough? Have you suddenly gone crazy here? I should think you'd be happy to be off the hook."

"I never looked at it that way and you know it. As least I thought you did." He looked from Rafe to Tyler and back again. "Something's not right here. I'm checking in with Kurt." Chad picked up the phone on Rafe's desk and punched in three numbers. "Yeah, hi, Nonie. It's Chad. Can I speak to the boss for a second? I'll be quick." He shoved his hand into his pocket, jingling his keys while he waited with barely leashed impatience. "Kurt? Listen, I need to ask you something. About Saturday night's event. Tyler said I'm not—"

Tyler saw the muscles in his face tighten as he listened and the jingling stopped.

"But—" He blew out a breath. "Kurt, do you —Okay, okay. You're right. If you say it's her decision, then I guess that's that. I just don't understand. I thought we—Fine. Yes, I'll still be there. Okay. Whatever you say." He replaced the receiver with more force than necessary and looked at Rafe. "I don't know what the fuck is going on, but she's all yours, Ortiz." He glared at Tyler. "I don't like being screwed over."

Tyler tensed at the obvious edge of bitterness and resentment in his voice. She couldn't embarrass herself by telling him she had seen it as an opportunity to please her father, hoping that it would soften his attitude.

Maybe if I hadn't gotten drunk each time and made a fool out of myself and sometimes him, too.

"You're not getting screwed over as you put it, Chad," she said in a tired voice. "You're being let off the hook. Now you can get your own date, someone who really wants to be with you."

Should she have said that? A dark flush spread across his face, although he didn't say a word, just clenched his fists. She looked over at Rafe, who stood there calmly, watching Chad.

"We square now?" Rafe asked. "You understand the situation has changed?"

"You think you're such hot shit," Chad sneered, "just because you were one of the boss's bright boys on the field. If you fuck this up, whatever is going on here, you'll be out on your ass. Keep that in mind."

He looked at his clenched fists for a moment, as if ready to throw a punch. Then he just turned and strode heavily from the office.

"Well." Tyler just stared at the now-empty doorway.

She wasn't sure what else to say after that. She'd always had the feeling Chad would be happy to get her between the sheets but otherwise saw her as a gigantic pain in the ass.

Rafe gave her one of his penetrating looks. "Was there something between you and Sinclair that I should know about?"

"Are you kidding?" She flipped a hand in the air. "I'll never understand why my father chose him as my official escort but that's all there ever was. He doesn't appeal to me any more than Dewey from Tequila Sunrise."

"That the name of the guy who trapped you in the restroom?" Rafe asked. She nodded.

"I'm definitely putting his name at the top of the list, Tyler," he instructed. "Chad's, I mean. And Ed's, too."

"I hear you, although you'd think Chad would be able to get enough women on his own without pushing me into something. I mean, as good-looking as he is and all."

Rafe lifted an eyebrow. "You really think he's good-looking?"

"Oh, can it." She flipped a hand at him. "The man does not appeal to me at all. Why do you even care, anyway?"

"Just making idle conversation."

"Okay." Tyler shrugged. "I guess he could be the one, only to what point?" She shivered at the thought.

"You have a history with him. Maybe he wants more," Rafe suggested. "Maybe he's got a thing for you and wants you to turn to him for help.

"As if."

"After all, like Chad said, it wouldn't be such a bad thing to hook up with the owner's daughter." He watched her through narrowed eyes, studying her face.

Something ugly raced through her for a moment. "Is that why you're doing this, Rafe? To curry favor with my father? I know it's not because you think I'm the love of your life."

"Let's leave the personal out of this," he said in an uninflected voice. "I'm more concerned right now to find out if Chad's your stalker."

"You can find out, right?"

"I'm going to do whatever it takes to nail this guy, whoever he is." He glanced at her phone. "None of those texts you read while you were waiting happened to be from our stalker, did they?"

She sniffed at him. "Wouldn't I have told you if they were? I'm irritated, Rafe, not stupid."

"Just checking." He paused as he picked up some more folders from his desk. "About the calls, not the stupid part, so don't get your panties in a wad." He stuffed his laptop and other things into a big messenger bag and zipped it up. "Come on, we can go. I'm done here."

She stuck her phone back into her pocket and hooked the strap of her purse over her shoulder. Rafe stopped her just as she reached the open doorway. He surprised her by cupping her chin in his warm palm and tilting her face up to him. "He's right about one thing. You look a hell of a lot better without all that war paint you insist on wearing." He dropped his hand. "Let's get out of here."

Tyler's skin tingled where he'd touched her, the feeling spreading to all her nerve endings, and her damn pulse took off at a gallop. She was stunned both by the gentleness of his touch and by his words. Everything she felt for him, everything she'd kept tamped down all these years bubbled to the surface.

She smiled to herself as she rode down in the elevator with him and followed him out to the parking lot. Yup. This cluster fuck might have a silver lining after all.

* * * *

They stopped at Rafe's house on the way back. He hustled them in and out in fifteen minutes. He really didn't want her presence imprinted on it anywhere. This job was irritating him enough as it was. Then a quick stop at a grocery and a deli and they were at her town house.

"I'm going to set myself up in the den," he said after he hauled all his stuff inside. "Then I'd appreciate it if you'd show me where I'm going to bunk down."

This is a bad idea, he said to himself, not for the first time. A very bad idea. Being alone in a house with Tyler Gillette spelled ten kinds of trouble. The woman had made it overtly obvious that she wanted to have sex with him. He was just as determined it was never going to happen. Screwing the boss's daughter might not be the worst thing he could do, but it was right up there in the top five. Especially this boss and this daughter.

Tyler tossed her purse on a chair in the great room. "Knock yourself out. I'm going to fix myself a cup of coffee. You want one?"

"Sure, but I'll get it in a few. As soon as I'm set up."

"Fine. Whatever." She stomped off to the kitchen.

Okay, he knew she wasn't happy about this. In her place, he wouldn't be either. No one wanted to live with a threat hanging over their head or have their privacy invaded this way. He'd have to find some way to make her okay with this. A pissed-off woman could create a dangerous situation, much more dangerous than him getting naked with her.

He'd had to go open his mouth about her situation and tell her father. It had been the right thing to do. He knew it. It was a sure thing she wouldn't take the kind of precautions necessary on her own, not when she lived her life on the edge the way she did. The last thing he'd expected was for Kurt to insist he do this himself.

That insane attraction—no, more than that, something he refused to identify—that ignited the first time he'd seen her still simmered beneath the surface, ready to erupt. It was always there, in her eyes, in the looks she gave him, in his reaction to her. Now he was going to be living here with her for the foreseeable future, and how the hell was he going to handle that? Because no matter how he looked at it, they were just two very different people, with no future between them.

Just keep it in your pants, he told himself. *Use your famous discipline and you'll get through it.*

Tyler's town house wasn't at all what he'd expected. He'd been prepared for ultramodern with uncomfortable furniture and bizarre colors. It was, in fact, the opposite. She'd chosen polished wood furniture with lots of warm colors. The den had an intimate, welcoming feel to it. Honey-colored wood shelves lined two walls and a matching carved desk sat in front of a small bay window that looked out on a manicured yard. The desk chair and the big armchair next to it were upholstered in honey-colored leather but neither looked as if they were used very much. Not a shock. Tyler didn't impress him as a work-at-your-desk kind of person.

He moved aside the small laptop sitting on the desk. If Tyler needed to use it, they'd figure it out. He set his own up, along with his external hard drive, and stacked his working folder beside it. He needed the password to Tyler's Internet, and he wanted to dump his suitcase. He looked for her and found her on the patio that ran off both the great room and the kitchen. She was standing under the overhang, drinking coffee and staring off into space.

"You okay?" he asked.

She jerked, startled, and coffee sloshed over the rim of her mug.

"Damn!"

She shook the liquid off her hand. Holding the dripping cup away from her, she carried it inside to the sink.

"Sorry," he said, following her back into the kitchen, fascinated by the flash of her purple fingernails as she cleaned the mess with paper towels.

"Aren't you afraid you might stab yourself with those?" he asked. When she gave him a questioning look, he indicated her nails.

"Oh. Well." She looked at the nails and then back at him. "A girl can't have too many weapons."

"I'd think the color itself would be a killer." The moment the words were out of his mouth he wished them back. How she looked and dressed was really none of his business. And he wasn't here to make snarky comments, just to do a job. Besides, today she was dressed like, well, a normal person. And what was up with that?

When she turned to him, he waited for one of her usual comebacks, but for one very brief moment she was completely unguarded, the look in her eyes one of someone who was so lost she needed a roadmap to find her way home. Well, hell. Something plucked at him and it wasn't the tentacles of sex. Then she blinked and it was gone.

"Sorry," he told her, and he actually was. "I was out of line. Paint your nails any color you want. And I'm sorry I startled you."

"What do you need?"

"The password to your Wi-Fi and a place to put my suitcase. In no particular order."

"I'll show you to your room first so you can get, uh, settled."

Before she could move, they heard the familiar staccato drum beat from her cell phone. Tyler's face turned pale. She put down her coffee mug and she pulled the phone from her jeans pocket with a shaking hand. Staring at Rafe, she held it out.

"I-I can't answer it."

"No problem."

He took it from her and pressed Talk, then held it to his ear, listening. At first, he heard nothing, then the faint sound of heavy breathing came across the connection. When Tyler opened her mouth to say something, he held a finger to his lips and shook his head. He wanted to see how long it would take before whoever this was either said something or hung up. He kept his eye on his watch, timing it. After exactly sixty seconds a voice whispered, "Bitch." Then the call was disconnected.

"D-did he say anything?" Tyler's face was nearly white.

"Just heavy breathing." He didn't want to tell her what was said. She was upset enough as it was. "Look. Changing your number hasn't done any good, so we need to try something else. I'm going to call the Lone Star office and see if they've had any luck finding the source of the phone. Where it was bought. Anything."

"What will that tell them? How does that identify the person?"

"Sometimes people are stupid enough to purchase them at a location right near where they live, or where they work. If we're lucky enough to get that information, we can move forward from there." He spoke as calmly as possible. "Meanwhile I'm here so no one will get to you. Let's get my belongings put away and I'll get to work on this. I know this sounds stupid but try to relax for the rest of the day."

She managed a weak smile. "Okay."

She led the way up the curving staircase. Watching the flex of muscle in her nicely curved ass didn't do one damn thing to keep his libido in check. He thought it a good thing she was in front of him and couldn't see his unruly cock pressing hard against his fly to get out. God! This whole thing was going to be harder than he thought. And speaking of harder—

"This way." Thank God her voice interrupted his train of thought.

He followed her down a short hallway to a door on the left and into a large and pleasant bedroom. A comforter in yellows and greens covered a king-size bed. The headboard had similar carving to the desk downstairs and matched a long dresser against one wall. He recognized the wood now as mesquite and figured she'd bought it from a Texas artisan.

"No television," she said, interrupting his thoughts. "Sorry. But feel free to use the one in the great room. I hardly ever do"

"Because you're home so little?" Hell. He needed to put a muzzle on it. He wasn't going to make this pleasant with all his edgy little remarks. "Sorry."

Her eyes widened at his apology but then she moved on through the room.

"Closet." She pointed. "En-suite bathroom. Linen closet. All the comforts of home." She turned back to face him. "My room's across the hall. If you, uh, ever need me. For anything."

Oh, he needed her all right, but it was a need he wasn't about to give in to.

"I notice you don't have any Hawks memorabilia in the house." He cocked an eyebrow at her.

Her smile disappeared and her face became a hard mask. Whoa!

"What for? To remind myself that the team comes first, way ahead of me, where the famous Kurt Gillette is concerned? The team is the child he gives all his affection to." The words dropped out of her mouth like icicles. "I don't need crap around to remind me."

He wrinkled his forehead. "If you hate it that much, why do you go to the special events?"

"It's a condition of my trust. My father set it up for me when I was twenty-one with only one stipulation. I must attend all the team special events and the community ones like the fundraiser this Saturday. Otherwise I'm cut off, and I happen to enjoy my lifestyle."

He studied her face. Searching for—what? "Pardon my crass suggestion, but you could always go to work. I happen to know you went to college, even though you chose not to finish."

That same flash of pain he'd noticed the other night swept across her face but in a second it was gone.

"Then I wouldn't have time for all the fun I'm having," she reminded him.

He was sure she meant it as a joke, but the look in her eyes held anything but humor.

"Make yourself comfortable," she went on. "Feel free to use the coffeemaker and raid the refrigerator, although there isn't usually much in it." She looked at him. "Go ahead, say it. Because I never eat at home, right?"

"I'm not saying a word."

She snorted. "That'll be a change. But the answer for two hundred dollars, Alex, is because I hate to cook for myself."

"Maybe I'll cook for you while I'm here." Now why the hell did he say that? This wasn't a social gathering. He gave himself a mental kick. This had to be all business, all the way, even if it meant ordering pizza every night.

Curiosity flashed in her eyes. "You cook?"

He nodded and quickly changed the subject. "I'll bring up my things. I also need the password for your Wi-Fi."

"Oh. Oh, sure. It's not very original. It's my birthday."

Rafe shook his head. "Bad move. That's one of the first things people try if they want to hack an account. I'm going to change it." He gave her a half smile. "Okay?"

"Is this part of your safety procedures?"

"Yes. Let me get my act together and I'll take care of it. And I'll get the office started on a trace."

He'd had a hard time dragging his eyes away from her all morning. Without the makeup, she was a completely different person. He had a gut feeling, and not for the first time, this was the real Tyler Gillette. She looked so vulnerable that he just wanted to wrap his arms around her and hold her close. What a bad idea that would be.

At lunch, while they ate the deli sandwiches they'd picked up, Rafe quizzed her on possible stalker candidates, creating a list.

"As I said before, I'm putting Chad Sinclair on the list." He typed his name into his tablet he'd brought to the table with him. "He's a good place to start."

"Chad?" He heard the disbelief in her voice. "I already told you. I thought about him at the beginning, but I have the feeling Chad doesn't even like me. Why would he go to all this trouble?"

"Oh, he likes you alright." Rafe snorted. "He wasn't making noise about tomorrow night just because he lost his party date."

Tyler chewed a bite of her sandwich and swallowed. "Still…"

"Remember the message that said he could protect you? He might be using this as a means to drive you into his arms."

"Whatever." She flicked her fingers in the air in a dismissive gesture. "I just don't think he'd waste that much time on me but you're right. He needs to be on the list."

"Let's talk about your ex." Rafe glanced at her. "Nate Something, right?"

"Broder. But we've been divorced for some time. I'm sure he's had a slew of women since then."

"You never know. Has he been in contact with you?"

Tyler gave a heavy sigh. "Well, yes. I told you. He's had a campaign of flowers and candy going, which I throw out as fast as I get them."

"Then he's not giving up," Rafe commented. "He goes on the list, too." He typed Nate's name into the tablet.

She pulled some other names out of her memory, even though she considered them to be long shots. Actually it turned out she didn't date so much as hang out with people. And those people most frequently moved on to someone else when she ended it. If she was to be believed, the men she met in the bars where she hung out were barely pit stops. She didn't even remember most of their names.

At the end of an hour, he had little more to go on. He took the names of her two close female friends, although he didn't see this as being the work of a woman. No, it was going to be one of the men she knew. He'd get Lone Star to run a full check on the names she gave him. He'd also task them with doing a canvass of the bars where she wasted time. He knew some of them from the media, others from gossip. His people could ask subtle questions and find out if she'd kicked someone to the curb and left them plotting vengeance. Or if she'd run into someone with a possessive streak who didn't want to let go. Probably not, but he couldn't afford to ignore the possibility.

As soon as they were finished, Tyler headed upstairs and he went back to his laptop in the den. He was doing some searches of his own when he heard her behind him.

"I'm going outside for a while."

He turned and nearly swallowed his tongue. She was almost wearing what had to be the teeniest bikini he had ever seen and carrying sunscreen and a towel. The look in her eyes was a mixture of residual panic and hot temptation. He'd seen a lot of women in bikinis, maybe his share and a few other people's, also. He recalled most of those women being stick-thin.

Tyler Gillette was a whole horse of a different color. Or conformation, if you wish. Hiding beneath the dresses he'd seen her in was a lush body that made his mouth water so much he actually had to swallow. He'd gotten a hint of it in the jeans and T-shirt but the bikini exposed a woman that dreams were made of. He loved the shape of her breasts, the little curve of her tummy, the flare of her hips and the kind of thighs a man wanted pressed to his body. He had to drag his eyes away or risk embarrassing himself.

Obviously she had more in mind than just catching some fresh air. The damn little minx. Resisting her was easy enough when they only had rare contact with each other. But it seemed since her emergency call the other night, Fate was determined to throw them together, and Tyler had revived her mission to seduce him. He also noticed, coincidentally, that she'd removed the nail polish and trimmed her nails and he had to swallow a smile.

"Yell if you want to interrogate me." She winked, obviously trying for flippancy. "Or anything."

Or anything was exactly what he wanted.

"Where's your phone?" He had given it back to her with strict instructions to keep her calls and texts down to her most intimate friends.

She held it up for him to see. "Maybe he won't call again today, since I didn't even acknowledge him on that last call."

"That would be nice if true, but I think he's probably just biding his time. Maybe plotting his next move."

Her face paled, but then the snarky attitude was back like a cloak. "Gee, thanks for the reassuring words. On that note, I'm going outside."

"Try to relax and enjoy yourself," he called after her.

He figured she'd be out on the patio, on the portion not covered by the overhang. Instead, movement outside the window caught his eye and there she was, setting up a chair on the lawn in his direct line of vision. Maybe he shouldn't have told her to enjoy herself, because he knew exactly what she was up to. She made a show of squinting up at the sun to determine the best direction, positioned the chair so she would face him, and then arranged herself on it. There she was, all that mouthwatering flesh, perfect breasts barely contained by the bikini top and hardly enough material to cover her mound.

In a moment, she began applying the sunscreen. First, she dribbled some from the bottle onto each breast and used her fingers to spread it over the swells. She rubbed slowly, lazily, tantalizingly. The tips of her fingers just barely slid beneath the edge of the fabric. Rafe held his breath, waiting to see if she would reach her nipples. But then she pulled her hand away to pour some more lotion into it. Even at this distance, he could see the smile teasing at her lips. The little witch knew he was watching, and she was putting on a show just for him. Oh, yes, she knew exactly what she was doing. Apparently that was how she planned to enjoy herself.

When she bent her knees, spread her legs and began to lazily stroke the lotion on the inside of her voluptuous thighs his cock got so hard it actually hurt. Not to mention the agony of his balls. She tipped more sunscreen into the palm of one hand and rubbed the liquid into the crease where hip and thigh met. When she patted it into that narrow cleft, her thumb stroked the fabric over her cunt. She finished one side then moved to the other.

Holy fucking shit.

His work completely forgotten, he sat there barely able to breathe. His heart thudded heavily in his chest and he couldn't seem to get enough air in his lungs. Almost unconsciously, his hand dropped to cover his fly, his dick so thick and full it filled his palm. As Tyler continued to rub the sunscreen into her skin, he had an incidental thought that it was a damn good thing she'd cut her nails. He'd hate to see her stab herself in inappropriate places.

Jesus! Was he really going to get himself off right here in her den?

He yanked his hand back up and pushed away from the desk. Ice water. That's what he needed. Maybe he'd pour it on his crotch at the same time. He downed an entire glass standing at the fridge then refilled the glass with ice and water and returned to the den. If he'd hoped that in the interim Tyler had moved her chair elsewhere, it was a futile wish. She was still in the same spot, legs splayed, skin gleaming, bathed in the glow of the sun like some ancient goddess on an altar.

Only an altar wasn't where he'd like to see her. He wanted her inside, upstairs, splayed out on that big bed. Or maybe he'd take her into the shower and carefully wash all that sunscreen from her body. He'd pay special attention to her breasts and her thighs. Then he'd give in to temptation to just slide his fingers between the pouty lips of her pussy and drench them in her liquid. He'd strum her clit with his thumb while his fingers sought that inner sweet spot, watching her face the entire time so he could see—

Fuck!

He was doing it again. He clenched his fist and slammed it on his thigh. It was his dick he should be pounding instead, beating it into submission. Maybe he could tie a knot in it, or something.

If he was a different kind of man, he could just take her to bed and fuck the shit out of her. Satisfy the urge that had been simmering all these years. But that had never been who he was nor was it now.

Rafe's gaze lifted to the window again. As if she knew he was watching her, Tyler lifted one hand and gave him a flirty little wave. Yeah, she was relaxing and enjoying herself all right. He supposed if it got her mind off the situation he could deal with it, but putting himself through this was painful torture. He groaned. He must be out of his ever-lovin' fucking mind. Well, he wasn't her shrink so it wasn't up to him to find out. He was just here to protect her and find this douche bag.

Meanwhile, if he wanted to get any work done, he had to move somewhere with a different view. A man only had so much discipline. He disconnected his laptop from everything and carried it and a stack of files into the kitchen. Refilling his glass with yet more ice water, he set himself up at the kitchen table and went to work.

Without the distraction of Tyler and her too-sexy-for-her-own-good body, he actually was able to focus on what he was doing. He was so absorbed in it he had no idea how much time had passed until he heard the glass patio door slide open. He looked up to see Tyler coming toward him, noting that her body now had a nice soft coat of tan. He looked at his watch. Holy crap! It was nearly six o'clock. He'd been at this for four hours.

"Should you have been out there all this time? That's a long time to be in the sun."

"I'm good. I turned over every half hour." She grinned. "It wasn't as much fun without you watching me."

"I had work to do." He shifted his gaze back to the computer screen. "Not all of us have a trust fund."

"Is that so?" There was a sudden hard edge to her words. "Well, I happen to have it on good authority that Rafael Manda Ortiz socked away millions from his playing days in some very high-paying investments. Same difference." She trailed her fingers across the nape of his neck as she walked behind him.

Rafe gritted his teeth. Jesus! Kill him now. He was about ten seconds away from losing his shit, seized by an urge to lick every inch of that lightly tanned body. Pretending her touch didn't affect him took every bit of discipline he had. *Remember,* he told himself yet again. *Gillette's daughter and outrageously wild lifestyle.* He respected the first and disapproved of the second. That should have been enough to cool his jets, so why wasn't it?

"Well, okay," she said. "But it's almost time to quit whatever you're doing and figure out dinner. I'm thinking pizza since that seems to be everyone's universal meal. Delivered, because there's a movie I want to watch." She poked his shoulder. "I told you I hardly ever watch television in the great room but I'll make an exception tonight" She paused. "Unless I can convince you to watch it upstairs in my bedroom with me."

Rafe stopped typing and ground his teeth together as the image of a naked Tyler in bed with him threatened to destroy what was left of his rapidly degrading self-control. He kept his eyes on the computer screen, knowing if he looked at her, he'd do something stupid.

"I, uh, don't think so."

"Spoilsport."

She stood so close to him the warm skin of her midriff brushed his shoulder. He wished she'd move away from him. The combination of the heady scent of sunscreen, wildflower shampoo, and just plain Tyler was making him sensuously drunk.

Move, Tyler.

"So back to dinner, then. I'll call it in if you tell me what toppings you like. Then you can watch the movie with me."

"Thanks, but I don't do chick flicks." Type, type, type.

"Well, unbelievable as it may seem, I actually like other types as well. Tonight I'm watching *Lone Survivor.*"

Now he stopped and looked at her. "It hardly seems your type."

"See?" She brushed her fingers over his nape again. "Maybe you don't really know what my type is." Thankfully, she moved away from him. "I'm going to take a shower and wash my hair. I'll order the pizza when I get back downstairs. Don't work too hard."

She giggled. Actually giggled. Then she trotted up the stairs, humming off key.

He had finished the analysis he was doing by the time Tyler came back downstairs. She was barefoot, still makeup-free, her hair still a little damp and pulled back in a high ponytail. She'd pulled on a pair of very short white shorts and an oversize University of Michigan T-shirt. The shorts barely covered the cheeks of her ass and from the way her nipples pushed against the navy material, it was obvious she wasn't wearing a bra. His cock tried to stand up at attention.

Rafe read the legend on the T-shirt. "That's right. I forgot you're a Wolverine. Any special reason?"

"Yeah." She gave him a bitter smile. "It was about as far from Texas as I could get. You about done there, hotshot?"

"As we speak."

He hit Save, closed the file, and shut down the laptop. Picking it up, he stuck it under his arm and headed for the den.

"How come you decided to work in the kitchen?" Tyler's voice had a playful note to it.

"The sun got in my eyes." As well as other things.

She followed him into the den. "Are you sure it wasn't me distracting you?"

Yes, but he wasn't about to admit it. He set his things on the desk and turned, nearly bumping into her. There was that scent of wildflowers again, sending his hormones into overdrive. He shoved his hands into his jeans pockets to hide the fact they were tightly clenched.

"We need to get something straight, Tyler." He cleared his throat. "We need to set boundaries."

She gave him a look of curiosity. "Boundaries?"

He edged past her and took two steps away.

"We're not playing games," he told her. "I'm here for a specific purpose. I'm not one of your boy toys so just cut it out."

"Cut what out?" She gave him a wide-eyed, innocent look.

"You know exactly what I mean. This is strictly a business relationship and it's going to stay that way, despite your little show out there today." Even if he *did* have to tie his dick in a knot.

"Fine." She whirled and headed for the kitchen. "What do you like on your pizza?"

Rafe took as much time as he could fiddling around in the den. He half expected Tyler to sidle through the door and get playful with him. He should probably keep an ice pack in his boxer briefs if he didn't want to embarrass himself. How was he going to make her understand that this was just a business arrangement and they needed to keep their distance? Tyler was too used to getting what she wanted.

He was happy that she hadn't received any more calls since the last one, but people like this didn't keep to a regular schedule. They liked to keep their prey off-kilter, waiting for the other shoe to drop. Maybe it wouldn't be a call or text. Maybe another incident like the tires.

Maybe—

The ringing of the doorbell interrupted his mental wanderings.

"Pizza's here," Tyler called from the hallway.

Rafe hustled out of the den and gently moved her aside before she could open the door.

"I'll get it. I don't want you answering the door."

Her eyes widened. "You don't think—"

He shrugged. "Not necessarily, but let's not take any chances."

She waited while he paid for the pizza and reset the alarm then followed him into the kitchen. They were seated at the table, eating, when she brought the subject up again.

"I can't believe whoever this is would come right up to my door."

"He snuck into your driveway the other night, didn't he?"

Tyler picked a piece of pepperoni from her slice and popped it into her mouth. It was obvious to him she was trying to downplay this as much as possible. Much easier to handle that way. "You really think he'd try something, knowing you're here?"

"He made that phone call earlier," he reminded her. "I'm sure he's pissed off because he didn't know which of us answered the phone."

"Would that be enough for him to just say screw it and turn to someone else?"

He shook his head. "This is personal, Tyler. I think we can both agree on that. I hate to tell you, but he's probably biding his time, regrouping. If he was angry because he saw me arrive earlier, he's got to be even more pissed with my car in your driveway."

"Maybe we should put it in the garage," she suggested. "There's room."

"No, I don't think he'll sneak into your driveway again. He might have tried if you were here alone, but he knows you have company. That ups the risk factor."

The tension in the room was palpable as they ate the pizza and watched the movie. The room fairly vibrated with waves of pure sexual energy. Jesus, just watching her chew the pizza somehow became an erotic experience for him. In the great room, watching the movie, he had all he could do not to leap across the room and rip off her clothes. He was acutely conscious of every single movement of her body. When she sprawled on the couch, her already very short shorts rode up so high he could almost see her cunt. When she shifted her position and sat cross-legged, she positioned herself so that he could see all the way up the inside of her thighs to where that skimpy material barely covered her.

The aura of sex was so thick in the room he expected he could reach out and touch it. Periodically he shifted position in the armchair where he sat to ease the pressure of his throbbing cock. He wondered if all this was her way of dealing with the situation, putting on her public personality, or if she actually felt something for him. Not that he could do anything about it. He had to keep telling himself that.

By the time the movie was over, his balls ached so badly it gave him a headache. He couldn't recall a time a woman had affected him this strongly. He'd be taking an icy-cold shower before he went to bed. Or maybe using his good right hand to take the edge off this intense reaction of his body.

Rafe followed Tyler into the kitchen as she carried her nearly empty drink glass and dumped the remnants in the sink. He was right behind her, so when she turned she was right up against his body. The rounded swell of her breasts and the taut buds of her nipples were visible beneath the soft T-shirt she wore. And she smelled so damn good.

Tyler locked her gaze with his, searching in his eyes for—something. He had no idea what. But there was that vulnerability again, mixed with something that sure looked like sexual hunger and desire. *Move*, he told himself, and wondered where the red Danger sign was that should be blinking. But she was right there, warm, sweet-smelling woman with her full lips and her silky hair and her nipples that just begged for his mouth.

When she stood up on tiptoes, wound her arms around his neck, and lifted her face to his, he was totally sunk. Lost. Every rule he lived by out the door and down the road.

I am so going to hell for this.

The kiss started out so gently, just a bare brush of lips, a gliding of surface against surface. He skimmed his tongue over her lips before using the tip to trace the outline of her mouth. When he gently nudged her to open, she did so willingly, and he slid into her heat. He tasted pizza and soft drinks and very spicy woman, a heady combination. He pressed her back against the counter, banding one arm around her while his free hand gripped her ponytail and held her head in place.

Her tongue met his, doing a dance with it that began so gently but soon escalated into a hungry mating. He fed from her mouth like a ravenous beast, pressing his lips against hers so hard he was afraid he'd bruise her. He angled her head first one way, then another, never breaking the kiss, and she met him with a hunger that matched his own. He only lifted his head slightly when he ran out of breath.

He opened his mouth to protest what they were doing, reaching for a shred of sanity, but Tyler touched his mouth with the tips of her fingers.

"Whatever you're going to say, don't. Just…don't, Rafe. Okay?"

"You mean don't tell you this is a bad, bad idea?"

Which was exactly what he should say. Except when he felt the firmness of her breasts against his chest and the softness of her mound where his painfully demanding cock pressed into it, rational thought escaped his mind. Sliding one hand down her spine to her ass, he cupped one cheek and squeezed it. Oh, sweet Jesus! What he wanted to do with that delectable ass.

He took her mouth in another frenzy of a kiss, licking and sucking and tasting, rubbing his tongue against hers again. They were both panting when he lifted his head.

"We're not doing this—"

"I said don't say anything," she reminded him, pressing her hand against his mouth.

"—in the kitchen," he finished. "If I'm going to hell, I'm doing it in a bed."

He lifted her in his arms and strode to the stairs, Tyler's body warm and soft against his, her slender fingers stroking his nape in a way that lit up every nerve ending. Damn it, he was a man, not a monk. If he was going to hell, he was going to enjoy the trip. In the upstairs hallway, he stopped a moment, trying to decide which room to use.

"Mine," Tyler said, reading his mind.

Chapter 8

Tyler's bedroom was slightly larger than the one Rafe was using, but he wasn't interested in square footage or anything else right now. His only focus was getting to the bed—a wide expanse of orange-and-gold comforter that looked thick enough to wallow in—getting them both undressed, and sliding into her body. He had to stop for a moment and take a deep breath to slow himself down. He was so aroused that he wanted only to rip off her clothes and feel her wet heat around him. Standing Tyler on her feet, he yanked the comforter back and pushed the pillows up toward the headboard. Then he went to work unwrapping his present.

Easing the T-shirt up and over her head, he tossed it to the side. No bra, just as he expected. Thank you, God. Stepping back, he took a moment to enjoy the sight of her round, plump breasts with their dark rosy nipples. Needing to touch them, he reached out and cupped them in his palms, squeezing gently. He rubbed his thumbs over the pebbled tips, reveling in the feel of them. Tyler stood motionless with her hands at her sides and sucked in a breath at his touch. The pulse at the hollow of her throat pounded against the thin layer of skin covering it like a jackhammer. Rafe couldn't resist. He lowered his head, placed his mouth over the delicate flesh, and sucked.

Every hair on his body felt as if it had been singed. God, she tasted even better than she looked or smelled. She had a unique flavor all her own, one that woke up every one of his taste buds. He couldn't wait to slide his tongue into her warm pussy and drink from her elixir.

Her nipple hardened even more as he wrapped his tongue around it and sucked it into his mouth. She clutched his biceps, digging her fingers into the hard muscle as he dragged his teeth lightly across the beaded tip. He tweaked her other nipple with thumb and forefinger, rolling it and pinching it lightly. A tiny moan vibrated from her throat as she arched herself into his touch.

When he had given both nipples equal time, he trailed kisses up through the valley of her breasts and the slender column of her neck. With his tongue he drew a path beneath her jawline and over to the soft flesh beneath one ear. He treated himself to a light nip before sliding his mouth to the other side and giving that lobe equal attention. Her skin was so soft and smooth, like polished satin, he was sure he could spend hours just licking every inch of it.

Tyler's breath was a soft breeze on his neck as she reached down and tugged the hem of his shirt from his jeans, pulling it up to expose his chest. She lifted it high enough that he could press his naked skin against her breasts and—holy shit!—the sensation was incredible. Her breasts were soft and firm at the same time, the hard points of her nipples branding his chest.

He stepped back for a moment to yank his shirt off the rest of the way and toss it to the side. Banding his arms around Tyler's lush body, he pulled her hard against him as if trying to imprint her body on his. He took a good look at her face and was startled not to see the hard-ass Tyler who gave the world the finger. This was a Tyler with everything stripped away, with that same vulnerability he'd spotted earlier. With a need in her eyes so strong it nearly brought him to his knees. His heart stuttered and his breath for a moment was trapped in his throat.

What the hell had he gotten himself into here?

Well, it was too late to second-guess himself now. The barriers were down and someone would have to shoot him to get him to stop.

The two layers of clothing still between them did nothing to diminish the impact the outline of his engorged cock made against her mound. His eyes locked with hers, he lifted her hands to his mouth and sucked lightly on each finger, dusting each tip with his tongue. That pulse beating so hard at the hollow of her throat increased its tempo. He pressed a firm kiss to the indentation, feeling the beat of the blood rushing through her veins against his lips.

Impatient now to see the rest of her, he undid the zipper at the back of her shorts and pushed them slowly down her toned legs. She balanced herself with her hands on his shoulders as she stepped out of the material and kicked them to the side. The insubstantial bit of lace that remained barely covered her pussy, tempting him and making his mouth water. His eyes widened as he saw the smooth skin on either side of the little triangle. Waxed. Holy fucking shit. His greatest fantasy come to life.

Unable to help himself, he knelt before her, placed his mouth right over her mound, and trailed the tip of his tongue the length of her slit, fabric and all. He wanted to lick his lips at the flavor of her exotic taste, sweet and spicy at the same time. He did it again, gripping her hips with his hands to hold her in place. Her skin was so warm and soft beneath his touch he couldn't wait to run his palms over every inch of it.

He felt her tremble as he licked his way from top to bottom of her slit again, using the barely there fabric to rub the nerve endings in the tender flesh. When he couldn't stand it any longer, he used his teeth to peel away the tiny triangle. Then with his thumbs, he opened the lips of her cunt and treated himself to a feast. She was hot and liquid, drenched with her own honey, and he lapped like a man who hadn't had a drink in forever. He followed the hot line between her cunt lips up and down, up and down before taking her clit gently between his teeth.

Tyler dug her fingers into his shoulders, bracing herself to hold her balance. She was trembling from head to toe and the little sexy moans she made told him she was close to orgasm. He tugged and nipped her clit with his teeth, alternating that with swipes of his tongue. The way she pushed her hips at him was her silent indication that she wanted more from him. That she wanted him inside her, but he wasn't ready for that yet. He would give her layer upon layer of pleasure before he slipped anything inside her. They couldn't do this again, so he would make this one time memorable for both of them.

He worked her with his tongue and teeth again and again, excited by her little cries of, "Please, please, please." And then, shifting his hands to grip her hips tightly once more, he bit down more intensely on her clit and jolted her into a climax. She tried to squeeze her thighs together, to apply pressure to the spasms in her inner walls, but Rafe held her in place. As she shook and quavered, rocking back and forth and moaning one steady sound of pleasure, he continued to torment her clit until the last shudder subsided.

Tyler bent down and pressed her forehead against his, her breath whispering against his face as she drew in air and tried to settle her racing pulse. Rafe held onto her until her breathing settled, then rose, lifted her, and placed her gently on the bed. His own breathing was far from steady as he looked at her beautiful skin flushed from her climax, her eyes heavy-lidded with desire, her lips swollen from kisses. He couldn't remember ever wanting a woman as much as he wanted this one right now. And not just for a quick fuck, damn it. He was turning into an emotional hot mess over this woman.

He couldn't stop. He'd probably be cursed for it later but he wasn't turning back now.

"I think one of us is a little overdressed." Tyler's voice was slightly unsteady and heavy with desire. It electrified him to know that she was as shaky about what was happening as he was.

"All in good time," he assured her. If he took off his pants now, he was sure he'd come without even touching himself. And when was the last time that had happened to him?

Kneeling between her thighs, he bent her legs and planted her feet flat on the bed, positioning her legs as far apart as possible. Immediately the image of her out on the lawn smoothing sunscreen into the crease where her thigh met her mound slammed into him and he gave in to temptation. He indulged himself for a moment, caressing the smooth skin of her inner thighs and her calves, the feel of them beneath his fingers better than any aphrodisiac. He wanted to lay her down on his bed and stroke her forever.

Forever? Rafe Ortiz didn't do forever, at least not with someone like Tyler Gillette. Only, every nerve and fiber of his body was shrieking for him to lose himself in her body, to bind her close to him, to—

Jesus!

And there she was, naked before him, presented like a feast he'd never get enough of. Bending low, he traced the seam with the tip of his tongue, first one side, then the other. Just the simple act sent a shiver skating over his body. When he did it again, Tyler reached out to slide her fingers into his hair, anchoring them in the thick black strands and trying to guide his head.

He paused in his journey over her sensitive areas to drink in the sight of her exquisite cunt. Her soft, neatly trimmed pubic curls marched in straight lines down the length of her outer lips. Rafe wished he had the guts to take a picture, an image that could keep him warm on many cold nights. She was gorgeous. Exquisite. So tempting and beckoning. Then he drew in a breath, inhaling her incredible scent, exhaled, and stroked her entire pussy with the flat of his tongue.

"Ohhhhh." The sound blew out on an exhale, soft and breathy.

Rafe looked at her, his mouth curved in a ravenous smile. Rising to his knees, he curved his fingers around her wrists and lifted her hands above her head toward the headboard. Deliberately he wrapped her fingers around two of the spokes.

"Keep them there," he told her. "Right there. No matter what, don't move them."

She licked her bottom lip slowly, back and forth. In response, his cock pressed even harder against his fly. He swallowed a groan.

"Is that an order?" she asked, her voice low and sultry.

"Damn straight." He barely recognized his own voice. "And don't you forget it."

He set himself up again between her creamy thighs and took a long moment to drink in every inch of her exquisite pussy. Then went to work with his tongue. He stroked her labia, inside and out, drawing lines with a slow movement and then a fast one. She was so delicious, so tasty, he thought he could do this forever. He nipped the very tip of her clit and tugged it, scraping his teeth lightly against the ultrasensitive dark pink flesh. Up, down, tug, tug. It was like a choreographed ballet performed with his mouth, the music silent but playing in his head. Damn it, this woman was casting a spell on him, and he didn't seem to be able to do anything about it.

And all the time Tyler twisted and begged and pleaded, but she never let go of the headboard. When he reached the point where he needed to explore her wet passage he stiffened his tongue and thrust it deep inside her.

"Oh, God!" She arched her hips up toward his mouth, pushing just enough that he was able to thrust into her more deeply.

Her hot, wet inner walls clutched his tongue, and he drove it in and out. Those delightful little sounds whispered from her mouth again. Curling his tongue, he scraped it leisurely against the sweet spot, drawing another exclamation of pleasure from her. When the muscles of her channel began to quiver against the intrusion of her tongue, he plucked at her clit, thrust his tongue harder inside her, and pinched her clit hard.

Her release broke over her, so intensely her entire body shook. Rafe continued to stroke her channel with his tongue while he held her in place. Her entire body was consumed by the orgasm, shaking and shivering, unconscious little moans of pleasure erupting from her. He took his time easing her down from the crest, still working her with his tongue, now lapping both inside and out until her body stopped quivering. Then he shifted so he was looking directly into her eyes. His lips were barely an inch from hers.

"Don't move those hands yet," he cautioned.

"Bossy, aren't we." But he could tell she liked it.

"See how good you taste." He lapped the surface of her lips with the flat of his tongue, sharing her liquid with her.

Heat flared in her eyes as she very slowly licked her lips.

That was it. Rafe had waited about as long as he could. There was more—much more—he wanted to do with her. To her. But his self-control was at an end. He stood up beside the bed and rid himself of his socks.

Then he unzipped his fly and shed his slacks and boxers. When he turned back toward Tyler, her eyes were focused directly on his cock, engorged and pointing almost directly at her. The head was a deep purple and the vein twisted around it pulsed with the blood flowing through it. Tyler's eyes widened and she licked her lips, that little swipe with her tongue that set a match to him.

He reached into the pocket of his slacks for his wallet and took out the sole condom he carried with him. Rafe had never been one for indiscriminate sex, not even in high school. He always had enough protection for one encounter, but as a norm, he knew ahead of time what he'd need and prepared for it.

Tyler slid a glance over as he tossed the condom on the nightstand.

"Either you don't have much confidence in your staying ability or in mine," she teased, but her voice was still uneven.

He gave a rough laugh. "I had no plans for this, Tyler. You know that. It's a damn good thing I had one with me."

"Always prepared? Were you a Boy Scout?"

"I was a lot of things but right now what I am is…so ready for you." He drank in her body with a thirsty look. "You can let go of the headboard, Tyler."

He positioned himself between her legs again and reached for the foil packet, but Tyler released her grip on the headboard as he said and knocked his hands away.

"Let me."

She ripped the foil open and with her slim fingers slowly rolled the latex down his distended length. Rafe sucked in a breath, just the mere contact with her touch enough to nearly send him over the edge.

"Easy." He told her through clenched teeth.

She stared at his shaft for so long he had an urge to tell her to get on with it.

"You can take it," he promised "I'll go slow. Real slow. Besides, those two orgasms I gave you ought to have you primed and ready." At least he hoped so.

"You know I'd love to take this in my mouth right now." She wet her lips again, and his cock flexed in her hand, making her smile.

He could have said another time, but he was determined this was going to be once and done. He hoped he didn't spend a long time regretting this lapse in judgment and his total capitulation to his hunger for her.

It took every bit of effort to maintain control while Tyler finished sheathing him. Then he stunned her by flipping her over and pulling her up to her hands and knees. He pulled some of the pillows over beneath her body to support her.

"Relax," he told her when she tensed her muscles. "I know what you're thinking. We're not going there. Not that I wouldn't like to but—" Shit, He was about to get himself in trouble here. He just knew it. "But what I really want to do right this minute is take you from behind so you can feel me all the way to the heart of you."

Before she could say anything else, he grasped the root of his dick, positioned it at her opening, and eased himself inside. She was soaked from her two previous climaxes and her muscles were relaxed, so even as large as his cock was, penetration was fairly easy. He ground his teeth together, holding himself in check as he eased into her, until at last she had taken him all the way. When he was fully inside her, deep inside, he took a moment to close his eyes and haul in a steadying breath. He was so deep inside her he felt as if her entire body was clamped around him, that he'd reached every secret place.

Jesus, how was it possible for anything to feel this good?

He took a moment to appreciate the curve of her ass, the sweep of her spine, the flare of her hips. Then, gripping those very seductive hips, he pulled out just to the tip, then thrust back in again. Pulled back and drove into her. She was so hot and wet she scorched him even through the condom. He had mentally prepared himself to dig for enough discipline to bring her back to the edge again, but it seemed only seconds before she was rocking with him, arching back to him, tightening down on him like a hot, wet vise. They began moving as one, Tyler riding his thrust and retreat motion, pushing back when he drove into her harder and harder.

When his balls and the muscles at the base of his spine sent him the familiar signals and he teetered at the edge, he reached around to Tyler's swollen clit and pinched it, hard. And just like that they both exploded. It was everything he'd thought it would be and more, an experience that made fireworks seem tame and a hurricane mild. He lost all sense of anything except his body and Tyler's, clenching and spasming, shuddering in tandem, her pussy squeezing down hard on his pulsing cock as he emptied himself into the thin latex sheath.

He had no idea how long the orgasm went on, only that he finally was spent, his muscles limp. He rolled to the side, taking Tyler with him, their bodies still connected. He wasn't sure he'd ever be able to draw a full breath again or that his heart would settle back to a steady beat. He cradled the warm woman in his arms, one hand cupping her breast, relishing the feel of her body against his.

He was fully and completely drained, emotionally and physically, every bit of who he was emptied into this woman in his arms who was such a contradiction in terms. They lay there like that for a very long time, neither of them saying a word. What could he say? That this was the single most intense experience of his life? That this one taste of her wouldn't ever be enough? That what he felt for her went way beyond the sex itself. He'd buried his feelings for Tyler Gillette for a lot of years. A lot of *careful* years. Now they had all come flooding to the surface, threatening to strangle him. This woman was poison for him and yet here he was, totally lost in her.

Damn it all to hell, anyway. He was so fucking screwed.

* * * *

Tyler woke slowly from a very pleasant dream. She was lying in Rafe's arms, replete from the most satisfying, soul-shattering sex she had ever had. Every muscle in her body ached, her sex was tingly and sore, but it had more than been worth it. The reality had been so much better than the dream.

It had taken every bit of nerve she'd had and then some to pull off the teasing display in her yard. She'd felt like a stripper on stage, enticing one of the customers. It so wasn't her, no matter what people thought. But she wanted Rafe so badly. If she never had another chance, she was going to make the most of this one. And it was definitely worth it.

Finally, she'd been able to feast her eyes on him, taking in every bit of the reality. And wow, he was just big all over. *All over.* She shivered at the memory of his very large cock fully seated in her wet channel. She barely stopped herself from reaching down between her legs to stroke herself while she called up memories of the night before. Too bad he'd only had the one condom, but it had been put to memorable use.

She'd finally realized her dream. She'd gotten him into bed for one night of unbelievable sex.

It was more than just sex.

The little voice that always rattled on in her head whispered to her. It definitely was more than just sex. And Rafe had lost himself in her. She'd had enough sex—although not for a long time now—to tell the difference between pure physical and sex with heavy emotion laced through it. For a few hours, he'd let down all his shields, but she was sure they were back in place by now. She'd just have to figure out how to breach them again.

Because the joke, apparently, was on her. One night would never be enough with this man. She wanted more. She wanted it all. He could say he didn't feel the same thing but that would be far from the truth. They'd peeled back layers and delved into the deepest parts of each other. Now she knew she'd have to battle him to keep it that way.

She stretched lazily, and reached out a hand to touch him, finding— Nothing. Empty space. She opened her eyes and slid a glance to the other side of the bed. Yup. Empty. If not for the dent in the bedclothes and the pleasant soreness of her body, she might have thought she'd imagined the whole thing.

She lay back against the pillows and plopped a forearm over her eyes. Of course. Just as she'd thought. He'd let his libido overtake his so-called good sense and when it was over he'd rabbited the hell out of her room. Well, too bad. If he thought this was the end of it, he was very much mistaken. He could try to deny all he wanted that there was anything between them except sex, but she knew better. No one made the connection they had without something deeper involved. The problem was convincing him of that.

Would he even give her a chance or would he just pull on the ice-cold shield he kept around himself and act as if last night never happened? She could just hear him now saying, *"I'll take door number two."* Too bad, Mr. *Former Football Player.* She'd had a real taste of him now and she wasn't going back. She'd just have to change her game plan a little.

He wanted her.

But in what way and for how long? Obviously not long enough to stick around after the most incredible sex she could ever remember having. She was sure he would either pretend it didn't happen or try to explain why it could never happen again,

She grabbed one of the pillows he'd used and pulled it over to smash against her face. When she inhaled, she could still smell the traces of his scent, that warm leather that spread through her body and made all her secret places tingle. It occurred to her how absolutely stupid she was, lying here hugging the pillow of a man who had probably already wiped last night from his mind, but she wasn't giving up. Whoever this stalker was, he'd created a situation where she had a chance at connecting with Rafe. At realizing a dream she'd held onto for a long time. She wasn't giving up that easily.

Glancing at the little clock she kept on the nightstand, she realized it was after nine o'clock. Not so late for her but probably for Rafe. He'd have team business—security business—to take care of. Who knew how long ago he'd left the room. Okay, time for her to get up, too. She rolled out of bed and started to pull the top sheet around herself then laughed. Who was she covering herself over for? He'd seen just about every nook and cranny in her body already. Opening the door to the hallway a crack, she tried to listen for sounds downstairs. Rafe's voice floated up to her faintly, no doubt from a phone conversation.

Phone. Her brain clicked over.

She looked around for her cell phone, which had been strangely silent. Maybe because she'd left it downstairs last night when Rafe carried her up to her room. And wasn't that a delicious image to hold onto. Meanwhile, she wanted her cell. She was sure by this time at least Betsy had tried to get hold of her. They hadn't spoken since yesterday morning.

Had her stalker called again? Would Rafe have told her if he had? Time to get moving.

She quickly showered and washed her hair, taking a few extra minutes to lather all the places Rafe had used his mouth and his fingers and his cock the night before. She slipped on a pair of skinny jeans and a bright green T-shirt. Again this morning she left off her makeup, realizing with a shock how good it made her feel. Yesterday the ball cap she wore, along with the absence of her usual painted public face, had served to keep people from staring at her, so she dug one out of her closet and plopped it on her head.

For a moment, she was tempted to wear the one from Tequila Sunrise but that would precipitate a lecture from Rafe, and she was not in the mood for that. The waning of the postcoital glow was bad enough. She didn't need him destroying it altogether. Instead she found one with no artwork on it (And where had that come from, anyway?), stuck it on her head and pulled her ponytail through the opening in back. Then, still barefoot, she hurried down the stairs.

"Okay," she heard Rafe saying, "I'll get back to you but we'll probably be there late morning."

She followed the sound of his voice to the kitchen. He was hanging up just as she walked in. "Are we going somewhere?"

He nodded. "There's a game tomorrow. I have things to do at the stadium today."

Go to the stadium? The place she despised? Sitting in Rafe's office yesterday had been bad enough.

"Can't someone else do it for you?" She sashayed over to him and pulled out her most seductive smile. "My father said you could turn stuff over to someone else."

She reached up to play with the curl of hair peeking out of the vee of his soft-collar shirt, but he grabbed her wrist and tugged her hand away. When she looked up, his face wore that same hard, implacable expression she was used to. The one that said don't waste your time trying to tempt me. The one she'd seen every time except for last night. The hot, passionate man of the previous night had completely disappeared. In his place was a man totally in control of his feelings and not about to let that control slip.

Well, wasn't that what she'd predicted earlier? She swallowed the hurt that bubbled up and stepped away from him.

"Then I'm staying here. I hate that place and I hate the team. You go without me."

"Not happening." He said the words as if it were a done deal. "And don't bother trying to argue with me. I'm not letting you out of my sight until we catch whoever this is."

She tried on a grin again. "So does that mean we sleep together again?"

His fingers were like steel gripping her shoulders. "Last night was a big mistake, Tyler. It's the last time it's going to happen. Trust me on that."

She searched his face for some semblance of softness but his expression was hard as steel.

"You loved every minute of it," she reminded him. "Don't try to deny it."

"That doesn't matter. It can't happen again and it won't."

"Give me one good reason why it can't." She knew she was pushing his buttons, but she couldn't help herself.

He released his grip on her and took a step back. "I'll give you two. Your father and your lifestyle. I took advantage of you last night. It won't happen again."

Her jaw dropped. This was not the reaction she'd hoped for. Wanted. Craved. "Took advantage? But—"

"The subject is closed. Now go put some shoes on. We have to leave."

"Leave? I told you I'm not going." She had a childish urge to stamp her foot.

A muscle in his jaw twitched. "You're going if I have to tie you up to go. And we have to stop for breakfast first, since it's not your job to cook for me."

She shrugged. "We could order in. Or eat out."

"Well, we're taking option number two this morning. On the way home later, we're making a pit stop at a grocery store. It's bad enough that I'm stuck here. I don't intend to starve. We'll have to leave time for it."

"Time?"

"We have that fancy shindig tonight, remember?"

"Oh, right." He had no idea how much she didn't want to go to the function.

He rubbed his face as if he could rub everything away. "Get me the invitation. I need to check everything out, and we'll have to stop by my place to pick up my tux. Fuck." He picked up his keys from the counter. "How the hell did I let myself get talked into this, anyway?"

Tyler turned away, unwilling to let him see how his words hurt her.

"I'm not leaving without my phone. Where is it? I need to talk to my friends. They probably think I've run away or something."

"Yeah?" His voice was edged with sarcasm. "I thought you texted with some of them yesterday."

"That was yesterday. So, phone?" She held out her hand, palm up.

With obvious reluctance he pulled it from his pocket. He studied it for a long time, frowning.

"Is there something wrong?" Fear clutched at her. "Oh my God. He called again, right? Didn't he? Let me see that." She reached out, but he held it just away from her.

"Before I give this to you, yes, he called. I have to leave everything on there because we're using it to backtrack to your carrier and get at least a serial number of the burner. Just like I told you yesterday. Don't freak out too badly when you see it."

"See what?" She wiggled her fingers. "Gimme."

Rafe handed over the phone and she began to scroll through missed calls. Several from Betsy and three of her other friends. And five of them from the stalker.

"I didn't answer them," he told her. "I was hoping he'd leave a voice-mail message."

"He's probably too smart for that," she pointed out. Next she checked her text messages. Again, a slew from Betsy and her friend Lynn, which she knew she'd have to answer before they invaded her place. And one from her stalker. She nearly dropped the phone when she read it.

"Did u fck hm?"

She looked up at Rafe, who was watching her through narrowed eyes.

"He knows you slept here." She hated the way her voice shook. "I told you not to leave your car in the driveway."

"Yeah, well, apparently it's not as much a deterrent as I'd hoped. Instead it pushed his hot buttons. Whoever he is."

Tyler frowned. "Is there more?"

"Put your shoes on and I'll show you. We need to get going so I can get my work done. We have to be back here by four."

"Why? What's going on?"

"Shoes," he said again. "Then I'll tell you. In the meantime I'm calling the Lone Star offices so they can get someone over here to beef up the alarm system."

"Beef up? Exactly how?"

"Add more sensors, especially outside. We don't want this guy to get so close to the house anymore. Next time he might not stop in the driveway."

A little chill raced the length of her spine, but she did her best not to show Rafe how upset she was. At all costs, she was going to keep her cool. Shoving the phone in her pocket, she raced up stairs and stuck her feet into flat sandals. Rafe was waiting for her at the door. His up and down glance seemed to strip her of all clothing and made her body heat rise.

She waited for him to say something, but he just motioned for her to precede him to the driveway. She stood there while he reset the alarm and locked the door. She hurried down the walk toward his car—and stopped.

An uneven line ran the length of the car, from the front fenders to the rear, along the doors. Forcing her feet to move, she walked around to the other side where the same damage had been done. She looked over at Rafe, who nodded.

"Yes, I saw it earlier when I went out to get something from the car. What really pisses me off is that he managed it right under my nose."

While we were in bed. Having sex. Fucking.

She wanted to tell him to go ahead and just say it. Get it all out in the open, but the words wouldn't come. It was bad enough that he'd already been regretting it. Now he'd have a good excuse to avoid it altogether. Well, too bad. She'd just have to figure out a way around his barricades.

In the next moment, the anger was replaced by a surge of fear. "Pretty bold of him, walking right up here knowing you were here with me."

"I'd venture a guess that might have been what lit another small fire under him." The muscle twitched in his jaw again. "I called the Lone Star office and asked them to send over an alarm service. They'll be here later this afternoon to upgrade the system you have and extend it to the outside areas."

She wasn't in the mood to argue with him anymore about this. If she did, she was just being stupid, ignoring her own safety. She might want to be independent, she might still nurse a major hurt where her father was concerned, but she was smart enough to know she should not put herself at risk. Independence only worked to a certain point.

She wet her lips. "Okay." *See how easy that was, Tyler?* "And, um, thank you."

He shrugged. "Your father is the one you should be thanking. We'd better get going here."

She was so many kinds of nervous by now she even forgot to ask him where they were going to breakfast. It didn't surprise her, however, when they pulled into a place called Bacon and Eggs. It was not only a favorite spot for the Hawks players but for most of the social and financial players in the city. What started out as a mom-and-pop restaurant had morphed about ten years ago into a comfortable but well-appointed restaurant that served everything from the food in its name to breakfast quiche and practically any exotic breakfast dish you could name.

It used to be one of her ex-husband's favorite places to eat brunch on a Saturday. He could rub elbows with everyone from football players to bankers to hedge fund managers to reporters and pretend he was a major player in the city. Crap. It would be just her luck that he'd be here today.

"Could we go someplace else?" she asked as Rafe pulled into a parking space.

"Why? I like the food, and I enjoy the people who come here for it."

"Well, what if I don't?"

"Unless you have a very valid reason for that, I'm getting out of the car now. I'm hungry, and we're burning daylight."

She put her hand on his arm, trying to ignore the way he tensed beneath her touch.

"Why are you suddenly being so mean to me? Why are you acting this way? I thought—"

He jerked his arm away. "You thought what? That some hot sex would change things? Get real, little girl. And get out of the car. I'm hungry."

She stared at him as if he had suddenly turned into a stranger. Rafe had been cold to her before, the few times she'd seen him, but not like this.

He blew out a breath. "I'm sorry, Tyler. That was uncalled for. I apologize. I—" He paused, then shook his head. "Never mind. *Now* can we please get some food?"

Tyler wasn't sure which stunned her more, his insult or his apology. She opted not to say anything, not that she knew what she'd say anyway, and climbed out of the car. All she needed to top this morning off was to run into her ex here.

And yup, the bad luck gods were having a laugh at her expense. They had barely settled into the booth they managed to snag when a voice she'd hoped never to hear sounded in her ear.

"Well, hey, Tyler. I'm glad to see you in here. This must be my lucky day."

She looked up from her open menu and yes, indeedy, there he was. Mr. Metrosexual Broder himself. Today he wore gray slacks with a black V-neck sweater on his slender build, the one she'd been attracted to because it was so different from the huge musclemen on the football team. Any football team. The sleeves were pushed up as if copying the habit of men obviously more masculine than he was. His hair was gelled and styled, and he sported a gold Rolex on one wrist. He'd always told her it was a symbol of his success.

If she hadn't been so reluctant to defend the athletes she saw as competition for her father's attention, she would have told him they could each buy a hundred Rolexes without dipping into their lunch money. What had she ever seen in this phony anyway?

She looked up at him and pasted on a fake smile. "Hello, Nate. Too bad I can't say the same." She hoped he caught the vinegar in her words.

She heard Rafe mutter under his breath, "Speak of the devil."

Nate frowned, and waved a finger back and forth between her and Rafe. "So, are you two an item now?"

"Yes." She said it for sheer meanness.

"No," Rafe said at the same time.

Nate laughed that weird laugh that after a time had grated on her nerves like steel on slate. "Shouldn't you get your stories straight?"

"What can we do for you?" Tyler asked. "I'm sure you must have much more important or interesting people to talk to."

"I always have interesting people to talk to." He looked at Rafe again, then back at Tyler. "Tyler, I'm really glad to see you. Why have you stopped answering my calls?"

"Because I don't want to talk to you." She met his gaze head-on. "Don't you get that?"

"Come on, Tyler." He pulled out what she was sure he thought of as his charm and that she found sort of smarmy. "I hate the way we left things."

"We left it the way it should be." She was doing her best to control her irritation with him. Their marriage had been a disaster from day one, at least as far as she was concerned. She had no desire to rehash it now. She just wanted him gone.

"I don't think so. I've really missed you." His mouth curved in what she always called his client smile, the one he used for, well, clients.

"Sorry, I can't say the same. And you can kill the orders for flowers and all that crap. I only throw them out, so you might as well save your money. Stop calling me. We're done, Nate. Finished. Get the message."

He frowned. "I haven't sent you flowers in a while, Tyler. Not since you yelled at me over the phone about them."

Her stomach knotted and she lowered her hands to her lap so he wouldn't see them shake. "Y-you stopped sending them?"

"Uh-huh. So if you're still getting them, you must have a new admirer." He shoved his hands in his pockets. "I'm not sure I like having competition."

Even as she fought the sudden wash of fear, anger surged through her. "Listen to me, Nate. Really listen. You are nothing to me. We are done. Over. *Finito.*"

"Come on, Tyler. We really need to sit down and talk." His voice softened. "As a matter of fact, a client of the firm is having a gallery opening next week." He pulled out that smile again. "I was hoping I could talk you into going with me. You still appreciate art, right?"

Calm, she told herself as she tried to bite back the anger. *Stay calm.* She needed to be firm but nice. That was difficult to do with Nate. However, getting into a spat with him here in the restaurant wouldn't do anyone any good. Maybe if she was polite but firm he'd go away.

"I still do, but that's a big no on the invite."

"Do you have plans?" He looked again at Rafe, who sat silently while this little tableau played out, then back at Tyler. "I can call you with the details." His smile faded. "Please listen to me. You know I was never happy with our split. We were good together. Very good. And you know it." He reached for her hand, but she jerked it away.

"The 'we were good' part lasted about a week and you know it." She forced out the next sentence. "By any chance have you been around my town house lately?"

He narrowed his eyes. "What—Why—"

"Have. You. Been. Around. My. Town house. Lately." She enunciated each word carefully. She glanced across the table at Rafe, who was watching the conversation intently, ready to step in if he needed to. "That's a simple enough question, right?"

The muscles in his face tightened. "If I happen to drive by once in a while, what's the big deal?"

She could hardly believe what he was saying. "You don't even live anywhere near me."

He shrugged. "Maybe I have friends in the area." He shifted his gaze to Rafe, then back to her. "What's going on here? What's this all about, anyway? Is something happening to you?"

He was either sincere or a very good liar. Right now, she couldn't afford to cross him off the list.

"Nothing's going on," she said at last. "But don't call me anymore and don't drive past my house. And now, if you'll excuse me, I want to study the menu."

"What about next weekend?" he persisted. "I'm not giving up here. We had something special together."

Rafe finally put down his menu and looked at Nate. "Apparently not special enough. The lady asked you more than once to leave her alone. It would be smart of you to do so."

"Or what?" Nate challenged. His voice was hostile now but his face held a look of desperation. "You'll get some of your football goons to beat me up?"

Rafe stated to rise but Tyler held out her hand. She was already tired of Nate. If he turned out to be her stalker, she'd be happy for them to lock him up far, far away.

"Enough, Nate. If you ever want to be able to score private suite tickets for a Hawks game again, you should just shut up and walk away. Now."

It was obvious by the way his entire body tensed up that he was far from finished, but he finally nodded his head.

"If that's the way you want it, I'll go. For now. But I know all that snark is just a front you put up to keep people away. I'm not finished yet." He started to leave then stopped. "I'll say it again, Tyler. We were damn good together. You just need to be a little more open to the situation, and we can be good together again."

"Over my dead body," she muttered as she watched him stride toward the rear of the restaurant and slide into a booth.

She noticed there was no one else sitting there, which she thought a little strange. Maybe he was meeting someone, because Nate never did anything without an audience. Not even eat a meal.

"I might need more than coffee after that." She forced herself to relax and nodded at the waitress. The woman had avoided the confrontation but now arrived with a full pot of coffee.

"Some of your football goons?" Rafe repeated. "He doesn't have a very high opinion of something that he obviously doesn't mind taking advantage of. He gets free guest-suite invites?"

Tyler lifted one shoulder and let it drop. "He got them as a perk of our marriage and kept them as part of the divorce settlement, such as it was. Thanks, Dad, for your wonderful generosity. He keeps using them to impress clients. I guess I should put a stop to it. I don't know why I haven't before this."

"It concerns me," Rafe said, "that he's been able to get your new phone numbers and has been driving by your house. What's this about flowers and calls?"

"I told you about it. After we divorced he started on a campaign to, as he put it, win me back." She nibbled on a fingernail. "The flowers and candy started again about the same time I began getting the strange calls. Except he says they aren't coming from him."

Rafe gave her a hard look. "Don't dismiss him as harmless, Tyler. He's still got a thing going for you, which makes him dangerous in my book. We almost had to throw him out of here to get him to leave."

She shuddered. "No kidding. But what can I do?"

He gave her a tight smile. "That's what you have me for." He slid out of the booth. "Order me a number seven. I'll be back in a few."

Tyler turned to look over her shoulder, frowning. He'd damn well better tell her what he was talking about when he came back. She was no dimwit to be kept in the dark. This was her life and her safety they were discussing. She turned around again and picked up her coffee, sipping at the hot liquid. Too bad it wasn't hot enough to melt the chill that had suddenly settled right in the center of her body.

Chapter 9

While they finished breakfast, Rafe told her about the call he'd made.

"I wanted Lone Star to be sure they put Nate Broder's name right up there with Chad Sinclair and Ed Spinelli. I'd originally put Chad at the top but Nate's almost running neck and neck with him after this morning's little display. And we can't forget Ed. Before we're through we'll know everything there is to know about them," he assured her. "Not that it's my business, but what the hell did you ever see in those assholes?"

She took a sip of her coffee. "I still ask myself that."

No way would she ever tell him marrying Nate had been her attempt to make herself acceptable to her father. She'd thought for sure a well-connected, successful attorney would do the trick. But Kurt had ignored the situation except to grant the request for game tickets. And once Tyler realized she was actually going to have to live with Nate and put herself through some very boring sex, she'd tossed him out. Kurt hadn't made a single comment, just sent her to a shark of an attorney so her trust fund was protected.

Rafe studied her over the rim of his mug. "We need to expand on the list you gave me yesterday. I need to know everyone you've come into contact with on a regular basis. That even includes the guy who does your landscaping who might have a secret fetish for you. So take a minute while you're sitting there, make another list of every male in your life no matter how insignificant, and I'll have the agency check them out. Do it when we get to the stadium."

His phone rang while they were finishing their coffee. From his side of the conversation she assumed it was about Nate and that Rafe wanted whoever it was to dig deeper. His comments were so terse she finally gave up trying to make sense of them. She pulled out her own cell, which she'd silenced, and scrolled through missed calls and texts. She caught Rafe looking at her, one eyebrow raised in question, silently asking if there was anything from her stalker. She shook her head and busied herself texting Betsy and Lynn.

As soon as Rafe finished his conversation, he signaled for the check. The drive to the stadium was accomplished in silence. Rafe's face gave away nothing of his thoughts, but she could tell he was deep in concentration. She went back to exchanging texts until they pulled into the stadium parking lot. Phone still in hand, she followed Rafe to the on-site Lone Star security office. It was on the ground floor where it served as the base of operations on game days.

"Do you want anything?" Rafe asked. "I need to get my team together and discuss tomorrow."

"I'm good." She flipped a hand at him. "If I want something, I can go look for it."

"No."

"No?" She gawked at him. "Are you telling me I can't wander around my father's stadium?"

He nodded. "I'm not taking any chances."

"For God's sake, Rafe. Surely you don't think any of those guys would be dumb enough to try something here."

"I'm not taking any chances. Until we nail him down—whoever he is—I want my eyes on you at all times." He waved at a chair in the corner. "Make yourself comfortable for the moment. We'll be going out into the stadium itself shortly. Meanwhile, work on that list for me."

Tyler didn't know whether to be pleased he was so concerned about her safety or pissed because he was acting as if last night had never happened. She plopped down in her chair and took out her phone. Betsy had texted her again.

"R u serious? That hot man is in yr house? Alone with u?"

"He's not all that."

The answer came back in a minute. *"If that's what u thnk you are seriously insane."*

"So I gss I'm nuts."

"Cn u talk? I want deets."

"None 2 tell u." She added a little smiley face.

"Ha-ha." Betsy added a grinning devil with a pitchfork.

While she was texting, the security guards filed into Rafe's office. The room was fairly large but the size and number of the men quickly gave it a crowded feeling. Rafe did not introduce Tyler nor did she make it a point to greet any of them. She finally stowed her phone and made herself as invisible in the corner as possible, curious to watch the man at his job.

She found it interesting the way he handed out assignments. She got the idea that most of the men had been with him for a while so this was more just checking their to-do lists. She was interested, though, to hear the changes that had been made.

"Tomorrow we play the Mustangs," he told his staff. "That's always a highly emotional game. Last year we had some fights erupt that we luckily managed to break up before anyone got seriously hurt. But between that and the episodes of violence around the country, management has decided to increase personnel on game day."

"Are they trained?" someone asked.

Rafe nodded. "Just not by us. But they have worked athletic events before. They'll be part of the yellow vest crew."

Tyler knew enough about it to know that Rafe's top crew wore soft-collared polo shirts in red with the Hawks logo. The rest of the men wore red Hawks T-shirts with bright green vests over them. Rafe believed in maximum visibility for his men at all times. She also knew that only Rafe and two other men were armed. The orders were never to use firearms except in extreme circumstances. Tyler had no idea what those would be, but she didn't remember an incident with a shooting ever happening at Southern Bank Stadium.

She passed the time trying to create the list that Rafe wanted. About the time she was finished, had e-mailed it to Rafe, and scrolled through her texts from Betsy and Lynn again, the men began to move out of the office.

Rafe motioned to her. "Come on."

"Come on? Where to?"

"The stadium proper. We do a final check and a walkthrough for the new guys." He looked at his watch. "I'll be as quick as I can. Let's go."

"I'll wait here."

"Did you already forget what I said before?" He took one of her hands and tugged her from the chair. "Come on. Up."

She was tempted to make an issue of it, but the sooner they finished the sooner they could get out of here. There was nothing about the stadium that made her enjoy being here. It represented everything she'd hated all her life, her competitor along with the team for the affections of Kurt Gillette. But she just let Rafe pull her to her feet. He kept her hand enclosed in his as they made their way along the concourse that circled the inner part of the facility. On either side of the wide expanse, she saw the shuttered kiosks of the food and merchandise vendors. Tomorrow the lines would be ten-deep everywhere.

They came to an access point and Rafe led her up the incline to where the second tier of seats began. A man stood there, obviously waiting for them.

"This is Tony," Rafe said. "He wants to keep you company while I finish doing my thing."

Tyler looked up at Tony and actually laughed. The man was doing his best to keep his face expressionless, but the thin line of his mouth was a good indicator that babysitting the owner's wild child—especially a thirty-two-year-old wild child—was not on his happy list.

"I can sit by myself," she assured him. "I'll be fine. What can possibly happen here in all this emptiness?" She waved her arm to illustrate her words.

"You never know who's going to show up." Rafe spit the words out like nails as he gazed over her head.

Tyler turned to see what had caught his attention. Chad Sinclair had just emerged onto their level but two entrances away. He had two people with him who she assumed were media. They were looking at the team on the field, both sides of the ball, going through a final walkthrough of the playbook. Chad motioned for Tyler to come join them, but Rafe had a firm grip on her arm.

"Tony's happy to sit with you." His words were completely uninflected, a sign she'd discovered of seething emotions underneath. She imagined it was the kind of control he'd learned on the field to work his assignments in each play. He looked at the man beside him. "Right, Tony?"

"It would be my honor, Miss Gillette." His voice was formal but he was fighting a smile.

"Tyler," she said. "Call me Tyler."

He was as tall as Rafe, but considerably older. Who on earth was he, anyway? Was he part of Rafe's team?

"Okay, Miss—Tyler."

Impishly she hooked her arm through his. "I'll bet you'll take very good care of me."

"Tony has his instructions." Rafe's voice was tight with barely leashed control.

"Oh, look," Tyler teased. "Here comes Chad with his reporters."

Rafe looked at Tony, who nodded and said, "I got this."

When she thought about it later, Tyler had to appreciate how smoothly Rafe had managed the whole thing. It seemed like only moments later that she was seated several sections over with Tony, watching the team on the field. Chad Sinclair, to her left, was walking down the steps to the field with his media people in tow. And Rafe, to her right, was on the walkway at the top of the first tier of seats with his very large security crew.

Wow!

And now here she was with Tony, whoever he was. He was slightly taller than Rafe, almost as bulky and with touches of gray in his hair. He had a very masculine face, square-jawed with thick eyebrows. The look he gave her now was warm and friendly, but she had the distinct feeling that same face could turn into a hard mask in seconds. Whatever, she was apparently stuck with him. Before she sat down, she stuck her hand in her jeans pocket and thumbed her cell to Off. She didn't even want vibrate. She didn't need to get calls while she was here with a stranger and then have to explain everything. If she heard from anyone else, she'd call them back later.

"It's nice to see you at the field, Tyler." Tony's voice caught her attention. "You don't come here very often."

"Football's not my thing." She tried to keep the bitterness from her voice. "Especially this team."

"Maybe you should learn a little more about them," he suggested. "The Hawks are a really hot team. For example, did you know that Dan Ochoa is on track for best defensive player of the year, not just in the conference but in the league?"

"Uh, no, I had no idea." Nor did she care.

"As a matter of fact, Rafe won it twice when he was still playing for the team. They were still the Bisons then. And if anyone asks, I like the name Hawks a lot better."

"I'm sure my father will be ecstatic to hear that." Then, out of some unwanted curiosity she asked, "What makes Ochoa a candidate for that?"

"Well." Tony gave her a smile. "The season is only half over and he already has racked up twenty-three sacks and twelve quarterback hits." He paused. "And a bunch of other stats that if you aren't into football would be all garbage to you."

"I agree." She waved a dismissive hand. "I really know very little about the game. Um, so what position did Rafe play?"

"Oh, wow, he was just the greatest safety in the game during his playing years."

"Safety." She repeated it as if it were a foreign word.

To his credit, Tony didn't answer her as if she were a nitwit.

"Yes. He was what we call a strong side safety. It was his job to prevent the quarterback from completing a successful pass by swatting the ball or catching it himself. In a rushing play, his job was to contain the runner."

"Hmmm." She should let it go. She wasn't all that interested. But as long as she had to sit here she might as well make conversation. "So why do they call him a strong safety? Because he's stronger than someone else?"

Tony laughed. "In his case, yes. But the term refers to the defensive back who covers the stronger side of the offensive line. That's when—"

She held up a hand. "I think that's as much as my brain can handle. Thanks, though."

"You know, for several of the years Rafe played," Tony went on, as if she hadn't spoken, "Marko Spinoza was our quarterback. He always said a major reason we won two Super Bowls and that he won League MVP three times was because Rafe was one of the best safeties ever."

Tyler smiled at him. "You do know you might as well be speaking in a foreign language? I never learned about football, like I told you. Never much cared to."

He nodded. "Your choice."

They sat in silence for a while. Tyler found herself enjoying the warmth of the sunshine, the heat alleviated just enough by a smooth breeze blowing across the stadium. She tried to remember what it was like the few games she'd attended. Exciting, for sure. Noisy? Absolutely, but that was to be expected. Colorful. And there'd always been a crackle of electricity in the air that seemed to sizzle throughout the stands.

Below her, on the lush green football field, the team continued to move in specific patterns, stopping each time a whistle blew. In spite of herself, she was fascinated.

"What are they doing?" she asked.

"The day before the game they walk through each of the plays to make sure they've memorized the patterns."

"Oh." She nibbled on a fingernail. "This is a lot more complicated than I thought."

"Not really." He laughed again. "It's actually pretty simple. When we have the ball, we want to run it into the end zone or throw it. When they have the ball we want to keep them out of the end zone." He spread his hands. "It's that simple."

"Wow." She chuckled. "You're right. It doesn't sound complicated at all."

In point of fact, it actually sounded like something she might enjoy, if she could get past her whole hatred thing about the team and its importance to her father. Really? Enjoy? What was happening to her? Surely one little visit like this wasn't going to change years of a mindset. Of course, stranger things had happened.

"So," she said, breaking the silence, "what exactly do you do here except babysit the owner's daughter?"

"I don't consider it babysitting. I'm actually enjoying myself." He studied her face beneath the bill of the ball cap. "And if you don't mind my saying so, I like the daytime Tyler Gillette better than the nighttime one."

Tyler was startled. When had he seen the nighttime one?

"Have we seen each other at night?" she asked. "Because I don't think you frequent the same places I do."

One corner of his mouth tipped up in a half smile. "No, I'm sure I don't. But I've seen you at some of the functions you've attended for the Hawks."

She cocked her head, studying his face. "How come I don't recognize you?"

"I'm usually at Kurt's table, which you seem to studiously avoid." He cleared his throat. "Maybe you recognize my full name better. Anthony Castillo. Lone Star Security."

Taylor gawked at him, stunned. Rafe had the owner of the security agency babysitting her? Was he for real? She rose from her seat and started toward where Rafe was still working with his team, but Tony put his hand on her arm.

"Leave him. It's all right. He needs to go over game-day procedures with the security crew."

"I'd think they'd know what to do by now," she commented.

"You're right," he agreed. "But some games are more high profile and so the atmosphere is edgier. Like the one tomorrow against the Mustangs. People drink more beer and control themselves less."

"That's what I keep hearing. I guess Rafe does a really good job, though?" She made it a question.

"He does. I've had this contract with your father for a whole lot of years and Rafe is the best security chief I've ever had."

"Why doesn't that surprise me?" She slouched back down in her seat, wondering how much longer she had to be here. "I'm sorry you have to waste your Saturday here like this."

"Don't be. I have some things to go over with Rafe, some info to give him, and we decided this would be the most convenient place to do it." He gave her a reassuring smile. "It was my idea, especially when he said he was worried about leaving you by yourself while he put the crew through their paces."

"I can't believe him." Tyler rubbed her knee in irritation. "This was quite an imposition. I'm perfectly capable of sitting here by myself for a while."

"He doesn't want you alone anywhere until we nail this bastard that's got you in his crosshairs."

"I can't imagine someone could get to me here," she told him. "Or that someone with the Hawks is involved."

Tony shrugged. "You never know what goes on in someone's mind. Trust me. For example, Rafe said Chad Sinclair isn't too happy you aren't going to the shindig with him tonight."

"Chad?" She twisted her lips in a grimace. "I mean, he asked me out a lot between events and I turned him down, but he's a good-looking guy. I'm sure he could have all the women he wants."

"But the one he wants could be you," Tony pointed out. "Anyway, it may not be him, although Rafe said he got a little ugly about not taking you to the event tonight." Tony cast a sideways look at the man in question, now walking back inside with his guests. "But if he's got an ax to grind, real or imaginary, we have to follow it through."

"It just seems so unlikely," she mused.

She leaned back in her seat and tilted her head up to the sun, enjoying for a moment the fresh scent of the outdoors and trying to lose some of the tension gripping her. Who on earth could be doing these things? She knew a lot of people disliked her but to pull a stunt like this?

Then Tony's voice broke the silence. "You know, Tyler, I've known your dad for nearly thirty years. Ever since he became a minority stockholder in the Hawks and made a vow to end up owning the whole team."

She made a rude sound. "He certainly accomplished that. The Hawks are his real family."

He gave her a searching look. "Maybe that's an easier situation for him because he can hide his real emotions."

Tyler frowned. "I have no idea what you mean."

He studied her for a long moment. "I knew your mother, too. She was a lovely, lovely woman."

"Yes, she was." Tyler felt her throat close up as memories of her mother came flooding back.

"She was the great love of his life. He was truly devastated when she died."

"So was I," she told him in a small voice.

"Even after all this time," Tony said, "I can still remember you being so sad whenever I saw you."

"Water under the bridge." She didn't want to talk about it. At the time she'd felt as if she'd lost both her parents.

"I'm not excusing him, but he was consumed with so much grief he couldn't function. And he had no idea how to handle a little girl. That's why he buried himself in the team."

"I was just born the wrong sex." She tried for a flippant tone, determined to conceal her real feelings. "If I'd been a boy, it would have been different. He made that plain. A son to take over the team."

But Tony was shaking his head. "Not true. Not true at all."

Tyler looked down at her folded hands. "You could have fooled me. All these years, no matter what I did I couldn't get his attention. Anyway, I really don't like discussing it."

"Maybe it's time you did." Tony's voice was gentle and caring. "Maybe you need to bring all that up and deal with it."

"Why? It's over and done with. He still doesn't give a flip about me."

Really, Tyler? Then why did he involve himself in your situation?

"Why do you think he insists you attend functions related to the Hawks?" Tony went on as if she hadn't said a word.

"To show me he has control over me," she snapped. "He always threatens to cut off my trust fund if I don't go. Now, can we please change the subject?"

"Like I said, a lot of this is on him. He's handled things badly and admitted as much to me." He turned his head to look directly at her. "But I know for a fact he wants to try to heal this breach."

Tyler shook her head. "I don't know if that's possible."

"Tyler, anything's possible if people want it badly enough."

"Oh, look." She interrupted him, ready to be done with the discussion. "I think Rafe is through with everything. We'd better get over there."

She rose from her seat, but Tony put a hand on her arm.

"I'll leave it for now, but please just think about what I said, will you?" He pointed to where Rafe was standing. "You know, Rafe's a real good guy, too. One of my top men." He winked at her. "Try not to give him too hard a time. A woman could do a lot worse than Rafe Ortiz."

Tyler looked at him in shock. "Oh, we're not—" She shook her head. "No, absolutely not. You've got the wrong idea. Rafe's just guarding my body until we catch this nut."

Tony grinned. "If you say so. Okay. Let's go on over there."

The others were already dispersing by the time she and Tony reached Rafe.

"You didn't tell me you asked your boss to babysit me," Tyler said in an accusing voice.

"First of all," Rafe protested, "he wasn't babysitting, just making sure you were okay. And secondly—"

"Secondly," Tony interrupted, "I'm always up for spending some time with a beautiful woman." He gave Tyler a serious look. "Keep that look you've got going today. It *is* beautiful."

The compliments made Tyler uncomfortable, as had the short discussion about her father. She turned her attention to Rafe again.

"Tony said he needs to meet with you?"

He nodded. "When I called the office about the security system, Tony said he'd take care of the order himself, then go over it with me. He was going to be right by the stadium. We figured this would be the best place to get together. Let's go back to my office."

They were headed toward Rafe's office when she heard her name.

"Tyler! Hey, Tyler."

She turned to see Ed Spinelli jogging toward her. She wasn't really anxious to talk to him, but she didn't want to be rude. Who knew what he'd write about her and by extension the Hawks if she was. So she stopped, and Tony and Rafe stopped with her. Great. An audience.

Ed stopped in front of her, grinning. "Hey. Good to see you." He blinked. "I mean, really good to see you. You look terrific." He raked his gaze over her from head to toe and back again, his mouth curving in a hungry smile. "I like the new Tyler Gillette look."

She was really getting tired of this. She didn't think she'd looked so bad. So she wore a lot of makeup and spritzed a ton of spray on her well-teased hair. So what? It got her a lot of attention, didn't it?

But what kind of attention. And from what kind of people?

"Thank you," she said in a flat voice. "I think. What's up?"

Rafe had taken a step closer to her and Tony was on her other side. It was so ludicrous to think she needed protecting from Ed that she wanted to giggle.

Ed looked at the two men through narrowed eyes, and then gave her a smile.

"We didn't get a chance to talk the other day," he reminded her. "The Hawks are going great guns this season," he began, "and I'm doing a profile on the team ownership. Kind of personalizing it, you know?"

She held up a hand. "I'll tell you the same thing I would have said the other day. You're discussing this with the wrong Gillette. Go find the team owner."

"I did. He gave me an hour of his time, which I thanked him for. Now I want to talk to you." He looked at the two men again. "I was thinking we could have lunch or dinner. You know. Maybe talk about old times."

Tyler curled her fingers into the palms of her hands, hanging on to her temper. She didn't want or need this right now.

"Listen, Ed. I don't—"

"Miss Gillette isn't giving out interviews." Rafe's voice was uninflected yet at the same time powerful. A man you didn't argue with. "And we're late for a very important meeting." He took her arm and urged her toward his office.

"Are you her guard dog now?" Ed hollered after them as they moved down the concourse. "What's the matter, Tyler? Can't speak for yourself? You and I had a good time. We could have a good time again. And I can write a killer blog about you."

Tyler stopped, resisting when Rafe tried to keep her moving. She turned slowly and glared back at Ed.

"I can speak for myself if I want to, but I do not speak for the Hawks. I don't want a killer blog or any other kind written about me. And just so we are crystal clear, not only didn't we have a good time, it was barely tolerable."

Then she turned and walked away so fast the men had to hustle to keep up with her.

"I'm calling you," Ed shouted after her. "I'll talk to you without your bulldogs."

When they entered Rafe's office and he'd closed the door, she dropped into the chair she'd used earlier. Tony took a seat in front of the desk but Rafe stayed on his feet, watching Tyler who was nibbling on her lower lip, an indication of her nervous state.

"They're all the same," she blurted. "It's like they're all reading from the same script. I want you, I'll have you, if I can't no one will. Rafe, I know I'm not an ugly mud dog, but surely these men can get any women they want. Women much better-looking than me."

"They do seem to have a sense of entitlement where you're concerned," he agreed.

"It's my father, you know." The words tasted bitter on her tongue. "They all think if they hook up with me they can be the crown prince. They don't even realize I'm not the princess."

"Oh, I don't know," he drawled. "It seems to me this morning he was stepping up and acknowledging you are."

She shrugged. "Maybe. We'll see how it goes. I'm not giving him awards yet."

Tony said nothing, just sat there observing.

Rafe unfolded his arms and stood upright. He glanced over at Tony.

"Let's make sure the profiles we run on our suspects cover everything including how many hairs they have on their chest. I don't want to miss anything."

Tony nodded. "If he's computer savvy, he might have some hacking skills. That would allow him to get Tyler's new phone number each time." He pulled out his cell and made a note in the memo section. "Okay, ready to fill me in about the new security system?"

While they were talking, Tyler pulled out her cell and turned it on. She caught her breath as she scrolled through missed calls and texts.

"R-Rafe?"

He turned to her, scowling. "What?"

"H-he called while I was out in the stadium. I had my phone turned off."

Rafe grabbed the instrument from her. "Damn. Five fucking calls. He's getting impatient. Let's look at the texts."

Tony had pushed himself out of his chair and come to look, also. Tyler moved to the other side of Rafe, drawn by a sick fascination with what she might see. She peered over Rafe's arm when she felt him tense beside her.

"R u fcking hm? I want 2 kno."

"Where r u? U belong with me."

"U don't need hm. Gt rd of hm."

"U R only safe with me."

Tyler looked up at Rafe, swallowing hard. "Does he really think he can frighten me into going to him? I'm not even sure who he is. But it couldn't have been Ed," she pointed out. "He's right here."

"But he could be making his calls from his office," Rafe said. "From the concourse. Hell, from the men's room. Son of a bitch." A muscle worked in his jaw.

"He'll make himself known," Rafe assured her in a tight voice. "He's building up to it." He handed the phone to Tony who made some notes on his own. "Tyler, did you make that list I asked for?"

She nodded. "I e-mailed it to you."

"Send it to Tony so he can forward it to the office. They can get started on it."

Tony watched it come through on his cell. "Okay, off to one of the day guys. I'll get on this myself, also, as soon as I'm back in the office."

In less than fifteen minutes, the two men were finished and Rafe had made several notes in his phone.

"I e-mailed you the files on Broder and Sinclair," Tony said. "I'll have someone get started on Spinelli."

"Thanks very much. Let me know what you find. Tyler, let's go." He held a hand out to Tony, who had risen from his chair. "Thanks for making the trip. I appreciate it. I could have stopped by the office if you wanted."

"No problem. Besides, I got all this additional info." He smiled at Tyler. "And I got to spend some time with a pretty woman."

Tyler swore she felt herself blush.

"Thanks, anyway." Tony started to walk away but at that moment his cell phone rang. "Yeah? Uh-huh. Uh-huh. Yes. Take them away. Thanks for the call." He thumbed the phone off and turned to Rafe and Tyler. "That was the crew who just finished the new security system at your place, Tyler." He glanced at Rafe. "A florist delivered a vase full of flowers big enough to fill a funeral home. Rafe, put someone on this."

Rafe nodded. "Already on it. Got the name of the florist and I have one of the guys checking it out."

"Good. All right. Tyler, we're on top of this. Don't worry about it."

Ha, she thought. Easy for him to say.

"See you tonight," Rafe told the other man. Then with his hand at the small of her back, he urged Tyler out of the office and toward the parking lot.

Chapter 10

It wasn't bad enough that this asshole trying to scare her to death had stepped up his game today. But, he'd thrown her off her own game. She had made up her mind that tonight she would go as what she thought of as the new Tyler Gillette. She changed clothes four times before she was satisfied with her look. Or at least as satisfied as she was going to get. She'd finally settled on a silky navy cocktail dress that clung to her body without looking like she was stuffed into it. She left her hair loose, and instead of teasing it to death, she just used a blow-dryer and a brush to get it to curl softly around her face. And she had a very light hand with her makeup, settling for smoky eye shadow, a soft blush, and a tinted lip gloss. She looked in the mirror when she fastened her earrings and hardly recognized herself.

Okay, Rafe Ortiz, prepare to be wowed by the new Tyler Gillette.

Rafe was waiting in the front hall when she came down the stairs, looking so elegant in his tux she wanted to lick him all over. That was if she could get the stick out of his ass he'd shoved up there after last night. She swallowed her satisfaction, however, when he looked at her and his eyes nearly fell out of his head.

"I take it you approve?" She tried to hide her smile.

"You look…very nice."

"Wow! My head might turn with such high praise."

Something close to hunger flashed in his eyes for a moment. Then they shuttered and he looked at his watch. "We'd better get going."

Just as they were about to walk out, the sound of staccato drums echoed in the air A call, not a text. She took her phone out of her little skinny purse and looked at the screen.

"Blocked." She held it up to show Rafe.

"Answer it." That muscle was twitching in his jaw again.

"Really? Now?"

"Now."

She pressed Talk. "Hello?"

Silence.

She repeated it. "Hello? Who's there?"

Then a voice that sounded like it came from the bottom of a well said, "Did you fuck him?"

Tyler's hand shook and she dropped the phone.

Rafe picked it up and held it to his ear, listening intently. Finally, he disconnected the call and handed the phone back to her. Then he took out his own cell and sent a text.

"Just letting the office know to check the cell towers on this latest call."

"It doesn't seem like they're getting very far with this." She could feel the erratic beat of her heart. Every time this idiot called it shook her up.

"It doesn't always, but we'll damn sure keep trying." He handed her the phone. "Turn it off, put this back in your purse, and let's get going."

"Turn it off?"

"We probably wouldn't hear it at dinner, anyway. Let's give ourselves a break for a few hours."

"Fine by me." She pressed the Off button and dropped the phone back in her purse.

They were silent on the drive to the Conquistador Club. So much was running through Tyler's brain. She wanted to know what Lone Star had dug up on Chad and Nate, if anything. Rafe had given her very little information after he'd checked the files. Why did he think geeky Ed would be a danger? But right now she knew she had to put the whole thing out of her mind, or she'd be a basket case when they got to the club.

If conversation was absent, a thick cloud of tension certainly wasn't. It was so heavy it was palpable. Tyler would bet every single one of the false eyelashes she hadn't put on tonight that more than half of it had sexual overtones.

He wanted her. It was right there in his eyes every time he looked at her, until he got control of himself and blinked it away. She'd seen it that morning. He was determined last night would never happen again if he had to lock her in her room. Well, she'd just see about that. Last night had been about way more than sex, and she wanted to see if it was real or just her overactive imagination making it into something it wasn't.

As they drew closer to the club, a swarm of butterflies decided to take up roost in her stomach and beat their wings to the tempo of a Latin dance. She wondered if Rafe knew just how nervous she was. Without all her outrageous makeup, her equally outrageous outfits, and at least three drinks in her system, she felt totally and completely vulnerable. How would people react to her? Would she know what to say to anyone?

Never let them see you sweat.

An old adage but one that she kept silently repeating to herself.

Rafe's friends would be there. The same friends who had seen her year after year doing her Tyler Gillette imitation of a woman with too much money and too few brains. She wondered how they'd react to her tonight, without the war paint and cold sober, her first major appearance as the new Tyler Gillette. If only her knees would stop knocking.

God! She was making herself so nervous she was afraid she'd throw up.

Then they were at the club and a valet was opening her door. He had just helped her out of the car when Rafe came around and cupped her elbow with his hand.

He glanced down at the needle-thin heels on her shoes. "I don't know how you walk in those things. I'd fall on my face."

Oh! A joke! She relaxed infinitesimally.

"It takes years of practice. Trust me."

And then they were inside and the butterflies began the next dance. Rafe gave their name to the woman at the door but she apparently didn't need it.

"Always so good to see you, Rafe." She smiled at him. "And you, Miss Gillette." The smile wasn't quite as warm now.

"Thank you. I'm happy to be here."

And you'll be a lot happier to see me when you find out I'm not going to act like an out-of-control bitch tonight.

The woman cleared her throat. "May I say you're looking very nice tonight."

Tyler barely kept her jaw from dropping. "Oh, um, thank you."

Well, she thought. *Another person who thought she'd looked like a painted whore before?* Funny, she mused, how we never really see ourselves as others do.

But I'm not going to regress. I'm finally starting to like myself.

Well, she'd gotten past the first obstacle tonight. Next came Rafe's friends.

She looked around as they entered the huge dining room. The room was nearly full with people chatting and drinking. There was hardly an empty seat anywhere. She'd paid so little attention to what the event was about before that she'd been stunned to learn it was a scholarship fundraiser. But now she saw the banner stretched across the top of one wall with a podium in front of it. On an easel to the right of the podium was a huge poster, also with the name of the event, and with a picture of Joe Reilly.

She took a good look at the picture for the first time and wondered if all football players were gorgeous. She'd ignored them as a group, all except for Rafe, who definitely gave gorgeous new meaning.

"Where are we sitting?" she asked Rafe as he guided her toward the front of the room.

He nodded to a table not far from the podium. "Same place I always sit."

"With your friends," she guessed. Of course. Other years she'd deliberately ignored him, or pretended to, putting on her very stupid act. "I hope—" She stopped.

"It will be fine." His voice was a little less harsh and held the first note of sympathy and understanding she'd heard from him.

He guided her easily through the crowd of people standing around, chatting, sipping drinks. Several people greeted Tyler, most of them with stunned looks on their faces before they got themselves under control. She managed to give everyone a cordial greeting and tell them how pleased she was to be representing the Hawks tonight.

"They must think I sent a clone tonight," she whispered to Rafe.

"Actually, I think they're stunned at the real thing." He squeezed her arm. "Are you doing okay?"

"So far." She gave a shaky little laugh. "But the evening's far from over."

"You can do it," he murmured. "And I'm right here."

Yes, but as her bodyguard, her keeper...or what she really wanted?

Rafe nodded to everyone and exchanged smiles as he kept them moving. She faltered a moment when she spotted Chad sitting at a table off to her left. Although a very attractive woman was sitting next to him, his eyes were glued to Tyler and followed her progress through the room. She shivered slightly at the look on his face. There was something just so ravenous about it. And possessive. Where had that come from?

"Problem?" Rafe murmured in her ear and turned to look over at Chad. "Just keep moving and be thankful we have to behave tonight."

"Why?"

"If he makes a move in your direction, I might have to deck him and that would destroy the line of my tux and ruin my reputation for self-control."

"Oh, ah, well..."

"Come on, we're almost there."

Then finally they were at their table and everyone was looking at her with great interest.

"Say hello to Tyler Gillette," Rafe said as he held out a chair for her.

A few jaws dropped and a couple of people frowned momentarily before smoothing out their expressions. Apparently they had seen her previous performances here. But they all nodded and there was a smattering of friendly hellos as Rafe introduced her to everyone. She tried to file away all their names away for later. Joe Reilly, the guiding force for the event, and his wife Shay. Jake Russell and his fiancee, Erin Brody. Mike and Shana Lazarus. Jilly and Jason Mackenzie.

"Nice to meet you." Okay, now what? She wasn't quite sure how this new Tyler should act.

"I'm pleased you're sitting with us this time." Joe Reilly smiled at her, a warm smile that did a lot to ease her nerves. "On behalf of the scholarship fund, I want to thank the Hawks for their incredible contribution. It will greatly increase the number of scholarships we'll be able to award."

She hoped her own smile didn't look as stiff as it felt. "We're happy to do it. My father has always believed in supporting young athletes. I think everyone should be thanking you for your commitment to it." Then she unfolded her napkin in her lap and reached for her glass of ice water, taking a slow sip.

"I'm going to hit the bar before they bring the food." Mike Lazarus stood up. "Can I get anything for anyone?"

Only one person took him up on his offer.

"Tyler?" he asked. "Something for you?" He winked at Rafe. "In case Rafe forgot to ask you."

"Nothing, but thank you."

Rafe looked surprised when she didn't order a drink, but he shook his head also.

Tyler inhaled and let out a slow breath, calming her jittery nerves. She was stunned when Rafe actually reached for her hand beneath the table and gave it a gentle squeeze. She glanced sideways at him but he was engrossed in conversation with the man to his right. Jason? Right, Jason Something.

She took a moment to look around the room, taking it all in without the haze of alcohol. Tony Castillo's words about her father suddenly popped back into her head. Was it possible he hadn't known how to deal with his grief? But they could have grieved together, couldn't they? If he didn't know how to raise a daughter as opposed to a son, they could have stumbled through it together.

People could change. She knew that. Look at what she was doing with herself. Did the gruff Kurt Gillette want to change, too? Was this whole setup with Rafe protecting her a way for him to reach out to her and try to build a relationship? Difficult as it might be, she'd have to give it some thought, and see what his next move might be.

She was still lost in thought when Rafe nudged her and whispered, "Wake up, Tyler. Someone's talking to you."

She blinked. "Oh, sorry."

One of the women, Jilly, if she remembered right, laughed, but it was a friendly sound, not disparaging.

"So it seems Rafe has been hiding something from us," she said.

Tyler frowned. "Excuse me?"

"He hasn't brought a woman around us for a long time," she explained, a smile teasing her lips.

"Right." This was Shana speaking now. Yes, Shana. At least, Tyler thought. She was pretty good with names. "I even tried to fix him up with my sister but they were never more than friends."

"Oh," she protested, "We're not—We're just—" Just what? What should she tell them? She wished Rafe would jump in.

But when he did she was stunned.

"She's definitely something, isn't she?" he asked.

Okay, that was about as noncommittal as it could get. But he didn't deny the whole thing and she wondered why.

"Are you a big football fan, Tyler?" Shay asked her. "I think all of us are immersed in it one way or another."

Great. Just great.

"I, um, well, that is—" Could she sound any more like an idiot? She should just lie, for heaven's sake.

"Tyler hasn't been as involved in the team as she'd like," Rafe broke in smoothly. "But that's going to change pretty soon."

It was? She turned to him and hoped the shock she felt didn't show on her face.

"You should get Rafe to bring you to some of our get-togethers," Shana said. "These guys like to pretend they're still in high school and relive the glory years. And we like to laugh at them."

Tyler didn't know what to say. "That's very nice of you to offer."

"I'm sure she'd enjoy it," Rafe said. "I'll make sure it happens."

And wasn't he just full of surprises tonight.

"Maybe Shay will give us another of her impromptu performances," Mike said with a grin.

Shay Reilly smiled but a red flush crept up her face. "You guys ever going to let me forget it?"

"Not if we can help it." He turned to Tyler. "First time Joe brought her to the house we were having a pickup football game in the backyard—"

"Which they do whenever it's possible," Shana broke in. "The boys and their toys."

"Anyway," Mike went on, winking at his wife, "Shay used to try to get Joe and her brother Hank to let her mix it up with them when they tossed the ball around in her yard. So when someone tossed the ball and it headed toward her, she just jumped up, caught it, and ran it to the end of the yard for a touchdown."

Everyone at the table laughed, including Shay. Tyler wondered what it would be like to feel that easy and relaxed with people. Not that she couldn't let it all hang out with Betsy and Lynn, but there was an altered feeling to the connection between and among these people. A different flavor. And when she glanced at Rafe she saw him looking at them the same way.

It amazed her that these men had been friends since high school. That had to be at least fifteen years ago. Where was that school? Oh, yeah, Granite Falls. About an hour from San Antonio, she thought. She and Betsy and Lynn had formed what she called a defensive friendship. Their bond defended and protected them against the lack of a real family environment and parents too involved in their own lives to care about their children. But these people had come together because of a milestone and bonded as friends.

"I guess you'll be sitting in the owner's suite, right, Tyler?"

She looked up, startled, as Shay called her name. "Excuse me?"

"Rafe said you'll be at the game tomorrow."

"That's one you definitely don't want to miss." Erin grinned at her. "Jake played for the Mustangs and Rafe and Jason played for the Hawks. Um, when they were the Bison." She looked across at Joe.

"You'll be sitting with your dad, right?"

Tyler wasn't even sure how to answer that. *It's bad enough I have to go to the game. I'm not sitting in the owner's suite? My father and I barely speak.* Holy shit. How was she going to get herself out of this one? *Thanks a whole hell of a lot, Rafe.*

She searched her brain for some kind of logical answer. "I, uh, think you get a better flavor of the game sitting in the stands, don't you?"

"Oh, absolutely," Jilly agreed. "Rafe, is her ticket anywhere near us? Maybe you can get someone to switch."

"Maybe next time," he said in a smooth voice. Then he leaned over and whispered in her ear, "Anything I can help with? You seem really distracted."

She lifted her glass of ice water and took a sip. She thought what she really needed was a glass of wine to calm her nerves but not tonight.

"I'm fine," she assured him. "And I'll pay better attention."

Somehow she held it together, the new Tyler without the false front and without a drink. Especially since it seemed all they talked about was football, the women as well as the men. She was proud of herself for actually carrying on a conversation about a game she had little knowledge of.

Fake it till you make it.

How many times had she heard that in more different circumstances than she could count? Now she knew what it meant. And while Rafe said very little to her directly, he made sure to give her hand a squeeze just enough to let her know he was there for her. She tried not to read anything into it.

As the evening progressed, to her astonishment Tyler actually found herself enjoying the event. She'd forgotten how to have real conversations with anyone but her closest friends. Certainly at the public events she attended, she'd been more interested in making a spectacle of herself and embarrassing her father. But tonight people who knew who she was actually stopped by the table to say hello and pass along their gratitude to the Hawks for their support. She even fell into the rhythm of the conversation at the table, enjoying the easy give and take of these people who were Rafe's friends.

And a funny thing happened on the way to dessert. Listening to the other women, it occurred to her if she could divorce football from her father, she might even enjoy watching a game. Maybe tomorrow would be a good time to find out.

She sat through the speeches and the announcement of the funds raised, still worried that before the event was finally over she'd do or say something to embarrass Rafe in front of his friends. At one point, he reached for her hand again and gave it a gentle squeeze. Her heart gave a little skip and she turned her head enough to whisper to him.

"Why are you being so nice to me?"

"How would it look if I wasn't?" he asked.

Of course. It was all a front, everything tonight. An act. He was behaving exactly the way her father would expect of him, an attentive escort. Certainly not as a bodyguard, someone who would attract questions neither of them wanted to answer. The tiny bit of hope that he was remembering how good last night had been was immediately extinguished.

At last it was over and she was saying good-bye to Rafe's friends. Joe and the woman who chaired the scholarship fund thanked her profusely again for the Hawks' contribution. The women, who she supposed had now gotten it into their heads that she and Rafe were an item, insisted she exchange cell-phone numbers. She really liked them, just on such short contact. Would she ever see them again? Would she ever see Rafe again when this was all over, except in passing?

As they headed out of the dining room, she felt a hand on her shoulder and turned to see Chad Sinclair smiling down at her.

"It wasn't the same tonight not being with you." The smile he gave her was polite but tinged with traces of both want and irritation.

"It's just an event," she pointed out to him. "I mean, it's not like we're a couple or anything."

He leaned down and put his mouth close to her ear. "We could be."

Tyler tried to figure the best way to answer him without making a scene. Then Rafe jumped in.

"She's otherwise occupied Sinclair." He laced his fingers through hers. "She's off-limits."

Chad scowled. "Really? How's that?"

Tyler opened her mouth to say something, but Rafe put an arm around her and gave her a gentle squeeze.

"I don't see that it's any of your business," he said in a deceptively mild voice. "If you'll excuse us."

He guided Tyler out the door so smoothly she hardly realized it was happening. As they stood waiting for the valet, she gave him a look filled with curiosity.

"That's twice you gave people the indication we're some kind of item. Aren't you afraid it will tarnish your image?"

He was silent for so long she wondered if he was going to answer her at all.

"We have a situation here that requires both of us to play a part." He said the words in an even, measured tone of voice. "It's better than telling them the truth. And if Sinclair is the stalker, I don't want him getting a heads-up."

"He already thinks it's strange that the head of security is hanging out with me. Won't he get even more suspicious?"

"If it's him, I don't think he'll put it together. He's too egotistical. But if he does, maybe he'll step up his game, make a mistake and we'll nail him."

Before she could say anything else, the valet drove up with Rafe's car. Rafe tipped him, and then they were headed home. Once again, a heavy silence filled the car. Finally, she couldn't stand it anymore.

"You don't like me much, do you, Rafe?"

She could almost hear him digging around in his brain for an appropriate answer.

"Let's just say I wasn't crazy about your lifestyle or the image you chose to show the world." He studied her face with heated intensity. "But if I've learned anything since this all started, it's that there's a real person beneath the masquerade. A person, if I'm not mistaken, who is really beginning to like herself."

Yes, but it was a daily struggle. She had such a mountain of insecurities to climb. And his next words did nothing to dispel them.

"We have to forget about last night, Tyler. I overstepped my bounds. It's a given you're off-limits to me and it's going to stay that way. I'm here for one reason and one reason only."

"Bodyguard, right?" She twisted her hands together. "And finding out who's trying to scare the crap out of me."

"I'm going to do just that," he assured her in a tight voice. "But that's all I'm going to do."

Tyler wet her lips and tried again. "You didn't feel that way last night."

"I told you. Last night is last night," he shot back. "Last night was—"

"If you tell me it was a mistake, I'm going to shove you out of this car and run you over." Anger bubbled up inside her. "Do not diminish what last night was."

"It was sex. Just sex." Each word stabbed at her.

"It was a hell of a lot more than that and you know it." She couldn't believe he could dismiss what happened so easily. "I don't care what you say or how you try to blow it off."

That said, she crossed her arms and turned as far away from him as she could get with the seatbelt latched in place. Neither of them said another word on the way home but Tyler did a lot of thinking.

When they pulled into the driveway, lights immediately went on from small spotlights on the little bit of lawn and from the roof of the town house, startling her.

"The new sensors," he reminded her.

"I don't guess we'll have anyone sneaking up the driveway again."

"Or anywhere else around the house." Rafe pressed a button on the extra remote she'd given him, and the garage door slid up smoothly.

She was so wrapped up in the aftermath of their hostile conversation the dark sedan gliding down the street with its lights off only pricked the edge of her consciousness.

Chapter 11

As soon as they came in from the garage, Tyler headed for the stairs. She wanted nothing more than to get to her room and clear her brain. So he wanted to insist what they had was just sex? Screw him. She knew the difference and the difference had been there last night. Tonight she was going to remind him of that, with words and actions. First, she had to get her temper under control, or she wouldn't get past the first quarter. Maybe not even get to the first. She'd fumble the kickoff and that would be that.

Oh, God! Am I really using football speak? How do I even know it?

She started up the stairs but Rafe put his hand on his arm and stopped her.

"Where's your cell?" he asked.

She stopped and turned. "My cell?"

"I know you turned it off before we left the house," he reminded her, "but turn it on now. Let's see if there's been any activity tonight."

She yanked the phone out of her purse and handed it to him without looking at it. She was beginning to hate the thing. "Well?" she asked as he scrolled through it.

But the familiar twitch of muscle at his jawline told her what she needed to know.

"Calls and texts." He delivered the information in a controlled voice, but she saw anger spark in his eyes.

"What do they say?" She held her hand out. "Give it here."

"You don't want to see these," Rafe told her. "And I haven't listened to the voice mails yet but there are four of them."

Tyler held out a shaky hand. "Yes, I do. And I can listen to the messages myself. Rafe, I need to know how bad this is getting."

She could tell he was battling with himself over it. Finally, he showed her the texts. Her stomach roiled as she read them. The worst one was, *"U shld be with me. Make it hppn. If I can't have u no one else wil, ether. Btch."*

"Oh my God." She felt as if her whole body was shaking. She looked up at Rafe. "Was he there tonight? Was he watching me?"

"That's what I have to try and figure out. He could have been an invited guest, or somebody's plus one. But the only person we recognized was Chad."

"Does that pinpoint him by process of elimination?" Chad Sinclair. God. She thought of his parting remarks as they walked out of the club.

"Not necessarily. Whoever this is could simply have watched you tonight, just followed us to the Conquistador."

"Oh my God." Tyler sank down to the stairs, her fingertips pressed to her mouth. She was determined not to fall apart but every bit of her self-discipline was being taxed to achieve it.

Rafe pulled out his cell and punched in a speed dial, she assumed to Lone Star, and quietly gave whoever answered some instructions. Then he turned to Tyler and held out his hand.

"I'll keep this tonight."

She stared up at him. "I should get another one tomorrow."

"Tyler, you can't just keep getting a new phone. This guy, whoever he is, keeps finding your new phone number."

"Then what can I do?" She trembled as the magnitude of the situation washed over her again.

"I asked the agency on-call to see if he can find out where our three top suspects were tonight. Well, two. We know where Chad was. And check the cell towers to see where your call was pinged from."

Her stomach clenched. "What if it isn't anyone we've focused on? Not Chad, or Nate or Ed?"

"I sent that list we put together to Lone Star. They're working on it." He took her icy hands in his warm ones. "We'll get him, Tyler. I promise."

The contact between them was charged. When his gaze met hers, she saw that he recognized it, too. But she also could tell the damn man was pushing it down deep and choosing to ignore it. Well, not her. With all this crap happening to her she needed that connection, and she needed to make him admit the depth of what was happening between them.

"I'm going upstairs," she said, pushing herself to her feet.

"Ditto," he said. "Busy day tomorrow. We both need to get some rest."

"Speaking of tomorrow." She turned and looked at him. "What arrangements have you made for me for tomorrow? You know I hate going to the game to begin with. Surely you don't expect me to sit in the damn owner's suite."

"I've got it covered. Now let's get some rest. I'll see you in the morning." He turned off the light in the hall and followed her up the stairs.

Before, she had just been mad at Rafe's attitude. Mad and hurt. But now she needed the feel of his body, the heat of their physical connection. She badly wanted the emotional link that he insisted wasn't there, even as she knew he was lying and so did he. He wanted to see the real Tyler? Well, okay, he was going to get her.

She stripped off her clothes, draping the dress over the little upholstered chair, kicking her heels into the closet, and stashing everything in the hamper. In the bathroom, she turned on the shower while she took off her jewelry and scrubbed off the minimal amount of makeup she'd used. Then she climbed into the steaming shower and lathered herself with her favorite creamy floral soap.

She would show him. She'd make him see what they *could* have. What they *did* have after last night. She would not let him dismiss something so easily that was about to impact the way she looked at everything. Maybe she was overdue for a change in course, and this stalker thing was the catalyst. But the real reason she wanted that change was Rafael Ortiz and she wasn't about to let him go that easily.

Out of the shower, she dried herself thoroughly and smoothed cream into every inch of her skin. She was so nervous about this—shocking for her—that she dropped the bottle of lotion twice. Her hands were shaking again as she brushed her hair, then dabbed a dash of cologne at all her pulse points and took one last look at herself in the mirror.

Okay, she was ready.

After pulling on the silk shorty robe she had hanging in the bathroom, she opened her bedroom door and peered out into the hallway. There was no light coming from beneath the guest-room door, and when she pressed her ear to it, she didn't hear a sound. Okay, if she was lucky, he was in bed but not asleep. No one could fall asleep that fast.

She cracked the door just enough to slip in and walked over to the bed. The blinds on the window were open and a wide shaft of moonlight shone on Rafe, lying on his back with his hands behind his head. If he was asleep, she'd just have to wake him up. And she knew exactly how to do it. She stood still for a moment and took a calming breath, inhaling the pure male essence of him. God, just his scent made every part of her body sit up and beg.

She had to do this carefully. She knew he'd resist her, even try to force her to go back to her room. *Not happening*, she told herself.

"What do you think you're doing?"

His deep voice pierced the darkness and startled her.

"I came in to say good night." His eyes were open, gleaming in the moonlight.

"Good night, Tyler." He kept his hands in place and his body still. "I think you need to get to your own room."

"I wanted to give you a proper good night," she told him.

Before he could stop her, she had dropped her robe and slipped beneath the covers. Wow! He slept commando. She should have known. She tried to lie down but before she could manage it, Rafe shifted positions and clasped her upper arms.

"Don't do this, Tyler. This is a very bad idea. You'll be making a big mistake."

She locked her gaze with his. "The mistake will be if I just get up from this bed and walk out."

"This can't go anywhere," he reminded her. "I told you. Just pretend last night didn't happen. Go back to your room. I'll see you in the morning."

"What are you afraid of, Rafe?" She wished she could see his face better in the moonlight, or read the expression on it. Of course, Rafe was famous for being unreadable. "Are you worried all those feelings you keep locked down will come bubbling up like before?"

"Damn it, Tyler." He growled the words and dropped back down onto his pillow. "Don't make last night into something it wasn't. Go ahead. You'll see it means nothing and you can go back to bed and wipe this from your mind."

"Not happening," she whispered. "I need you, Rafe. Tonight I really need you."

She had to peel back those layers tonight. Get to the heart of him. She might never have another chance. She placed her hand on his body, so warm it was giving off enough heat for a furnace. The warmth wrapped around her as she eased down beside him. Except for a slight jerk when her skin touched his, he hadn't moved at all, not even his hands.

"Do you think if you don't touch me, don't react, I'll just walk out of here?" she asked. "I'm not giving up that easily."

"Neither am I."

She slid her own hand across his chest coasting it over the crisp curls of chest hair, every muscle in his body tensed. She wondered if he could feel how much she was shaking.

He wrapped his fingers around her wrist.

"What is it, Tyler? What's going on tonight?"

She wet her bottom lip. "I don't just want you, Rafe. I really need you. I need to be with you, like we were last night. Please."

God how she hated begging, but she spoke the truth.

"Tyler." His chest rose and fell as he exhaled. "We cannot do this. There's nothing between us, no matter how much you want there to be, and there can't be. That's the plain truth."

"Go on, keep telling yourself that, as if you really believe it." She continued to sift her fingers through his chest hair, still trembling. She looked directly into his eyes, hoping he could read hers. "We both know you'd be lying. Damn you anyway, Rafe."

She waited, watched the severity of his masculine face in the moonlight. She knew he was fighting an inner battle. He was trying to reconcile all the things he disliked about her with all the things he wanted from her. And with that unexpected emotion connecting them.

Finally he let out another long sigh.

"I'm going to hell for this," he said between clenched teeth, as he grabbed her and dragged her mouth to his.

The kiss scorched her, seared every nerve in her body. His tongue probed, touched, tasted, until she lost all sense of self and still he held her. When he finally broke the kiss, she was dizzy from the intense feeling of arousal.

"Fuck." He closed his eyes for a moment. "Goddamn it to hell." He started to say something else then just shook his head.

"Nobody kisses like that when it's just sex," she whispered. "I can tell the difference. So can you if you'd quit being so stubborn. Please, Rafe."

She had to make him believe. Sliding her hand over his hard abs and the flat plane of his stomach, she tangled her fingers lightly in the nest of curls surrounding his cock.

His nostrils flared and fire blazed in his eyes, caught by the soft moonlight. She threw back the covers, exposing him, and wrapped her slim fingers around his very hot and engorged cock and gently squeezed. When she placed the flat of her other hand on his stomach the muscles beneath her touch tightened like a drum.

He grabbed her wrist again. "Yes, goddamn it. All right. So I—have feelings for you. Damn it. Feelings I don't know what the fuck to do with. Feelings it would be better for both of us to ignore." He looked at her as if he were trying in the pale silvery moonlight to see beneath her skin. "Like I said, I'll go to hell for this, but I have to have you."

He released her wrist and hissed a loud breath between his teeth.

Fisting his hot erection, she leaned forward and touched her lips to his. The contact was so electric she felt as if lightning zapped through both of them. This was way more sexy than a hot, sensuous kiss.

He didn't move and they stayed that way for a long moment, lips connected in the lightest of contacts. The now familiar scent of his leathery aftershave invaded her nostrils and actually made her sex tighten in response. Then she let the tip of her tongue peep out and lick along the seam of his mouth, light and feathery as an angel's wing. Back and forth, both of them barely breathing. She swiped her tongue lazily over the surface of his lips, teasing him.

When his tongue inched out to meet hers with the faintest of contacts, Tyler felt shivery all over, her nipples tingled and in the heart of her pussy, her inner walls vibrated with an aching need. Without breaking the kiss, she pressed her hands to his chest again, sliding them over the hard wall of muscle. When she found his flat male nipples, she lightly scored her fingernails over them and still he never broke that soft, erotic, sensuous kiss. It was more arousing, more erotic than the hungriest, most voracious kiss she could imagine.

Tyler pinched his nipples, squeezing them enough that his fingers tightened their grip on her arms and his breath hitched slightly. Beneath her palms, she felt the heavy thud of his heart as he silently responded to her touch.

She took time to run her hands over his muscular, toned body. She loved the feel of him beneath her palms, the soft dark hair sprinkled on his chest and abdomen, on his thighs and arms. Of the hard planes and dips and swells. He lay there, unmoving, except he wasn't unresponsive. When she touched his abdomen, his muscle contracted involuntarily, and when she brushed over his pubic crest, he sucked in a breath. But he held still, letting her explore him at her own pace, even though his body vibrated with the tension of restraint.

A little bolder she shifted one hand and coasted it over his flat abdomen again down to where his cock rose from its dark nest. When she closed her fingers over the base this time, she slid them gently up and down. The thick vein that wrapped itself around his shaft pulsed as blood raced through it, responding to her caress. She did it again and again, her efforts rewarded when his entire body tensed and the rhythm of his breathing increased.

"Lie back," she whispered. "Let me do this."

She increased the pace of her strokes, pausing now and then to rub her thumb over the velvet softness of the head. She felt slickness right at the slit, the seeping of the precum telling her as much as anything else that he wasn't as unmoved by any of this as he wanted her to think. Eyes still focused on him she shifted position and knelt beside him.

Sliding a quick glance at him, she lowered her head once more and took him into her mouth. His hard thickness was covered with skin as soft as silk and rubbing her lips up and down on it was an outrageously sensuous experience. When she had taken him so deep that the head of his erection hit the back of her mouth, she slid her lips back up and let him pop free. Then she slowly stroked her tongue up and down the length of him, swirled the tip around the head and licked again.

Rafe groaned. "Fuck, Tyler. You have the most incredible mouth. Don't stop, whatever you do."

She had absolutely no intention of stopping. She wanted him to feel this, not just physically but deep inside the way she did.

He reached up a hand and brushed her hair back, winding it around his fingers. Then he tilted her head just so to give him an unobstructed glimpse of her with his cock in her mouth. She glanced at his face, the harsh planes of it outlined in the moonlight. The sight of him watching her was so erotic it made her even wetter.

She swept her tongue over the head of his cock again before once more taking the entire length of him into her mouth. Easing her other hand between his thighs, she cupped the sac with his balls, manipulating them with her fingers and gently squeezing. She gripped the root of his shaft with her hand and set up a steady rhythm, her lips sliding up and down with an increasingly rapid pace.

The faster she glided her mouth along his length the tighter he wound his fingers in her hair, tilting her head this way and that. Rafe's body vibrated with tension, his hips thrusting now up to her mouth as she took him deeper and deeper. She forced herself to slow down, now dragging her teeth gently up and down the texture of the skin covering his cock. Every time she did, she made sure to sweep her tongue across the head, once even pulling back enough to probe the slit.

"More. Faster." His voice was hoarse, sounding as if it came from a deep cavern.

From the rigidity of his body and the erotic sounds he made, Tyler knew he was close. She was having trouble hanging onto her own control, the pulsing in her pussy at a fever pitch and her thighs wet with her juices.

"Jesus, Tyler. Oh, Christ! Hurry. Fuck!"

His hand gripped her hair harder, guiding her head. She increased the pace, taking him deeper still, until she felt his balls tighten and his entire body tense. Then he erupted in her mouth, spilling himself into her. She squeezed the base of his shaft as she sucked him dry, swallowing every bit of him. Little by little his body relaxed, his breathing settled, until finally his cock softened slightly and she slid her mouth up and free.

She rested her head on his chest and he lazily stroked her hair, tucking the long strands behind her ear so he could expose her cheek to him. He trailed his fingers over her cheekbone and the line of her jaw while beneath her ear she could hear the erratic beating of his heart.

"You wiped me out," he said at last. "Jesus, Tyler. You have the most incredible mouth. I don't know if it's an angel's mouth or a devil's, but it does unbelievable things to me. Holy fucking shit." He tugged her head toward him, her hair still wrapped around his fingers. "Kiss me with that very sexy mouth," he growled. "Let me taste myself on your lips."

She touched her mouth to his, expecting him to be satisfied with just a soft contact of lips. Instead he used his grip on her head to bring it close to his and took her mouth in a kiss even hungrier and more voracious than the one earlier tonight. His tongue invaded her mouth like a marauder, sweeping every inch of the inner surface. Tyler felt as if a hot flame was searing the tender skin and lighting up every erogenous zone in her body. The impact of it reached down deep inside her, a connection that was far more than a mere kiss. It sucked every bit of breath from her and still she didn't lift her mouth from his. Only when neither of them could breathe did they break the contact.

Rafe cupped her face in his palms, holding her head in place while he studied her intently. She never took her eyes away from his, knowing he was searching for something and hoping she was sending him the right message.

We can do this, Rafe. Just give it a chance.

If only he could read her brain. If only she could read his. She could tell he wanted to say something, and she hoped it would be what she wanted.

"I like to taste myself on your mouth," he said at last.

Not what she wanted but at the moment she'd take whatever she could get. "Good," she told him. "That's good."

She bent to the task again, touching her lips gently to his but then deepening the kiss. He didn't back down from it, instead holding her to him while their tongues dueled and they drank from each other. Again it lasted until they were gasping for air. But this time when they broke there was a different look in Rafe's eyes. It wasn't hunger this time, but more a look of confusion. Shock, even. As if he'd been hit by a thunderbolt and had no idea what to do with it.

She wanted to say, *I told you so,* but instead she just stroked his cheek and kept her gaze locked with his. Then, as if he wanted to lock the whole thing away and pretend whatever he was feeling wasn't there, he grabbed her and in a swift movement had her straddling him. Whatever had been in his eyes before, now there was only raw hunger. Sexual hunger.

Fine, but she was determined to make it about more than that no matter what she had to do.

He palmed her breasts, kneading them and brushing his thumbs over the nipples back and forth. Her sex pulsed and her blood raced as that simple movement aroused her beyond belief.

"Mmm," she hummed, and rocked back and forth on him.

He tugged her breasts, drawing her closer to his face, and closed his mouth over one of her nipples. He scored one taut peak with his teeth while he pinched the other between thumb and forefinger. Then he switched, giving equal attention to both beaded nubs. He used the tip of his tongue to trace the areolas on each breast, paying careful attention to each one. Every lash of his tongue, every scoring of his teeth only added to the heat already surging through her body.

She closed her eyes and gave herself over to the feeling, the rasp of his tongue a sensuous caress. By the time he had licked his fill she was shivering with need and he hadn't given attention to anything but her breasts.

"My turn," he said suddenly, and flipped her over.

"T-turn?" she stammered. "For what?"

"For you to lie there and enjoy yourself and just feel. Don't do anything but feel."

She pillowed her head on her arms and closed her eyes. She could still smell the lingering trace of his aftershave, only now it was mingled with the scent of male and sex and heat. A mixture more volatile than any cocktail.

She felt him straddle her, his knees on either side of her hips holding his weight from her body. Lifting her hair away from her neck, he trailed a series of little feathery kisses down her nape and across her shoulders. Every few kisses were punctuated by a tiny flick of the tip of his tongue. Everything inside her body wanted to uncoil and explode. She was so aroused she was sure he could smell her musk.

Still holding the bulk of his weight away from her, he began to sprinkle kisses down her spine, placing one on each bump of a vertebrate. She felt him shift slightly and in the next moment, he was kissing the sides of her breasts first one, then the other. Again he punctuated the kisses with the tip of his tongue and she shivered in delight.

When he moved his mouth to the base of her spine she shifted a little, not sure what was coming next but Rafe leaned over so his mouth was close to her ear.

"Easy, Tyler. Just relax. I'm going to make you feel so good."

Going to? He already was.

"'K." She barely got out the one syllable.

He returned to peppering her body with kisses and strokes of her tongue. When he reached the curve of her ass, she tensed again, but he stroked the curves of both cheeks with the flat of his palm until she settled down. Oh, wait. Settled down? Who was she kidding? By now she was melting into a puddle yet at the same time anticipating the next touch, the next caress.

He smoothed his hand over her buttocks again, just a gentle sweep of flesh over flesh but so erotic she felt more moisture seeping from her pussy. She felt the movement of his body when he shifted and wondered what was coming next. Not what she expected, certainly. He trailed a string of very gentle kisses over every inch of each cheek, not in any pattern or in any rhythm, which made it even more erotic. When she felt the soft press of his lips against one curve of her buttocks electric shocks zipped through her followed by a rush of fiery heat, all of it heading straight to her sex. She squeezed her legs together against the thrumming in her inner walls but the more he placed kisses on her the more intense the thrumming became.

Tyler hugged the pillow tightly to her body and clenched her fists and fire uncoiled deep inside her, surging through her, pushing her toward that elusive precipice she craved. When he trailed just the very tip of his tongue along the edge of that hot crevice, she lost it. The orgasm roared through her like a whirlwind, shaking her, the walls of her pussy contracting with intense spasms. Her heart beat wildly and she could barely breathe with the intensity of the shudders consuming her.

Rafe continued to string kisses along the curve of her buttocks while his hands held her in place. When the last spasm died away he peppered her with more kisses, smoothed more caresses on her until she was again limp and pliant. Then he rolled her to her back again.

"Don't move," he whispered. "Just…Just stay right there." He climbed off the bed.

"Where are you going?" she asked. Was he going to just leave her there or what?

He paused then gave her a slow, hungry smile. "I did a little extra shopping in the store today, so don't move. I'll be right back."

As he turned toward the bathroom, she noticed that his cock was nearly at full mast again. Her body responded to the sight, her hungry sex clamoring for him to fill it. In a moment, he was back, dumping a handful of condoms on the nightstand. Her eyes widened.

"Do you plan to use all those?"

He straddled her, his gaze locked with her, the look in his eyes indefinable.

"We'll see," he answered, his voice nearly unrecognizable. "Jesus, Tyler, you have the sweetest body." He leaned down and placed a soft kiss on the sensitive hollow of her throat.

Her pussy throbbed in response.

He ripped open the foil packet and sheathed himself without ever taking his eyes from her. Tyler licked her lips, watching as he rolled the latex down his swollen length. Then, lifting her legs and bending them back to open her to him fully, he nudged her opening with the head of his cock. Eased into her slowly, one inch at a time. She was so wet that his passage was easy and it was mere seconds before he was fully lodged inside her.

Oh God!

Already she could feel another orgasm building inside her. His gaze pinned her and she could not look away. The way Rafe's look penetrated hers she felt as if he could see clear inside her. Maybe he could. No one ever had before. She didn't think anyone had ever wanted to. Certainly none of the men she had been with. Not any of them. It made her feel more completely exposed than just being without her clothes.

She desperately wanted him to like what he saw, what he felt. He said he had feelings for her, even though the admission hadn't come so easily for him. She hoped it was as strong as the one that wrapped itself around her and inside her. She realized as she lay there, connected to him in the most intimate way, that he was the only man she'd ever permitted to see her stripped of everything including her defenses.

I'm so glad I got rid of the old Tyler Gillette. I want Rafe to love this new one.

Surprisingly, she had discovered she was actually beginning to love herself. What a startling revelation. If only they could catch whoever was after her, she could move on with her new life with a sense of freedom she'd never felt before.

They stayed that way for so long Tyler wondered if Rafe was ever going to move or just hold them in this position all night. She pressed her feet flat on the bed to push her hips at him, and he pulled back slightly and then thrust into her hard one time. And holy shit! The climax swirling low inside her burst to the surface with nothing else except that one movement.

"Oh God!" The words drifted out on a heavy breath as the spasms rippled through her like waves on a pond.

Rafe braced himself, holding still, until the contractions seized. When she lay there, panting, he began a slow in-and-out movement, thrust and retreat, driving that big erection hard into her body. Unbelievably, her body was ready again.

"Wrap your legs around me," he ordered.

She wound her legs around his hips, locking her ankles at the small of his back and digging her heels into him. And hung on for the wild ride.

If she thought last night had been good, it was insignificant compared to this. She lost all sense of self, completely immersed in this man who was in her, around her, in her body and her senses. She wanted to close her eyes as he pushed her higher and higher to the top of the wave but she was unable to break away from the intense look in his eyes.

Harder and harder he drove her, up, up, up to the top of that wave. With a breathtaking suddenness it crested and she tumbled over the top, whirling and swirling, her entire body in the grip of intense shudders. His cock pulsed inside her in giant throbbing swells and her body clutched at him as if to never let him go.

At some point, she had no idea how long, everything subsided like a wave as it ebbed and slid back to the ocean, leaving the sand swept clean but with the outline of it imprinted on its surface. No matter what happened next in her life—or ever—Rafe Ortiz would be forever imprinted on her body.

He eased himself down on her, catching his weight on his forearms, and rested there until they could breathe normally and their heartbeats settled into a normal pattern. She waited to see what he would do next, knowing it would be the footprint of where their relationship went. Or if it went at all. She was prepared for a brief, obligatory kiss, or maybe no kiss at all. Perhaps a repetition of why this could never work between them. Anything, except for the reality.

He slid his hands to cup her face, lowered his head and took her in a kiss so demanding, so voracious, she felt it in every corner of her body. He devoured her mouth, tasting every inch of it with his tongue. Coaxing her tongue to duel with him then licking everywhere again. Like the orgasm, it went on forever. She didn't care if she ever drew breath again as long as he never stopped.

Finally he lifted his head. Tyler's mouth was dry as she forced herself to look into Rafe's eyes and see what was there. He held her gaze for so long she was afraid of what he might say. He eased from her body, still without a word, and made his way to the bathroom to dispose of the condom. Tyler lay rigid, clenching her hands at her sides, just waiting. She tried her best to figure out if that kiss was a good-bye or a step in the right direction.

Rafe padded across the floor, slid into bed beside her and pulled the covers over the both of them. Then he tugged her into his arms, cradling her against his chest, gently stroking her hair.

"You're right," he said at last. "It isn't just sex."

Happiness coursed through her like warm syrup, seeping into every nook and cranny. But she didn't give herself over to it completely. She sensed there was a "but" coming here.

"And?" she finally prodded.

He studied her face, looked into her eyes as if trying to find the real her deep inside herself.

"And I guess walking away from it just isn't going to work." He rested his chin on her head. "Shit, Tyler. I think you turned my life upside down."

Her breath came out in a whoosh and she tucked her head into the crook of his neck, her arm coming around his chest. "Then we're even, because you did the same to me. We can make it work," she promised him. She wasn't going to lose him, not when she finally had someone who could complete her. Give meaning to her life.

He looked down at her, his face serious. "You think so?"

She nodded. "I know we can. I-I'm feeling good about myself now, Rafe. More like I have something to offer someone. Someone I can feel good about. Someone—" She knew she was babbling.

"And you should." He placed a gentle kiss on her forehead. "Tyler, it isn't about makeup or clothing, you know." He shifted his head and grinned down at her. "Although I definitely vote for those changes."

"I-I...want this to mean something to both of us."

"Listen to me, *cara.*" He stroked her cheek. "I'm not sure either of us is ready for this, but I guess we have to give it a try."

"Oh, yes. Please."

"It won't be easy," he told her. "I was definitely not looking for or expecting this. And we come from two different places."

She was silent as she pressed herself against him. Then she said, "So what are you saying?"

He sighed, his breath ruffling her hair. "I'm saying…Yes, I want this, too. So let's take it one day at a time and see how it goes."

She hadn't expected him to jump feet first into a relationship, especially when she had so much baggage she was dragging with her. But he was willing to try and she could live with that. The new Tyler Gillette could be hopeful about anything.

Chapter 12

Tyler came awake slowly, memories of the previous night washing over her. Eyes still closed, she smiled, remembering every moment, especially when Rafe decided to stop fighting her and give in to what was so intensely there between them.

Rafe!

God! Last night had been so magnificent. They hadn't quite used all the condoms on the nightstand, but they'd made a good dent in them. She hadn't thought it possible for a man to have that many orgasms in one night. Maybe Rafe was an exception but she didn't care, as long as he was *her* exception.

This morning she didn't have to stretch out an arm searching for him as she had yesterday. Instead, today he was curled around her spoon fashion, one muscular arm banding her to his big, toned body. And nudging the cleft of her buttocks was his equally big cock, standing at full attention if she was any judge. How much better it was to wake up like this than to an empty bed he'd run from because he didn't want the involvement. She just hoped in the light of day he wouldn't have another attack of conscience or whatever it was and push her away again.

"I can smell your brain burning." He chuckled and his warm breath teased her ear. "Hope those are pleasant thoughts."

"Mmm." She snuggled back against him. "Very pleasant."

"Mine, too," he said in that warm as molasses drawl of his.

He turned her to face him and stared at her for an intense moment. Then, with a caress as light as a butterfly's touch, he brushed his lips against hers, back and forth, before using his tongue to urge her mouth to open for him. Little by little he eased that educated tongue of his inside and licked her inner surface, sliding it over her teeth and the inner flesh of her lips. Every single nerve in her body leaped to attention as he deepened the kiss, tilting his head this way and that.

The kiss was hot and hungry, and she swore she could feel the tip of his tongue deep inside her. This was a different kind of kiss than all the others. More intense. More demanding. More—She couldn't even think what else because the kiss was so all-consuming.

"Well," she said, licking her lips when at last he broke the kiss. "That's some good morning."

He grazed his mouth over hers again. "There's more where that came from. More of everything."

He proved it by taking her mouth in another equally ravishing kiss. There might as well have been a string directly tied from his tongue to her pussy because the throbbing in her cunt was suddenly so intense it reverberated throughout her body.

"I'm so hard," he murmured against her lips, "that I don't think an hour would be long enough for me to fuck you. And damn it, we have to get up."

"We do?" She gave him a quizzical look.

"I have to be at the stadium well before game time, and I want to get some breakfast."

"You didn't tell me when I asked, but exactly where will I be sitting? I happen to know the games are all sold out."

"Not a problem," he assured her. "The agency has a few tickets for special circumstances."

"And that's me?" she asked, grinning. She'd decided it wasn't worth the effort to fight this anymore. Hating something took more energy than she wanted to expend now. "Special circumstances?"

"Uh-huh. For today anyway." He nuzzled her neck with his nose, then gave her a light smack on her ass. "Much as I want to stay here and explore that incredible body of yours for the rest of the day, duty calls. Let's move it."

Tyler swallowed hard and reached out to touch him.

"Rafe? Thank you for last night. It was—special, on so many levels."

"Special for me, too." He brushed his mouth over her lips. "You know I never gave anything between us a chance, Tyler, but maybe something good will come out of all of this."

"Something good," she agreed.

"Now," he said, "we need to get moving."

Sliding out of bed with great reluctance, she pushed to her feet and headed for the bathroom. Shower first. She needed to wake up. Too bad she'd have to wash away all those delicious smells at the same time. She let the water run, heating up, while she brushed her teeth, then stepped into the enclosure. She stood there with her head back, surrounded by the hot steam. She was just letting the water pour over her when the glass door slid open and suddenly Rafe was behind her, pulling her against his body. God! He was so big and so ripped, and his cock was so huge, pressing against her wet backside. She leaned back against him, reveling in the feel of him.

"I think you might need some help here," he murmured, taking the bottle of shower gel from the little alcove in the wall. "Besides, I didn't want to start my day without this."

He poured a liberal amount into the palm of one hand and worked it into a generous lather. Then, slowly and deliberately, he bathed the front of her body. His hands moved at a leisurely pace along her throat, over the slope of her shoulders, back to her breasts where he tweaked the nipples and circled the very tips of them with his fingers. Her waist came next followed by the flare of her hips, his hands meeting over the slight curve of her tummy. He moved his hands slowly, unhurriedly, in lazy concentric circles, soothing as much as bathing her. She closed her eyes and pressed her head back against him, enjoying the feel of his touch.

When he eased his hands lower still, cupping the top of her mound, she tried to part her legs but Rafe bracketed them with his own, forcing them together.

"Not yet." He voice was a low rumble in her ear. "Some things should not be rushed."

He knelt behind her to finish soaping her legs from thigh to ankle and back before arranging her so she faced forward with her hands braced against the tile wall. Then he began again, stroking her shoulders, her back, tracing the length of her spine. He used the tip of one finger to move lazily from neck to waist and then slip easily through the crevice between the cheeks of her ass.

Tyler sucked in her breath and curled her fingers into her palm. She felt the glide of his hands down the inside of her legs and up along the back, shaping them over her buttocks before he rested them at her waist and drew her back so she was again leaning against his body. She did her best to ignore the thick length of his shaft pressing into the cleft between her cheeks. When she pressed back against him harder, though, Rafe just laughed that low, sexy rumble.

"Don't be in such a rush."

But she was. She wanted him inside her. Now. Right now.

This time when he slipped his fingers down between her labia, and she parted her legs, he moved his own feet on the inside of hers, nudging her legs apart. A little pressure and he was holding her open for his pleasure. His soapy fingers fondled and caressed and played, swirling around the nub of her clitoris, sliding easily into her very wet channel.

It only took a few thrusts of his fingers inside her before she clamped down on them and her orgasm overtook her. Holding her with one arm banded around her, he stroked in and out as he rode her through the spasms.

Her inner walls were still fluttering when he slid open the shower door and reached out to retrieve the condom he'd stashed on the vanity counter. It amazed her how deftly he opened it and rolled it on with his fingers still so slick with soap. It surprised her even more how quickly he turned her around, lifted her with his powerful hands, and lowered her onto his erection.

Oh God!

It was all him from then on, and she could do nothing except hang on. Rafe braced her against the wall, took in a deep breath and plundered her. That was the only word for it. He drove in and out in an ever-increasing, ever-harder rhythm. It seemed they were both primed and ready because barely seconds passed before he plunged one last time. And they exploded, in a climax so intense it shook both of them from head to toe. She didn't know how Rafe managed to hold both of them in place while shudders ripped through their bodies.

Aftershocks still rippled through her body as he rested his forehead against hers, water sluicing down on both of them. Finally, with strength Tyler never would have believed he had, he lifted her from his cock and lowered her until her feet touched the floor. Deftly he removed the condom and disposed of it in the wastebasket.

Tyler let out a long slow breath when he wrapped his arms around her again and just held her beneath the steady stream of water until the aura of the climax faded. She looked up at him, his body blocking the water temporarily, searching for something in his eyes. Thrilled to see hunger and need and want and yes, even happiness glittering there.

As if she'd said it out loud, he smiled and nodded. "It's all good, Tyler. Really good. Let's finish our showers. You make a man work up an appetite."

* * * *

Breakfast at Potrero's was delicious and the atmosphere between them was easy as they ate and joked and laughed. But Rafe also took the opportunity to study the woman across from him very carefully. If someone had told him he'd be feeling this good and all because of this woman, he'd either have called them a liar or decked them. He was seeing an entirely different side of Tyler than she'd shown since the first day he met her. There was a softness and a vulnerability he had never seen before. Now as they headed toward the stadium all kinds of thoughts rambled through his mind.

He'd always been so careful about his relationships, but Tyler had landed like a whirlwind, literally shaking up his life. And shock of shocks, he not only liked it, he wanted it. Maybe even craved it. She was a woman who made every part of him come alive. Someone who he thought had gotten lost in the image she'd created for herself.

He loved her new look, minimal makeup, hair in a ponytail with a navy ball cap, a blousy navy-and-white T-shirt, and plain jeans. She bore no resemblance at all to the woman he'd hauled out of Tequila Sunrise. He would make sure to tell her as often as possible how much he liked this woman. Loved. Loved? Yup, loved. Just the sight of her made him feel good.

After the first night with her he'd sworn never again. He'd known the danger when he was obligated to take this assignment, and he'd expected to regret that one night for a long time. But after last night he knew what a big fat lie that was. Much as he'd hated to admit it, last night actually had been about more than just sex. Emotions had come into play, hers and his, and walking away from her was not going to be an option.

He'd give his left nut—well, figuratively, not literally—to know what went wrong with her father that set her on the life course. He was just glad he was the one enjoying the transformation.

Tyler's amused voice interrupted his thoughts.

"I can hear your brain from over here," she teased. "Thinking about the logistics of game day?"

Should he tell her what he felt? Would he say things the right way? This wasn't just any woman he'd gotten himself tangled up with. This was *Tyler Gillette*, for fuck's sake. This was complicated on so many levels.

He mentally shook himself back to reality and cupped her chin.

"Just thinking how glad I am that things happened between us the way they are."

Her face lit up with happiness. "Me, too, but you know that, right?"

"I don't know." He grinned. "Maybe you'd better tell me another ten or twenty times." Then he sobered. "Not to throw a damper on the day, but I was wondering why we hadn't heard from your stalker today."

"I was thinking the same thing." Tyler thumbed through her texts and missed calls as they navigated the streets. She shook her head. "Nothing. Not a word."

"Maybe he's regrouping, although I don't think so."

"You think he knows I'm going to the game today?"

"I spread the word around pretty good, just as we discussed," he told her. "That means Chad and Ed will automatically get the news. And if Nate is shadowing you he'll see where we're going."

"Wait, wait, wait." She looked over at him. "What do you mean, if Nate is shadowing me? Has he been following me? Us?"

He blew out a breath. "I hate to admit I didn't pay enough attention but a couple of times I noticed a car following us. I just wasn't tuned into this situation at the time. I'm sorry, Tyler. My screwup."

"Don't blame yourself," she insisted.

"But I should be paying attention to things like that. I have a feeling he tracked you to that restaurant yesterday morning. I know, I know." He held up his hand. "You said it's a favorite place of his, but I had one of my guys drop into the place casually, long after Broder had left. He asked after him and was told the man had been in earlier but otherwise they hadn't seen him in weeks."

Tyler was stunned. "You're kidding. Nate loves that place. Loved."

"I got the reports I had the agency run on everyone." He paused while he moved into another lane of traffic. "You probably aren't aware that his law practice is slowly going down the tubes. Or that the senior partners have him on a very short leash. He's not hanging out in his usual places anymore."

She didn't know what to say. "His place in that law firm was the gold star in his crown."

"Yeah, well, the gold is tarnished and his crown is crumbling." He slid a glance at her. "I don't know how you'll take this, but apparently when he married you he promised the partners he'd deliver the Hawks."

"What?" She jerked her head around to look at him. "Are you kidding me? God! That was his brass ring. I knew he never really loved me. I mean, he loves himself too much."

"But he loved what you could give him access to."

The more Rafe thought about it, the angrier he became. Maybe Tyler had been complicit in some way, looking to normalize herself in Kurt's eyes and gain some attention and respect. But from what the agency had learned in their investigation, when she didn't come through with the keys to the penthouse office for him, Nate had basically treated her like shit. And pitched an unholy fit when she'd tossed him out. Rumor had it that Kurt got her a shark of an attorney to make sure Broder didn't end up with even one penny of her trust or anything else. Now it seemed the man was sucking up to her, trying to hook up again.

Tyler sighed so heavily he almost regretted bringing the whole thing up. "I suppose."

He had one other thing to relate to her but he had to pick his time. He and Tony had agreed to have someone checking her street periodically at night. Last night three different cars had coasted down that street after he and Tyler shut the town house up for the night. Everyone, it seemed, was spying on Tyler after she went to bed at night. Where else had they been following her? And how had he not observed any of this before now, just because he'd formed his own prejudiced opinion of her. Discovering the real Tyler Gillette just made him kick his ass that he hadn't worked harder on this in the beginning. Some security agent he was, letting his prejudices affect his work.

Okay, then. Sending the flowers and candy made this more personal. By the sound of his latest text he was getting impatient. The problem was, how would they know which of their three suspects was pushing harder when they all wanted the same thing?

Fucking damn. Unreasonably he wished one of them would make a move that would narrow this down to one person. He wanted to get this out of Tyler's life once and for all. The more he thought about it, the more he felt the rightness of what they had discovered together. If none of this had happened, would she have decided to make major changes in her lifestyle? In herself? Would he have embraced the feelings for her he'd been fighting all these years?

Who knew? But now he wanted this done and gone so they could get on with their lives. Together.

When he pulled up to the employee gate at the stadium, a man wearing a Lone Star Security polo shirt stepped up to greet him.

"Hey, boss. Got your usual parking spot waiting for you."

"Thanks."

The man tried to peer into the car without looking too obvious.

Rafe chuckled. "Luke, say hello to Tyler Gillette. She's taking in the game today."

Luke was doing his best not to gawk. "Nice to see you, Miss Gillette. We don't see you out here too often."

"That's going to change," Rafe told him. "Okay, we're rolling."

He found his slot in the private section of the lot and ushered Tyler into the stadium. The concourse today was jammed with people, standing in line at the concessionaires, hurrying to their seats, or just chatting with friends. When he nudged Tyler toward an elevator, she dug in her heels.

"B-but I won't know anyone," she pointed out.

Rafe smiled. A slightly hesitant Tyler Gillette was completely new to him. "Yes, you will. Anyway, you don't have to talk to anyone if you don't want to. Just sit and enjoy the game."

"Enjoy the game?" She sniffed. "That'll be the day."

"You never know. You got into it last night." The elevator doors opened and he eased her forward. "This is our floor."

The man checking tickets nodded to him and smiled as he and Tyler walked up one entrance ramp to the section where the seats were.

She grinned when he guided her to their row. "Fifty-yard line, no less. You do treat yourself well."

"Not me. I don't get to sit down. This is where your date sits."

She stopped and frowned at him. "My date? Wait a minute—"

Just then the man sitting in the end seat of the row in front of them stood up and turned around.

"Nice to see you again, Tyler." Tony Castillo grinned at her. "Glad you decided to take in the game."

Tyler looked from one to the other. "But you—But I—But—"

Rafe took her hand and squeezed it briefly. "Don't freak. Like I said, these are Lone Star seats. Tony comes to a lot of the games, and he was happy to have you here with him today."

"Come on." Tony stepped back so she could take the empty seat next to him. "Let's sit down. Would you like a beer?"

"Yes, I—" She shook her head. "No. Thanks, anyway."

Rafe wondered if she was doing this, refusing the beer, for him or herself.

"Okay. I need to get moving." He was still holding her hand. "Remember what we discussed. Phone on at all times, right? Just in case?"

She lifted an eyebrow. "In case he decides to text me or do one of his crazy calls here in a stadium with seventy thousand people. Where I might not even hear him. Right?"

"Right." He nodded. "Anyone obsessed the way this guy is with you will do crazy things. We won't take any chances."

"I'll put it on vibrate," she told him. "I won't hear a ring but this way I'll know if a call or text comes in."

"Good enough." He looked from her to Tony. "If she gets anything, you tap me right away, got it?"

"Got it, boss." He winked. Then his face sobered. "We're good here, Rafe. Go on. Do whatever you have to."

"I don't think he'll try anything at the game," Rafe said, "but then with crazies you never know. And my money says this guy is unstable."

"We'll cover all bases," Tony agreed.

"You know what to do if anything off-kilter happens, right?"

Tony touched the little radio clipped to his belt. "All set.

"Okay. We'll meet up at my office later." He gave Tyler's hand one last quick squeeze. "Be careful."

He had to hold himself back from giving her a quick kiss on the lips. What the hell? Deliberately he turned and headed off to check on VIP security.

* * * *

"I think you have young Rafe's head in a spin," Tony commented as he adjusted his large frame to the seat.

Tyler made a rude noise. "Puhleeze. Rafe Ortiz is neither young nor spinning."

Tony chuckled. "I think everyone is young to me. I keep forgetting he's been retired for two years now, plus he played for ten."

"I'm surprised he's not still playing," Tyler commented

"He was at the top of his game when he retired," Tony said. "He decided to get out while his body was still in one piece."

Tyler scowled. "Isn't that unusual?"

"Not really. There are a lot of players who make that same decision." He shrugged. "They've had the adrenaline rush, the guts and glory, the excitement of the game. They're in a good situation financially and they want to start the next phase of their lives." He shifted in his seat. "I'll tell you another thing about that man. Unlike most of the players, he has never touched a dime of his signing bonus or his salary all these years."

Her jaw dropped. "You're kidding. What does he live on?"

Tony grinned. "His endorsement money. His agent got him some fat contracts, so he's just let his football money grow in the investment accounts. Even managed to buy his folks a new house, over their objections I might add. Neither of them are much for anything fancy."

"Neither is he," she commented. "Even his own house is really nice but not, you know, outrageous like some of the guys."

"That's just who he is."

She nibbled on a fingernail. "I'm surprised he's never married."

Tony winked at her. "Probably just never found the right woman. He's got some pretty old-fashioned ideas."

Tyler stared off across all the people sitting in front of them. "I guess that lets me out."

"Not at all." Tony took the hand with the nibbled fingernail and tugged so she had to face him. "That woman out there in the media?" He shook his head. "That's not you. Never was. The one sitting next to me today is the real Tyler Gillette. It just took you a while to realize that."

"I hope he feels the same way."

"If the look in his eyes means anything, I'd say he's definitely on your side of the fence." A loud roar went up from the field. "Oh, look. Here comes the team. Let's watch a little football and forget about stalkers and all that other crap for a while."

To her amazement, Tyler found herself enjoying the activity on the field. The pregame festivities intrigued her, but not nearly as much as the action between the two teams. Tony did his best to give her a crash course for newbies as the game progressed and she sucked it up. She thought again about the college classes she'd taken that required a lot of detailed study. One of the things all her professors had been in agreement on was the fact she was a quick study, learned easily and had a real skill for solving puzzles. Although she had wasted all that since she stopped taking classes, it seemed her mind had only been hibernating. Now it kicked into overdrive as she soaked up everything about a game she'd sworn she hated.

She found herself actually reading the patterns on the field, studying the plays, trying to guess what was going to happen. She screamed as loud as everyone else when the Hawks made a good play, and especially when they scored two touchdowns. By the time the first half was over, she was thoroughly and unbelievably juiced.

"They're winning." She grabbed Tony's arm and shook it. "The Hawks are winning."

He laughed. "That's what we want."

She plopped back down in her seat as the halftime show began. She had never expected to be infected with football fever. Now what did she do with it? That was the big question. She was about to ask Tony a question when she felt her phone vibrate in her jeans pocket. Fully expecting it to be Betsy or Lynn or maybe one of the others in their little circle she pulled it out and pressed the button to light up the screen. The number one perched on the message icon.

"Tony?" She nudged him.

"Yeah?" He looked at her face and suddenly was all business.

She could hardly make herself heard over all the halftime noise so she bent as close to him as she could get and showed him the phone. He started to take it from her, but she shook her head.

"I'll do it," she said in his ear. "I just want you to see it with me."

He nodded and she tapped the icon. The message of course was from Unknown.

"I told u I wanted u. U shld b at gm w/me. If I can't have u no one can."

As she stared at it another one rolled in.

"I wil keep u safe and happy. Otherwise u hv no future."

Immediately another text came through. *"U wil only lev hre with me 2day. Or not leave at all."*

And then a third.

"It's hlftm. Get up now and walk to elevator. Follow the crwd. Move."

Tyler was shaking so hard she nearly dropped her phone. Tony plucked it from her hands.

"He's watching me." She looked around, trying to see if she could spot any of the three men. "God, Tony, where is he?" Had this miserable bastard had eyes on her since she got there? Maybe even before?

Tony unclipped the small radio from his belt and hit the button. "Rafe, security office. Now." Then he urged Tyler up from her seat. "Come on. We're going to the main security office. My radio is set on a closed circuit to Rafe's so he'd get the message right away."

She could hardly make her feet move as he helped her up the steps. She thanked God that Tony had a firm grip on her. He hustled her into the elevator and punched the button for the first floor.

The elevator was jammed with the halftime crowd. She and Tony just barely managed to squeeze in before the doors closed and the elevator started down. She hoped the security guards who were watching the three men had a handle on who was doing what because she needed this to be over. Now.

The doors slid open and the crowd surged forward, practically pushing them out into the equally crowded concourse.

"This way." Tony reached for her arm.

Then something jabbed her in the back, a hand yanked on her arm and she heard a voice she'd learned to despise.

"Let her go, old man," he growled at Tony. "This is a gun I've got at her back, and I won't hesitate to pull the trigger. I've got nothing left to lose."

"N-Nate?" All the blood rushed from her head, and she was sure she was going to faint. "What's going on here?"

"I said let go of her," he repeated to Tony. When the older man still held onto her arm, she felt the gun leave her back for a moment.

A shot cracked in the air as Nate fired up at the ceiling, and then he grabbed her again.

"Let go of her now," he yelled, "or the next one hits you, old man."

Around them people were screaming and running in every direction.

"Okay, take it easy." She knew Tony's words were meant to be soothing, but he had to shout to make himself heard. He released her arm, giving her a reassuring squeeze as he did, and mouthed the words, *It will be okay.*

How could he think that? At the moment, she could only concentrate on not being shot.

Nate kept the gun pressed to her spine with one hand and clamped his other arm around her neck.

"Everyone?" he shouted. "Stay out of my way, or I'll shoot her and then anyone else near me."

She had no idea where he was taking her. Behind them were windows overlooking the parking lot. Every access was ahead of them and blocked by crowds, people all trying to get out of each other's way.

"Nate." She had to raise her voice to be heard. "There's no place for you to go. This is stupid."

"Stupid?" He tightened his arm across her throat. "Are you calling me stupid?"

Oh, hell.

"No. No, I'm not. I'm just trying to point out there there's no exit this way."

"They'll let me out." Every word was edged with desperation. "I've got an exit pass. You."

She wanted to tell him that if he shot her, the guards would just shoot him, but she didn't think that would help her cause.

"Everybody move," he shouted and again fired toward the ceiling.

People scrambled and Tyler could see now that in addition to Tony, others had appeared—some of the Lone Star security guards, her father... *Her father?* And where was Rafe? She didn't see him anywhere. Didn't he know what was going on?

Nate continued to drag her backward. The people to either side of them continuing to scatter, until suddenly he stopped.

"This is a gun pointed right at the nape of your neck, Broder."

Rafe! Oh, thank you, God. Rafe.

"Drop the gun or you'll be dead in two seconds. Do you know what a bullet in this exact spot can do to a person?"

"I'll kill her," Nate threatened again.

"And then you'll be dead, so what have you gained?"

"It's all her fault," Nate shouted. "She walked out on me. Divorced me. Ruined my career."

God. All this was because of his damn law career?

"And you thought threatening her would bring her back to you?"

"I thought..." Nate paused. "I thought if I scared her enough, she'd come back to me to keep her safe."

"If you want her to be safe," Rafe said, his voice unbelievably measured and calm, "then drop the gun now. While there's still time to end this safely."

"End it?" Nate's laugh was tinged with hysteria. "The minute I do you'll arrest me."

"But at least you won't be dead," Rafe pointed out.

Tyler held her breath for what seemed an interminable moment. Then, as if all the air had gone out of him, Nate released his hold on her and the pressure of the gun eased. Two of the Lone Star guards rushed forward to take control of Nate, and then Rafe swept her into his arms.

"Jesus, *cara.* I nearly had a heart attack." He was holding her so tight she could hardly breathe, but she didn't care. "I think I lost ten years of my life."

"H-How did you get behind him?" she asked.

"Tony radioed me and when I got here there was still enough crowd cover for me to slip behind the two of you." He tilted her head back and in front of everyone gave her a kiss so hot and passionate it curled her toes. When he lifted his head at last he said, "I may never be able to let you out of my sight again."

"Do you think I could give her a hug, too?" Her father's voice, but unfamiliar because it sounded so uncertain.

"Of course." Rafe released her with obvious reluctance.

Then she was wrapped up in a big bear hug from a man who hadn't hugged her since she was a tiny child.

"It's okay, Daddy." She patted his back. Daddy. She loved the sound of that word. "I'm okay."

He looked at her, his eyes actually damp with tears. "I'm so sorry, Tyler. I've been the world's biggest ass, but I'm done with that. I have a lot to make up to you for."

"How about starting with you taking her up to your suite," Tony suggested. "They need to clear the concourse here and I think everyone would like to get out of the public eye. Cell-phone cameras have been going off like crazy."

"Great." She frowned. "I'll be in all the papers and blogs again."

"And it won't matter a damn to me," Kurt assured her.

"Taking her upstairs is a great idea, Kurt," Rafe said. "The cops are on their way, and I need to clean up this mess here. I'll be up in a bit. I need to find out who that asshole bribed to get a gun into the stadium."

"I'm on it with you," Tony said. "Whoever it was better find a job in American Samoa. There won't be one any place else."

"Good idea." Kurt actually put his arm around Tyler to guide her. "Tony? You come along, too. The second half has already started. The stadium is flooded with cops. Some people hightailed it out of here, but a lot of the crowd is still here. I think some good old-fashioned football is just what we all need right now."

Tyler barely remembered the rest of the game. She sat in her father's owner's suite, protected and cosseted by him in a way she'd grown never to expect. She had to work hard to control the shakes, and she had no appetite for the food people kept trying to press on her. But somehow she managed to smile and nod politely.

Eventually, helped along by a glass of wine, the shakes subsided and she began to feel a little less tense. She was sure she'd have nightmares for a long time, though.

As she was sipping the wine and trying to relax in one of the seats, Kurt introduced her to a man he said was Nate's boss at the law firm.

"I'm so sorry about this," Colin Segar said.

"It's not your fault," she objected.

"Maybe yes, maybe no. Nate was on his way out," Colin told her, confirming the fact that the man had truly been in big trouble. "He promised he'd be getting back with you and bringing in the Hawks as clients." He made a disgusted sound. "I should have known better. No, I should never have hired him in the first place. I had a feeling he was a loser from day one."

Rafe returned eventually after handing over supervision of security to his assistant, never leaving her side until the game was over. Tyler wanted to tell him he could go back to work, but she was afraid if he left the suite, her hard-won control would shatter.

The game went right down to the wire, with the Hawks just barely edging the Mustangs seventeen-fourteen on a last-minute field goal. In Kurt Gillette's suite at the stadium, insanity reigned. The win moved the Hawks into first place in their division and people couldn't stop screaming and high-fiving each other.

Despite everything that had happened, Tyler soon found herself swept up in the celebration and the excitement. Part of it had to do with her sudden newfound absorption in the game itself. But a bigger part was the way her father had reached out to her. He took great pains to introduce her to everyone in the suite with unexpected pride and went out of his way to make sure she had a good time. But the thing that really made her feel good? During a time out on the field, he leaned close to her and whispered, "I have a lot to make up to you for. I'm not going to waste any more time getting to it, either, if you'll just give me half a chance."

Half a chance? She'd give him a whole chance. Tony Castillo had made a couple of comments that she'd had to think about. Looking at it as objectively as she could despite years of emotional pain, maybe her father hadn't been able to deal with his grief. And maybe his answer had been to shut her out completely. But he'd begun to reach out to her when the situation with her stalker had blown up. So maybe the "new" Tyler could try to meet him halfway.

Rafe explained to Tyler he'd have to take her to the police department in the morning to file an official complaint. He also insisted on telling Kurt about the episodes with Chad and Ed.

"I'm going to have a very long talk with Chad," Kurt said after Tyler told him everything that had happened with that man. "His behavior has been unforgiveable. If he can't get his head straight, I don't need him out there with the media."

"He really surprised me," Tyler said. "I don't know where that possessive steak came from."

Kurt grimaced. "I may have given him the wrong impression when I asked him to be your permanent escort to all those functions. I just thought the media relations director would be the best person. I had no ulterior motive where the two of you are concerned."

"I couldn't believe how antagonistic he got when I told him Rafe was taking me last night."

"I think it's a case of getting too big for his britches." Kurt shook his head. "We'll see how our little chat goes. Ed Spinelli is on my list, too. He doesn't work for me, but he knows I carry a lot of influence in the world of pro football. He won't want to get on my bad side."

At last the game was over. As Rafe led her away, her father came over to give her another hug.

"Tomorrow we're having lunch," he promised, "and I'm going to start making up for the fact that I've been the world's worst father for twenty-two years." He kissed her cheek. "You go home with Rafe now. He's a good man. He'll take care of you."

Which was exactly what she needed.

Chapter 13

By the time she and Rafe finally returned to the town house, she felt she'd been through ten wringers.

"I think I am beyond exhausted." Tyler flopped down on the couch in her great room.

"No wonder." He lifted her in his arms, sat down, and placed her in his lap, still holding onto her. "I nearly lost you today, *cara.* I'm not ashamed to say I was scared shitless."

"Me, too." She nestled her head in the crook of his neck.

"I wanted to tear that fucking bastard limb from limb." He sighed. "But knowing he'll spend a good many years in jail is almost as satisfying."

"I still can hardly wrap my head around it."

"I'm glad to see a change coming up in your relationship with your father," Rafe commented.

"Me, too." She smiled. "I'm having lunch with him tomorrow. He said we have a lot to talk about."

"I'd say he's right." Rafe nodded at her. "He made a lot of mistakes, for whatever reasons, but he knows it."

"I did, too," she admitted. "I'd like to think he and I can get past all this."

"You can if you want to," he told her. "I realized something else today, too." His words were soft, his lips pressed to her cheek.

"And what's that?"

"If I'd lost you, I would have lost the one woman who could give meaning to my life. They say it takes a shock to make you realize the truth. Today I believe it. My truth is, I'm in love with you, Tyler. Maybe I have been forever. I was just…" He paused, as if not knowing what to say.

"The past is the past, Rafe. Maybe this is the wakeup call we both needed." She curled more tightly against him. "I think I've always been in love with you. Does that scare you off?"

"Not even a little bit." He touched two fingers to her lips. "What's past is past. There's an old saying that out of death comes the affirmation of new life. I'd say the threat of death is almost the same thing. Let's go upstairs and celebrate it." He stood up with her in his arms, studying her so intently she wondered what he was looking for.

"I'm all for that." Yes, she definitely was.

"We've got something really good going here, Tyler. Sitting at the fundraiser the other night, I realized how much I want what the Reillys and the other couples have. I want to explore what you and I have and see if this is something that's going to stick."

"Me, too."

He carried her up the stairs and into her bedroom, setting her down beside the bed. Very slowly he lowered his head and pressed his mouth to hers. His tongue slid across her lips before he prodded them to open and swept inside. She slipped her tongue over his in an erotic dance, tasting every bit of his mouth, sucking hard on his tongue. Rafe captured her head with one hand, holding it in place while he slid the other down to the curve of her ass and pressed her body hard against his. His thick cock was a hard length pressed against her sex. Moisture seeped into her panties and her inner walls flexed as desire coursed through her.

When he lifted his head they were both breathless.

Everything that had been jumbled inside her settled in place and warmth spread through her.

"Something's going on with you." Rafe stroked her cheek with the backs of his fingers. "You always nibble that poor lower lip when you're not sure about something. Come on, Tyler. No secrets between us anymore."

"You'll probably think it's a stupid idea." She leaned her head into his shoulder, avoiding his eyes.

"Unless it involves throwing me out, I'm sure I'll fine with it."

She blew out a breath. "Okay, here goes. I want to go back and finish getting my degree."

Tyler waited for him to laugh at her or tell her it was dumb or any other put-down. But he surprised her. He tipped her chin up so he could look directly into her eyes.

"I think that's a great idea. A really great idea."

Her eyes widened. "You do? You don't think at my age it's stupid?"

"Tyler, honey, people twice your age are getting their degrees. I think it's great and I'm sure your dad will, too."

"I-I want to make you both proud of me."

"We will be. We are." He kissed the tip of her nose. "Any idea what you'd like to study?"

"Uh-huh. I was really good at my business courses, especially statistics, which I think is why when I started to understand the game today it fascinated me. And then…"

"And then?" he urged.

"And then I'd like to ask my dad if there's a place for me in the Hawks organization. I figure if he says yes we can be a real San Antonio Hawks family."

He studied her face for a long time. "This is quite a change in lifestyle for you. Are you sure it's what you really want?"

"I know what I don't want," she told him, "and that's to go back to living the way I was. That night at Mike's I was already regretting so much of what I'd done. I want you to be proud of me, like your friends are of their wives and significant others. I want *me* to be proud of me."

"*Cara*, I think that's great. And I know Kurt will, too." He pulled off her ball cap and tugged her ponytail loose. "But I won't love you any more because of it, because I don't think I could love you more than I do. Some might think us an unlikely pair, but as far as I'm concerned we fit perfectly. So. We ready for that shower now?"

She nodded. "The last one we took together worked very well."

Rafe laughed. "It did, so let's have a repeat."

In what seemed like seconds they were standing beneath the steaming cascade of water, her smaller body pressed back against his very large one as his big hands soaped her body. For a man of his size, his touch was unbelievably gentle as he spread the rich lather over her nipples, her rib cage, her tummy and down to her pussy. His thick fingers slid between the lips of her labia, sliding up and down, rubbing against her tender clit in a way that sent little electrical charges through her inner walls.

She squeezed her thighs together, trapping his hand between them, and his low laugh rumbled in her ear.

"You're so slick and so wet for me. I love sliding my fingers through you like this and feeling how tight you grip me." He nipped the shell of her ear. "I've never felt this connection with another woman, Tyler. I think you bewitched me."

She leaned back against him. "If I did I hope it doesn't wear off."

"Not a chance."

He murmured hot, erotic things in her ear as he continued to rub her swollen nub while pressing his cock into the cleft of her buttocks. Tyler didn't know if her body was ramped up because of everything that happened that day or if Rafe just pressed every one of her buttons by just touching her.

She had a sense of possession. His hands were magic, coaxing responses every place they touched. She was so aroused, so on edge, he'd barely stroked and teased her before a climax burst from deep inside her. She was glad Rafe was holding her so tightly or she would have fallen to the floor, as much as she was trembling.

"Well, damn," he murmured, "I must be better than I thought."

Her laugh was soft and shaky. "But not better than *I* thought. But what about you?"

"Coming right up." He bit her earlobe. "If you'll pardon the pun. But I want to be on a bed for this."

He hastily dried both of them, then carried her to the bed, stripped back the covers. In seconds he had rolled on a condom and knelt between her thighs. When he looked at her there was such love and passion in his eyes it made her weak all over again.

He entered her with one strong thrust, then held himself in place while her body adjusted to him. Their gazes locked and Tyler felt as if he could see clear to inside her soul. It gave her such a sense of belonging she actually felt tears come to her eyes.

Rafe stilled. "Are you okay? Am I hurting you?"

"No." She shook her head. "Far from it. I feel as if every part of me belongs to every part of you."

"Good. Because I feel the same way. I know I said I wanted to make slow, delicious love to you, but I don't think I can do that this time. I want you too badly."

"Then don't wait. We'll have plenty of time for slow later on."

Rafe began to move, slowly at first, measured strokes, in and out, his eyes never leaving hers. She wound her legs around his hips and locked her ankles at the small of his back, holding herself to him as tightly as she could. He never broke the rhythm he set up, in and out, slow and steady. Soon that was all that consumed her, their joining and the tempo of their bodies.

She clung to him, wrapped in the velvet of erotic pleasure, everything focused on the two of them joined together, on Rafe's plundering of her body, on the feel of his thick cock filling every inch of her. Everything they felt for each other seemed poured into this single act.

Tyler was focused totally on the feel of him, the thickness of him, the slick slide and retreat. She was so caught up in the building layers of sensation she was stunned when the orgasm rolled up, so suddenly it shocked her. Rather than the cataclysmic mating of the previous nights, this was more sensuous yet no less intense. Her inner walls gripped him like a vise while his cock flexed and pulsed inside her. The spasms gripped her again and again, ebbing and flowing like slowly rolling waves, on and on and on.

And then it eased, slowed and faded, until they were both left weak and limp and drained. Rafe dropped to his forearms and rested his forehead on hers.

"Incredible." His lips tilted in a slow smile. "Just damn fucking incredible."

"I agree." She unwrapped her legs from him, resting her feet on the bed, watching him as he slowly eased from her body.

He gave her a quick, soft kiss on the lips. "Be right back."

She watched the muscles flex in his magnificent ass as he padded to the bathroom to dispose of the condom. How, she wondered, had she gotten so damn lucky? Less than a week ago she was a hot mess on a self-destructive path with not much to look forward to. Now she had a future with an incredible man who actually loved her.

"You look like someone who is very pleased with herself," Rafe teased as he climbed back into bed.

"Just reflecting on the fortunate turn my life has taken."

"You know what pass interference is, Tyler?"

"Barely. Tony was doing his best to explain things to me today, but it was a lot to cram into my brain at once."

"In football it is when any player's movement beyond the line of scrimmage hinders the progress of an eligible receiver in an attempt to reach the pass." He rested his chin on her head and pulled her more tightly against him. "Here's how I look at it. The ball in your game of life got snapped, but on the way to you catching it shit happened. It's like a defensive player interfering with the receiver. You've been trying to get back in position to catch it again all these years."

"Is that what it was?"

"Uh-huh. Someone just screwed with your playbook. I'm the one who's going to straighten it out."

She lay there silent for a moment.

"I love you, Rafe. More than I can ever tell you."

"I love you, too, *mi corazon.* My heart. You own my heart."

"Good. Because you own mine, too."

Tyler relaxed in Rafe's grip and slowly drifted off to sleep, more secure than she'd felt in a very long time.

Meet the Author

Referred to by *USA Today* as the Nora Roberts of erotic romance, Desiree Holt is the world's oldest living published erotic romance author. A graduate of the University of Michigan with double majors in English and History, her earlier careers include agent and manager in the music industry, public television, associate vice president of university advancement, public relations, and economic development. She is three times a finalist for an EPIC E-Book Award (and a winner in 2014), a nominee for a Romantic Times Reviewers Choice Award, winner of the first 5 Heart Sweetheart of the Year Award at The Romance Studio, as well as twice a CAPA Award winner for best BDSM book of the year, and winner of the Holt Medallion for Excellence in Romance Literature. She has been featured on *CBS Sunday Morning* and in *The Village Voice*, *The Daily Beast, USA Today, The (London) Daily Mail, The New Delhi Times, The Huffington Post* and numerous other national and international publications. She is also the Authors After Dark 2014 Author of the Year.

Readers can visit her at www.desiremeonly.com.

Keep reading for an excerpt from the first book in the Game On series:

Get Ready to Play Rough

Shay Beckham grew up idolizing her brother's best friend, star quarterback Joe Reilly. There was no one in their Texas town who had the moves to match Joe on or off the field. Years later, he's still a player who has what it takes to drive any hot-blooded woman wild. But Shay isn't a kid with a bad case of hero-worship anymore. She's grown-up and independent, with her feet on the ground and a serious head on her shoulders. If she could just say the same for Joe.

It's been fifteen years, but Joe Reilly hasn't forgotten the skinny little kid who used to follow him around like a shadow. What he can't get over is that the skinny shadow has grown into one hell of an incredible woman. One any man in his right mind would kill to get his hands on. And one who seems to be completely immune to him. He knows he and Shay could have something special together. If he could only convince her he's about more than just the game.

A Lyrical e-book on sale now.

Learn more about Desiree at
http://www.kensingtonbooks.com/author.aspx/31606

Chapter 1

"Damn it, Hank. Why don't you answer?"

Shay Beckham pressed End on her cell phone yet again and sighed. She and her brother had been playing telephone tag for two days. When he called, she was in meetings. When she called, he was out of signal range. The only voices talking to each other were their voice mails. How godforsaken could it be in Wyoming, anyway? It was still in the United States, right?

And why was he trying so hard to reach her? They exchanged texts now and then, but they were both so busy they only called each other in case of emergency. The places he went, cell reception was spotty at best and talking to him was like playing leapfrog. Wait! Was he okay? Her heart stopped for a moment at the thought he might be hurt, but then she relaxed. If something had happened to him, his boss would have reached out to her. So what was on his mind that had generated this flurry of aborted phone calls? Obviously, he wanted something because he was the one who'd initiated this current game of phone tag.

She leaned back in the taxi as it turned from the airport access road onto the interstate. Less than half an hour and she'd be home, thank God, and she could get out of her sweatshirt and jeans that wore the remnants of her diet cola from the plane.

With the way her luck was running, maybe she shouldn't have accepted her complimentary beverage. On the flight out to New York a week before, a little turbulence had been responsible for her arriving with a huge coffee stain on her favorite yellow sweater. Maybe she should carry a bib with her. Or a large tarpaulin.

On today's flight, she had just set up her iPad and lifted her glass gingerly to take a sip when the plane hit an air pocket and everything bounced. Her iPad. The purse beneath the seat. Worst of all, her drink.

Her hand flew up, with it her diet soda and, most importantly, the ice cubes. Up in the air. Over the back of her seat. Into the seat behind her.

She could still hear the man behind her growling. "Shit!"

Then, "Damn it anyway."

She'd used the miniscule courtesy napkin to blot up what she could from her sweatshirt and jeans. Shay had cringed as the man behind her continued to mutter under his breath.

"Hey, you in front. Didn't you ever learn to pay attention on a plane? You got your damn drink all over me."

He hadn't seemed impressed with her mumbled apology so she'd just slid down even farther and buried her nose in her iPad again. And been damn glad to get to the end of the flight without further incident. When it was time to deplane, she'd avoided even looking back at the man, hustling up the Jetway into the terminal as fast as she could. Getting home was all she could think of.

Sighing, she brushed a few wisps of hair away from her cheeks and tugged on the brim of her red ball cap. A lean cougar prowled across the red background, a new graphic she'd created for Dazzling Designs. The company she worked for produced merchandise for college and professional sports teams. This prototype had been waiting for her when she flew in for four days at the main office and she'd decided to wear it on her trip home.

She was worn out from the long, intense days of discussions and brainstorming. This was her third round trip to New York since she'd made the move back to Texas. After five months, she was piling up plenty of frequent-flyer miles, which she hoped to use one of these days.

She realized with a start the taxi, which had slowed a moment ago, had come to a standstill. The driver's two-way radio crackled in the front seat, but she ignored its staticky sound as she checked her phone again. Still no answer from Hank. She leaned forward, seeing rows of vehicles stopped in every lane of the interstate as far ahead as she could see. Shit.

"Is there an accident ahead of us?"

"Yes, miss." The driver was nothing if not polite. "Dispatch radioed me a moment ago. Sorry, miss."

Well, crap. Just what she didn't need. She wanted a hot bath, a glass of wine, and pizza delivery.

She checked her watch again. Was it really only two minutes since she'd tried calling Hank? Maybe a text would reach him. Sometimes she had better success with that.

"In cab on way home from airport. What's up? Try a tin can for reception."

She hit Send and waited to see if he answered. In less than two minutes, her phone chimed.

"Good trip?"

"Yes. What's up with you? What's with all the phone calls?"

"Just wanted 2 let you know Laura had 2 vacate condo for repairs for 2 days. Told her she could stay at house. She knows where extra key is."

That was what was so important?

Shay snorted and wrote, *"I'll bet."*

"She'll be gone sometime 2day. Just a heads up." Shay ground her teeth. Damn it. Why couldn't the damn woman have gone to a hotel? And what was with giving out the location of the key? She loved her big brother and was grateful to him for sharing his house with her but she definitely needed to find a place of her own. She didn't need his females driving her crazy when he wasn't there.

"She'd better be out of there when I get home. Want peace and quiet."

"I'll text her now. Just wanted to get yr flight info."

"On my way home from airport now."

"Thx. I'll tell her. How was NY?"

"Same old same old. U home soon?"

"Maybe. Don't know. Take care."

"You, too."

Traffic was still not moving. Shay bit down on her frustration, sighed again, and unzipped the front pocket of her carry-on. She'd grabbed a sports magazine in the airport, planning to check the ads her company was running, but hadn't bothered to read it on the plane. Maybe she could use it to pass the time now.

Flipping it open, the first thing she saw was Joe Reilly's face smiling at her in full living color. Crap. Joe Reilly. Her childhood hero, her teenage crush, and the star of her adult erotic fantasies. The same Joe Reilly who'd called her squirt and pest when she tagged after him and Hank. The football idol who had been a babe magnet since his voice changed.

The man she'd been secretly in love with all these years, a love that stilted every other relationship she'd had. When was she ever going to admit that it was an impossibility? That she needed to stomp on it, bury it, and move forward?

In Texas, where football was the number one religion, high school stars wrote their own tickets. As the star quarterback for the Granite Falls High School Coyotes, Joe had had women hanging over him like so much drapery. During his outstanding career in college and then in the NFL, it seemed every time she turned on the television or checked sports online she saw his picture with one female or another. She was sure he had a black book that rivaled an encyclopedia in size. She might as well have been chopped liver for as much attention as he ever paid to her.

She'd wasted so much of her time studying football, until she could diagram games almost as well as Joe could. She could even point out the percentage of success for each play. Joe had always grinned and winked at her. Only in hindsight had she realized he'd tolerated her because she was Hank's baby sister, with the emphasis on baby, even as she stupidly wanted him to wait for her to grow up.

She needed to find a way to get Joe Reilly out of her head. For good. Certainly her obsession with him wasn't helping her love life. She needed to stop looking for Joe Reilly substitutes. The men she tried to build relationships with may not have been athletes, but they were ardent sports fans and that was what attracted her.

And look how far that had gotten her. One cheated on her with a coworker, one out and out lied about who and what he was, another wanted to move in with her and have her pay the rent. Thank God she'd never said *I love you* to any of them, probably because, in retrospect, she hadn't. All those experiences left her with a strong distrust of the male sex, Joe Reilly being no exception.

Yeah, she was the champion of stupid. What was with her, anyway? She was smart, savvy, successful at her work. She'd braved the Big Apple and found herself a dream job she loved, which paid her extremely well. People would be lining up to be her if she let them. Now she needed to find a way to get rid of this restless, unfulfilled feeling she hadn't been able to shake in years.

For weeks she'd been telling herself tomorrow she'd take the first step to build a new life here in San Antonio, back in Texas where her roots were. Reach out to old friends. Meet new people. Rebuild her life and shake the ghosts of the past. Stop burying herself in the house with her work and marathon sessions with old movies and popcorn. How pathetic was that?

What she needed was the right guy, one who understood emotion and who respected her. One who wasn't a Joe Reilly substitute. It wouldn't hurt if he was really hot and could make every one of her erotic fantasies come to life. And also didn't lie or cheat. Time to finally put the vestiges of her crush, her childish daydreams, where they belonged—in the mental Dumpster. She was through lusting after Joe Reilly.

Enough already.

If she was going to hero worship someone she should have stuck to Joe Montana. He'd be a lot safer. And better. Yes, way better.

She closed the magazine, putting Joe Reilly where he belonged. In her carryon.

Time to get on with life.

* * * *

Joe Reilly wheeled his rental car out of the parking lot toward San Antonio. Checking his cell phone for traffic alerts, he discovered an accident on Interstate 10 that had traffic at a standstill. He programmed the GPS for an alternate route and headed out.

He could still smell the traces of a soft drink on his slacks. He'd done his best to wipe away the stains but the rental clerk had given him the fisheye, probably thinking he was a real slob. It wasn't his fault some idiot who couldn't walk and chew gum, or manage to hold onto her drink on the plane, had dumped its contents over the back of her seat and onto him. Just another indication of how crummy his day was going.

He'd seen this trip as a chance to spend some quality time with Hank Beckham, who, despite geographical differences, was still his best friend. He didn't get to see as much of him as he'd like to these days. The last time had been three years ago.

Their schedules just hadn't allowed for any time together since then. Hank was an engineer who was always being sent to some assignment for his company while Joe ran around the country for Fox Sports One and for the Coaches Conference business he'd started. The latter was an important project for him, workshops for high school coaches on how to lead as well as coach. How to teach players personal values as well as diagrams and game plans. He'd seen too many kids come out of high school without understanding that playing was only half the deal. Personal responsibility was a big part of it. His programs were geared to help coaches pass that along.

Unfortunately Hank had texted that morning he was still in Wyoming working on plans to build a bridge, but Joe should make himself at home in the house.

"I'll try and catch a quick couple of days while you're there, buddy," Hank had assured him. "But if not, just make yourself at home."

He'd also hoped to spend some time with his parents, of course, who were happy in their new adults-only community, except they were away on a trip. Bad timing, but it couldn't be helped.

So he'd be alone in the house.

Joe shifted in his seat, trying to stretch out his left leg. The ache served as a constant reminder the glory days had come to an abrupt end.

His cell phone rang, interrupting his thoughts. He looked at the readout and swore. Lisa Margolin. No doubt calling for his help with Gina again. God. How had he gotten himself in this pickle anyway? Because his parents raised him to take care of people who couldn't take care of themselves. That was how. He let the call go to voice mail, not in a mood to deal with it right now.

He was aware the most recent company Gina worked for had gone out of business a few weeks ago. Employees had received a one-month severance package and Joe knew Gina was coming to the end of hers. She didn't deal well with uncertainty. Her dysfunctional family had set off her battle with the bottle to begin with and he knew the thread of sobriety was always very shaky.

Ten minutes later the ringtone chimed again and he knew without looking who it was. She was nothing if not persistent. Setting his jaw, he pressed Accept.

"What is it this time, Lisa?"

"You know I wouldn't call you unless it was important, Joe. Really." She always began the calls that way.

Except it was always important. "Yeah, okay. Just tell me what's up now."

"I hope you aren't mad."

She was as good at sounding tearful as Gina always had been.

"Lisa, I'm kind of busy. What's the deal?"

"Well, um…" She paused.

"Look." He chuffed with impatience. "Just spit it out. How much?" It was always money. Of course.

"She's got a few job interviews coming up and she could use a couple new outfits."

Joe squeezed the phone so hard he was amazed he didn't crush it. "What happened to the money I just sent her?"

Pause. "She got sick." Lisa's voice was very quiet. "I mean, really sick. She needed medicine."

He could only imagine. Medicine that came in bottles of cheap booze.

"She really wants to make a good impression at these interviews," Lisa added.

A headache began to burrow its way into his temples.

"Fine. Give me an hour and I'll transfer some money into your account."

"Can't you just meet me with a check?" she whined.

"No. I'm busy. It's the transfer or nothing."

"Whatever." Her heavy sigh was clear across the connection. "Sorry. I just want this to happen for her."

"We're coming to the end of the road here, Lisa. It's time Gina took responsibility for her own life."

"But you're all she has," Lisa protested, a familiar refrain. "You can't let go of her now. I-I'll make sure she stays clean. Gets a job. Goes to work."

"Do that. I'll check back with you to see what's going on." He disconnected the call in the middle of her thanks, grinding his teeth.

Gina Rivera. High school bombshell. Wild child who'd captured his virtue. He hadn't seen her, had even forgotten about her, until his third year in the NFL. She'd shown up at a game, waiting for him at the player's gate, all masses of blond hair and tight clothes. He'd been high enough on the excitement of the win to succumb to her sexiness and spend the night with her.

He hadn't thought much of it, not even when she showed up twice more. Then he'd discovered her secret, answered her one plea for help and after that he was trapped, just because he was basically a good guy. Occasional contact turned into regular contact. And when he'd stopped taking her calls, she'd had Lisa contact him with a sob story that plucked at his conscience.

How long was he expected to offer aid to a raging alcoholic who didn't help herself? He should have told Scott Manchin, his agent, about it from the beginning. By now so much time had passed if word got out, the media wouldn't look at him as doing something kind for a friend. They'd want to know why he'd kept her hidden all this time. Did they have a child together? All that shit. He'd seen it happen to others and hadn't been smart enough to protect himself. It would be gossip fodder for weeks and kill all the work he'd done to clean up his act. He really had to cut the cord here.

Okay, enough of that.

Following the GPS directions, he pulled off the interstate and into an attractive neighborhood of larger homes and mature trees. A little farther on and the GPS directed him to turn left into the long driveway of a two-story colonial. *Nice digs, Hank,* he thought. But the guy was making big bucks. He deserved a good place to come home to.

He parked in front of the garage door. Maybe when he got inside he could grab the opener from Hank's car and use it while he was here. The key was right where Hank had said it would be. He opened the front door, pulled his suitcase inside, and headed toward the room Hank had said was his to use. On the way he passed a room that looked far too feminine to be Hank's. He wondered briefly whose room it was. Hank hadn't mentioned anything about sharing the house with someone.

Too much for him to think about right now. He wanted a shower, and then he'd see about ordering some dinner. Less than five minutes later he was under hot, steaming water, washing away the grime of the day.

* * * *

The taxi moved forward with a jerk and Shay's eyes popped open. She leaned forward and tapped the driver on the shoulder.

"Did they clear away the wreck? We're finally moving, right?"

"Yes, miss." He shrugged. "But slowly."

She rotated her neck, trying to work out some of the kinks. She'd been sitting in uncomfortable seats since she got in the shuttle to the airport and every muscle in her body ached. The hot shower was looking better and better. Or maybe she'd fire up the hot tub Hank had installed on the rear deck.

Hopefully, with all this delay caused by the wreck, by the time she got to the house Laura would be packed and gone. They pulled off the interstate and she mentally crossed her fingers and silently chanted, *Let her be gone*. But bad luck was still with her. When they turned onto her street and she spotted the car parked in the driveway, she swore under her breath. Laura Whoever was still here. Well, she'd better be getting ready to leave. Shay was in no mood to put up with bullshit. Sighing, she hauled her suitcase into the house, closed the door, and headed through the living room to her bedroom.

And stopped.

A hissing sound came from the shower in the bathroom connected to her bedroom and the guest room. Damn it! The least Hank could do was tell his little friends to use the master bath and leave hers alone. He had, after all, promised her that she'd have complete privacy.

"I travel a lot," he'd told her. Then grinned. "And I'll keep the sleepovers to those times you're in New York."

Yeah, yeah, yeah.

So how come this female hadn't gotten the message she was supposed to be gone?

Crap! The door wasn't even closed. Clouds of steam billowed in the bathroom and obscured the figure in the frosted-glass shower enclosure. Okay, enough was enough.

Shay stepped into the bathroom and banged her hand on the glass.

"This is my bathroom," she ground out. "I've had a tough day and you don't want to mess with me. Next time use Hank's bathroom. This one is off-limits. Get your ass out of here in five seconds, or I won't be responsible for my actions."

She turned away, not the least bit interested in a glimpse of Laura Whoever's nudity. She just wanted her out of the house.

The water stopped and the door slid open.

"Okay. I don't want to cause you any more stress. But Hank said I should use this one."

The deep voice shocked her and she turned around before she even thought about it. And nearly swallowed her tongue. A very wet, very naked Joe Reilly stood in her shower stall, grinning at her.

Just when she'd finally made up her mind to stop thinking about him and obsessing over him.

At that exact moment her cell phone chimed. A message from Hank.

"BTW, Joe's in town. Take good care of him."

www.ingramcontent.com/pod-product-compliance
Lightning Source LLC
Chambersburg PA
CBHW020446270626
47155CB00022B/1705